BRIGHTSIDE

MARK TULLIUS

VINCERE
P R E S S

VINCERE
P R E S S

Published by Vincere Press
65 Pine Ave., Ste 806
Long Beach, CA 90802

Printed in the United States of America
First Edition

ISBN: 978-1-938475-00-9
Library of Congress Control Number: 2012936980

Cover design by Florencio Ares – aresjun@gmail.com
and
Salvatore Lo Medico – www.onesheetstudios.com
Book cover photo by William Dudziak. ©William Dudziak,
http://www.dudziak.com

For Jen and Olivia, who make the bright side so easy to see.

And to my dearly missed friend who wasn't able to.

Brightside

"Let freedom ring with a shotgun blast!"

- Machine Head

Ajax,

I hope you
can always look
on the bright side.

CHAPTER ONE

They call us Thought Thieves, but it's not like we have a choice. All the sick, twisted things rolling around in people's heads, we can't help but hear. God knows I've tried to turn it off. The sexual perversions, the violent fantasies about your boss, that annoying neighbor you want dead, even those unfortunate thoughts about your kids. I've had to stand there and listen.

I'd never wish this upon anyone, not even my mom, the woman who's been over-sharing since I slid from her womb.

You wouldn't believe the awful shit I've heard.

Imagine if you knew every dark thought people had about you.

Trust me, it's not pleasant. In any given moment, the person you love is thinking about someone else she'd like to screw, how fat you've gotten, how unbearable it is to hear you chew. Later, she'll hold you and kiss you and regret most of it, and you'll fall asleep hating yourself for having all the same thoughts.

Secrets keep the world from burning. I know this now more than ever. The secret I have left could get everyone killed. One person's already dead, more are sure to follow. All because I couldn't keep my stupid thoughts shut.

So I understand why they rounded us up, Thought Thieves like me, and took us to this little town on top of a mountain with drops so steep there's no need for a fence. It keeps the country functioning, lets everyone feel safe, knowing we're up here in the sky, far away from everyone's thoughts, except our own.

They call our town Brightside because, as they like to remind us, things could be worse. Some Thought Thieves weren't so lucky. They were beaten and hanged, shot in the streets. Others were wrapped in straightjackets and locked away in squishy-walled rooms.

Brightside was our chance to start over. We could hold jobs and have apartments; we could even go on dates and shop in the little stores. It wouldn't be so bad, they told us. As long as we never tried to leave.

But now it's Day 100, the day it's all going to end. Guess we'll find out how bad it can get.

My bedroom window's right in front of me, but I've got my eyes closed. The warm glow of the sunrise is trying to make me peek, but I can't look at the jagged crack running down the center of the glass. I can't look at the pool of blood on the chair, the tiny drops on the ceiling.

Eight pounds of power rest across my thighs. My Mossberg 12-gauge. American metal. Dad's special gift.

Odds are this is my last sunrise. I open my eyes, take in the absolute beauty. I wonder if Danny and Sara are awake and seeing it, too. If I can somehow help them escape, it might make up for some of the things I've done.

Not Rachel, though. What happened with her is beyond redemption; I can't go back and change it. If I'd just given her what she needed, told her what she wanted to hear, she'd be coming with us. I know what happened to Rachel goes beyond Day 39, but that's when it all started.

* * *

It was seven hours before Day 39 officially began. Rachel and I were in our office, the only one with two desks. They put us there because of our shitty sales record. Jobs in Brightside were based on the ones we held in our former lives. I used to sell BMWs. Here, I sold timeshares. At BMW I never missed a quota, never blew a sale, but I was always within six feet of the customer, the range I needed to hear someone's thoughts. On the phone, I was next to worthless.

The clock on the wall showed the same time as my computer. All the clocks in Brightside were perfectly in sync. No reason to be late. No reason to think this wasn't all perfectly normal.

They even hid the security cameras to help us relax. They put them inside light fixtures, behind bushes in the Square, where we have a bakery, a bar, and even an electronics store. All built for us. To make us believe this is just a regular town, a place like any other. No reason to ever escape.

Rachel got hung up on before she could finish telling the guy how close the condo was to the beach. We had five minutes left of work, enough time for her to make another call, but she just opened the bottom desk drawer and pulled out a bottle of lotion. She squirted it onto her palm and rubbed her legs that were spilling out from under the desk.

Rachel and I had been dating for close to three weeks. Long enough for Rachel to decide I was the one. Long enough for me to give her a key to my place, to convince myself I loved her back.

Everything gets accelerated in Brightside, because you can't lie. Everything's exposed. Normal couples take six months to admit how they feel. Brightsiders do it on the first date.

Rachel rolled back in her chair and looked at me like I'd just said something. It made me feel sorry for all the people I'd done this to over the years. Taking whatever I pleased.

She got up with a smile and walked over to my desk. Her red skirt stopped mid-thigh and was tight enough to be painted on. She didn't need to listen to my thoughts to know I liked it.

The last couple days, Rachel only saw me at work, and she knew I was ready to break up with her. It's not that things were bad. They were just too intense. Rachel was the first Thought Thief I'd ever been with. I had no idea how exhausting it could be. You can't just say you're tired or that nothing's wrong.

Rachel knew everything, even though I never said a word.

That's why she sat on the corner of my desk, crossed her legs so I couldn't focus on my computer screen. She'd put her dark hair in a ponytail so it looked less Jewish. I'd only thought that once, but she never let it go.

Rachel smiled and took off the glasses she didn't need. The ones that looked exactly like Mom's.

She took the part of the frame that rested behind her ear and put it in her mouth. She sucked on it a bit then spoke around it. "You got plans tonight?"

I noticed Rachel had gotten contacts, her eyes so fucking blue. Just like Michelle's, my last girlfriend before Brightside.

Rachel turned her legs toward me. They were shiny and smooth and smelled like piña colada. "I just shaved," she said.

We both knew I wanted to feel the inside of her thigh, run my hand up to see if she was telling the truth, but I just mumbled that they looked nice and powered off my computer.

Rachel rubbed her calf against my knee until I looked up at her. "I need to see you tonight," she said.

I adjusted my khakis, pointlessly trying to conceal the fact her plan was working.

"We can go out," she said. "Something nice. I'm thinking Oscar's."

Oscar's meant a lot of money, something I wasn't making in Brightside.

Always staying one step ahead of me, Rachel said dinner was on her. She wanted me to know things could be different. She was willing to change. It didn't have to be so intense.

"Come on, it'll be fun," she said. "And I don't even need to stay over tonight. Unless you want me to?" Rachel took hold of my collar and pulled me in, her red lips so close.

I could feel the security camera zooming in from its hiding spot. I pushed her back and said, "Fine, we'll go to Oscar's."

Rachel smiled and spun off my desk. She let me watch her ass as she picked up her purse and walked out the door.

Oscar's was only a few blocks from my apartment and, even though I was dressed and ready, I waited until the last possible minute to leave. I didn't want to get there before Rachel.

I passed under the bronze archway and entered the park with its enormous pine trees. Someone had decorated them with little white lights to make it look like a winter wonderland. There were no rules about sticking to the path, so I cut across the grass, staying far away from the edge where the mountain dropped off. A full mile, straight down. Heights threw my stomach around in my chest and made me shake like a little girl. I passed the pond and took deep breaths to clear my head. The air was cool, everything silent.

The Cabin was high up on the hill, with its big red logs and long bay window. The curtains were always pulled back, so we'd see the residents who'd broken the rules. Some had refused to go to work or started fights. A few had slit their wrists too shallow.

In the common room, a small blonde in a nurse's uniform sat behind the desk reading a magazine. The rule-breakers sat in chairs, their faces pale, eyes ringed in black. They weren't allowed to talk during rehabilitation. They were given pills to keep them calm.

The Cabin was the big reminder in Brightside that our town was still a prison.

I focused my eyes straight, kept walking, went through the South archway and stepped onto Main Street. The six small stores were dark and closed, but everything else was lit. Every ten feet, a lamp post to wipe out any shadow. No place to hide.

I strolled down the deserted street as the American flag flapped high above the Square. The flapping like a goddamn slap in the face.

I knew I had to clear my head. I needed to blow out all the bad thoughts before I turned the corner.

Rachel was waiting for me on the bench outside Oscar's. She was wearing her fancy green dress. The one she'd worn under her robe at graduation. Back then it fit perfectly. Now, she had to suck in. Her hair was up in a French twist, and her makeup was thick. Especially her lips. Dark red. Her glasses were gone. She wanted me to know she'd been paying attention.

I didn't realize it was supposed to be that kind of dinner, but at least I had on my nice pair of jeans and my shirt had a collar. Rachel didn't care what I was wearing. She was just happy I showed.

I took her hand and said, "Let's go eat."

Oscar's windows were tinted just enough so you had to press your face against the glass to see the idiots paying thirty bucks for the same steak they could buy for ten across the street. Brightside liked to remind us we could still be special.

The hostess was going to seat us in the back, tucked away in the corner. Rachel asked if we could sit at a table.

She knew I wouldn't break up with her in the open. We sat in between two couples silently engaged in conversation.

Rachel wanted to talk though, wanted me to feel this was a normal date. She knew I was thinking about The Cabin and that fucking flag. She told me to order anything I wanted. She asked about my day, even though she'd been sitting next to me the entire eight hours.

Our steaks arrived, and Rachel kept asking questions, like the first concert I went to and the last book I'd read. She was trying, and I felt like an asshole. I answered her questions and even asked a few of my own.

It made me think this is how our first date should have been. Not me sharing how much I hated my mom. Rachel sharing what her uncle did with her panties.

But by the time we'd finished dessert, we'd run out of things to say. We were like an old married couple after only three weeks. I took Rachel's hand and started to have the talk we'd been avoiding. She put her other hand on top of mine like it was a game.

"Let's just grab a drink."

She knew I wasn't a drinker. It's not that I have a problem with booze. The problem is when I'm buzzed I start thinking about shit I shouldn't. Back home in Ohio, I could get away with it. In Brightside it was a problem.

I said, "It's kind of late."

Rachel snorted. That's how she laughed. "We'll only have one." She looked so desperate sitting there, her hand squeezing mine. She just wanted us to have some fun.

"All right," I said, "we'll go for one."

We crossed through the Square and headed for Riley's, the bar where everyone knows your name and all the horrifying shit that fills your head.

It started out fine because that's how bars usually start out. Then an hour turned to two and I was somehow on my sixth Jack. All my thoughts started creeping out like cockroaches. Rachel handed me another shot. I talked louder to keep other things to myself, but some guy asked what I had against the flag. Rachel laughed and pulled me towards the door. Everything was spinning and I thought I might fall over. Rachel kissed me and kissed me.

And then it was Day 39.

I woke up to the darkness. The curtains were closed. I had no idea what time it was or how we'd gotten back to my place. Besides the pounding headache it seemed like every other morning with Rachel, but something was definitely wrong.

Rachel was sitting on the edge of the bed, legs dangling over the side. She kept pulling at her curls, over and over, again and again. Her right hand was clenched, her fingers pressing down on her thumb like she was trying to break it.

I put my head back on the pillow, tired and hungover. I was still halfway in my dream, and it was a good one.

Michelle and I were walking in the forest, its grass so green, Ohio's brilliant blue sky above. Michelle stopped at a clearing and laid down her red blanket.

Then she was underneath me.

Her eyes were the lightest blue with the softest shine. I brushed Michelle's sandy blonde hair from the side of her face, ran my thumb lightly across her cheek, around her ear, then cradled her head.

She reached behind my back and pulled me down. My heart covered hers. Her heart, my heart, beat to beat. "Can you feel that, Joe?"

And then I was inside her and we were white on red, all that blue above us. Beautiful colors back then.

Michelle. Michelle. Michelle...

"Are you fucking serious?"

The voice definitely wasn't Michelle's.

The dream was gone. I was awake, back in Brightside, darkness all around me.

I had no idea what I'd done, but I knew it wasn't good. "Come back to sleep," I said.

Rachel wouldn't face me, all her focus on those curtains, the ones I refused to open, the mile of Brightside beyond them.

I reached out and put my hand on her back. Rachel recoiled and my hand fell. Her mouth was a black hole moving in the darkness.

"You still love her."

I played dumb, what Mom wouldn't call a hard stretch. "Who?"

Rachel swung her knee onto the bed so it was up against my ribs, the thin white sheet the only thing between us. "Please don't lie to me, Joe. I'm not an idiot."

My eyes were adjusting to the dark. I saw Rachel's blue contacts, the black trails bleeding beneath them.

I took hold of her fist and eased it open. I rubbed her college ring, the emerald set in white gold. She'd gotten it a month before they brought her to Brightside. "You're not an idiot," I said. "You've got the ring to prove it."

She said, "You think this is funny?"

It wasn't funny. It was scary.

I said I was sorry. "I shouldn't have joked like that." I kept touching her ring, started picturing her in school, lying under all those guys.

Rachel's hand clenched back into a fist.

I couldn't control my thoughts. "Rachel, it's late." I looked over at the clock. "We've got work in three hours."

"Do you wish I was her?"

She knew I couldn't answer that. Not in one word. Not the one she was looking for.

Michelle was the woman I was going to marry. She found out the hard way about my secret. She was there when they took me away.

Rachel sat waiting for an answer, staring at me, peering inside. I took a deep breath, trying to clear my head, but she knew everything.

Everyone always did in Brightside.

I asked if she was hungry, mentioned the diner, some eggs.

Rachel just sat there. She needed me to say it.

But I couldn't.

Rachel reached over and grabbed my dick poking up under the sheet. My hard-on was news to me, but the proof she needed was in her hand. It looked like she'd captured the world's smallest ghost.

I said, "Let go. I have to piss."

Rachel spoke like I was a Special Ed student. "How about you just wait?"

"I'm not pissing the bed because you want to talk."

There wasn't much left of my dick to grip because getting treated like a child isn't my thing. But that didn't stop Rachel. "You're not walking away," she said.

I took hold of her wrist and pried off her fingers. "You need to stop this." And then real serious and slow so she heard me, I said, "Fucking relax."

Fucking relax?

Rachel's football player. His words coming out of my mouth. I hadn't meant to say it. Not like that, at least. Or had I? Cornered, what was I capable of?

Rachel wasn't the only one who could use thoughts against people.

I'd learned about the jocks, the Dartmouth boys, and all the other guys on our second date. She was drunk and underneath me. I thought she was moaning because of me, but then her thoughts started pouring, flooding her head, and then mine. She realized what was happening, and she started crying. She was ashamed. No one had ever seen these things with Rachel. I told her it was okay, that I didn't care.

All things considered, I'm not a bad guy. I don't try to hurt people on purpose, but just like Rachel, sometimes I can't let shit go.

Rachel got off the bed, moved to the other side of the room to get out of my range. She couldn't stomach the disgusting thoughts in my head.

Out of range, I could finally lie. "I'm over Michelle. It was just a dream."

But Rachel was bawling. I sat up all the way and asked her to please come back to bed.

Rachel wiped at her tears like she was mad at them. "Yeah, you're over her. You proved it to me, right? And it was so sweet. Carving my name on a tree. Just like we were in junior high."

It was stupid, something I did on Day 7. I'd used my key to carve out a big heart, put "Joe loves Michelle" inside it. I didn't think anyone would see it.

But Brightsiders see everything.

Rachel and I were coming back to my place one night, and my lock was sticking. I'd damaged the key by carving Michelle's name.

Rachel didn't say anything, didn't need to. I felt awful though, so I went out the next day and crossed it out, re-placed Michelle's name with Rachel's. It was childish, something an eighth grader would do, but it was better than what Rachel was doing back then, getting fingerbanged behind the gymnasium.

Rachel kicked the bed. She was back in range. "You got something to say?"

Fuck!

Thirty-nine days weren't enough to get used to this. From Day 1, we all knew we weren't alone. They told us being together in a group would make it easier, but it was so much worse. Everything on display, nowhere to hide. It's what brought Rachel and me together. We thought we could elevate past all the dysfunctional relationships, especially our parents', but we were even more dysfunctional, all honest and exposed, the little secrets and awful truths firing off like buckshot at anyone within range.

I'm not proud of it, but I couldn't stop thinking about the list. It was long. All the guys Rachel had been with, the depths she'd sunk.

"You're fucking sick," she said.

"What the hell happened last night? I remember going to Riley's and you ordering those shots—"

"Oh, so you're just drunk?"

"What's your problem?"

"I shouldn't care if you dream about her? That you gotta pretend I'm her to fuck me?"

As calm as I could, I said, "I don't do that."

Rachel's jaw clenched so tight I thought she'd break teeth.

I usually have a great memory, one of the things I hate about myself. Not on Day 39. I was having trouble thinking, let alone remembering. The walk home was one big blur.

Rachel's jaw relaxed. She was listening to my thoughts. I was trying to piece things together, grasping at vapors.

The smell of sex was stronger than my breath, and I guessed it was possible I imagined Rachel as Michelle. But I couldn't admit that and saying I blacked out wouldn't change anything. I put my hands over my head, as if that would block her out.

"I didn't do that," I said.

I heard her thought:

You're a liar!

"Rachel, I don't remember anything. If that happened, I'm sorry. I never should've had those shots."

"So it's all my fault?" She started pacing, moving in and out of range.

"Holy shit. Can you just stop? You're acting crazy."

Rachel smiled, breathed through her nose. "You want to see crazy?" Her voice scared the shit out of me. She was all the way on the other side of the room.

"Rachel, I know you're angry. But you need to calm down—"

"You want me to calm down? Should I get some air? Maybe we should take a break. That's what you want, right?"

Right then was my best chance of denying things, her by the door, both of us out of range, lights off so she couldn't look me in the eyes. But I knew we weren't going to work no matter how much I wanted it.

All I had to do was say it.

But I couldn't.

"Rachel, come on..."

"Where should I go, Joe? Should I go back home? Huh? Oh right, I can't. This is it." Her smile was creeping me out. "This is home."

I suddenly realized this was about so much more than Michelle. Rachel was cracking, like a dam ready to burst.

"Rachel, please, I'm begging—"

Rachel screamed like she was being burned. Her legs gave out. She thudded off the hardwood. She put her forehead to the floor. Her tiny fists strangled her matted hair and she just kept screaming.

The lights flashed on, the 120s blinding me even with the fixture over them.

"Rachel, come on, be quiet."

I looked at the clock. We still had an hour before morning lights. They never came on early.

"Rachel, please!"

Her throat wouldn't close, just kept spraying screams until I covered my ears.

"I think you're great, Rachel. I wouldn't be with you if I didn't. Just please be quiet."

She kept wailing.

And I knew they were coming.

Rachel knew it too, but she didn't seem to care, just curled up under the bright lights. Everything exposed. The scar on her collarbone. The two-inch wide birthmark on her lower back. She banged the floor with her head, pleading for someone to let her go.

"I just want to go home," she sobbed. "Why won't they let us go?"

My head was pounding from the lights and the hangover, but I kept my voice nice and quiet when I said, "Just come to bed, okay? We'll say you stubbed your toe."

The bootsteps were coming.

Rachel, get over here NOW!

I jumped off the bed, felt foolish because my dick was just hanging there. But Rachel wasn't looking at me. She was still crying to the floor, the voice not her at all. Broken and shattered. I yanked her arm, but she wouldn't move.

The Boots were here.

It was going to hurt like hell, but I had to get close, right up against her so my thoughts would sound like they were coming through a megaphone.

GET UP! THEY'RE HERE! PLEASE!

Rachel made herself smaller, pressed her fists against the sides of her face.

They didn't even knock, just opened the door. Two of them standing there, all calm, like they were here to fix the sink.

Rachel screamed, "Fuck you! You can't keep us here! You can't!"

I told Rachel to shut up.

She did, but only to spit in one guy's face.

The guy didn't even wipe it off, just twisted her arm, almost snapped it. She begged him to let her go. Then she clawed him in the eyes.

I stepped forward, my hands out to show them I wasn't looking for a fight. "She had too much to drink. Please, don't—"

The baton cracked off my skull and I fell. The boots walked right up to my face.

"You got anything else to say?"

I kept my face to the floor, listened as they dragged Rachel from my room, her screams slowly fading until they were gone.

CHAPTER TWO

It was Day 39 and I was alone in my office, just Rachel's desk to keep me company. I needed to look busy and pretended to type, my fingers tapping out nonsensical strings. I drank cup after cup of water so I could focus on my throbbing bladder, focus on anything but Rachel, the Boots dragging her from my room.

My computer dinged. A polite email reminding me of my quota.

Brightside required us to work. It wasn't for the money. The government funded most everything. But Brightside needed us to keep busy, to feel productive. They started the jobs program after the first month. Too many Brightsiders had jumped off the mountain, took the easy way out.

Quotas kept us from living in our heads.

Busy people don't kill themselves. That was the idea, at least.

I started dialing. Got twenty-four hang-ups, five don't-call-me-ever-agains, and one old woman who spent three minutes asking about the weather in Greece before she realized I wasn't her son.

I was one of the few Brightsiders allowed to make calls to the outside world. I'd been deemed a low risk. But everything was monitored. If I said one thing, like begged for help or told anyone the truth about this place, I'd be sitting in The Cabin dripping drool by night.

Finally, a guy actually sounded interested. I asked him if there was anywhere he dreamed of going.

The guy said, "Costa Rica. I've heard good things about that place."

In three quick clicks, I was on their homepage. "Oh, definitely. Costa Rica's great. Did you know the average temperature is seventy-two degrees?"

"I didn't know that."

"Yeah, and they've got active volcanoes."

"That's pretty cool."

"Yeah, Costa Rica is definitely the place to go," I said, "and we've got some incredible getaways available at great prices."

Brightside had given me a sales script, which was shit, but deviation was against the rules.

"I don't know," the guy said. "How much would it run me?"

"I'm sure you'd qualify for our no-down-payment plan. And our smaller suites are under two hundred a month."

"That's nothing."

"Exactly. Less than you probably spend on gas." I checked the screen. "Are you still in management, Mr. Crawford?"

"Yeah, home enjoying a sick day."

"Lucky man. How are your benefits over there? Do you have much vacation time built up?"

"Tons."

"So what do you think? Would you like to own your very own Costa Rican condo? Doesn't that sound like fun?" They told us to emphasize the word "fun" as much as possible.

"It does, but tell me this. Is prostitution really legal over there?"

The screen said Mr. Crawford had a wife and son, but that was none of my business. For all I knew, he'd gotten a divorce. The computers were never accurate.

I told him prostitution was legal and his laugh made me sick.

"Would you be looking for a one bedroom or two?" I asked.

"Just one. So tell me more about this. Are there brothels?"

"I believe so, now I've got some nice villas on the Pacific Ocean."

"And I heard there's no age limit."

"That's something you'll have to check. Now, the place is right on the water. Why don't we get the process started? If I can get your credit card number and verify a couple details, we'll be done before you know it."

"How do I know this isn't some kind of scam?"

"Good question. Goes to show what a smart man you are. Why don't I just email over a contract? Just click on the link and it'll take you to our site. Brightside Travel is a very reputable company."

"Holy shit, you're one of those guys? Tell me what I'm thinking."

"Uh...afraid it doesn't work like that. If you give me your email address, I'll send you the contract."

A door opened and closed on Mr. Crawford's end. A woman's grating voice said, "Paul, what are you doing on the phone? You're supposed to be sick."

Sounding nothing like the man he'd been when she wasn't around, Mr. Crawford said, "I'll be off in a minute."

I didn't know if he was still listening to me, but I kept trying. "Tell her it's a surprise. Tell her you're doing something special for her, but don't tell her what." As quick as I could, I said, "You make this decision, and she'll thank you."

But he'd already hung up.

I'd told Carlos, my boss, the website's name was hurting our ability to sell. Carlos said it reminded people Brightside allowed us to live productive lives. Again, I told him, it was hurting sales. Carlos said the P.R. was worth it.

Brightside wasn't very profitable, but we only needed to make enough to cover what the government wouldn't fund, like the ice cream parlor, movie theater, and electronics store.

If this had been BMW, I would've had papers everywhere, stacks of sales contracts, important phone calls to return.

My Brightside desk had one piece of paper, a blue Post-It Carlos had stuck on my phone. A completely unnecessary reminder of our three o'clock meeting.

I'd never worried about a review before Brightside, got salesman of the month five times in a row. Worst thing my ex-boss, Saul, ever said to me was slow down a little.

Leave something for the other guys. Some of them have families.

Here, I shared an office because I sucked so hard.

I made another call, but it just kept ringing. I stared at the door, waiting for it to open, to see Rachel and that red skirt, her legs glistening with the piña colada lotion. The only thing that entered the office all morning was a note card, slipped under the door. It told me I had an appointment with Sharon, Brightside's resident shrink. Sharon liked to say there was beauty in everything. Look at it all. Breathe it in.

But she could keep her fucking Kool-Aid. Self-help wasn't going to save me. It was too late for that. It might have worked when I was a kid, when everything started.

* * *

It was winter and I was in kindergarten, my very first day. The bell rang and class began. Miss Parker assigned us seats. Corey thought I smelled like a girl. Tameka asked to be moved because her dad told her never to trust a honky. Jennie thought I looked weird and stupid.

I knew all this before naptime, and it only got worse.

I'd been hearing other people's thoughts for a few months, but never this many at one time. Miss Parker had told us to be quiet, to try and fall asleep. The ones who couldn't would just lie there and think. A million voices blasting straight into my head. It was like standing behind a jet engine. I covered my ears, mashing my palms until I thought I'd crack my skull, but that's not how thoughts entered me. They just shot in, and I screamed. Miss Parker ran over, thinking I was having a nightmare. She saw my pants covered in piss. Some kids laughed, they all thought I was a baby.

I kept my hands over my crotch. Miss Parker told everyone to be quiet. She took my hand. Her skin was dry and scaly, covered in chalk. She took me to the bathroom to get cleaned up. She said there was a change of pants in the teacher's lounge. This sort of thing happened a lot. I remember my little pecker rubbing against the corduroy because the school didn't carry underwear. Miss Parker had to cuff the legs because they were too long. I wondered how many other peckers had touched this zipper.

Miss Parker held my hand again, her skin cutting into mine, and we went back to class. The kids were quietly thinking I was a retard, except for Steven, probably the only Chinese kid in Columbus. He thought the other kids were jerks, but he just sat there, said nothing. I would've done the same.

When the day finally ended, I waited for everyone to leave the room then slipped on my red rain boots because Mom said comfy winter ones were a waste of money. I put on my puffy blue jacket that was my Hulk jacket when I wore Dad's green sweatshirt over it and growled at the mirror. I left my gloves in my pocket and headed to the door. I hoped it wasn't too cold out. I hoped I wouldn't have to wait long. Mom had promised she wouldn't forget. But she said not to worry enough times for me to know better.

The snow was coming down hard, the sky a dark cloud. I put on my gloves that were only just mittens, the kind without fingers because they were cheaper.

Over half the class had already been picked up, their parents waiting out front. The rest of the kids were lined up along the fence with Miss Parker folding her arms and hopping up and down looking like a skinny Big Bird. She had the same puffy yellow hair, too, but hid most of it under her brown hat with the giant ear-flaps.

She said it was the rule to wait by the fence, but there were kids spilling out by the street. I headed over to the end, squeezed in between Steven and the giant mound of snow.

Steven was dressed for success, a bright blue snow coat and matching vest, a light blue button-down beneath it. No one had told his parents dressing like that came later in life. Maybe they knew Steven's life would be a short one.

He never looked up from his six-inch tall Superman, the strongest man on the planet.

I had both hands in my jacket pockets, holding each other and my belly because the lining was ripped and Mom didn't sew. I kicked away a circle of snow. My boots were too thin and I was going to be there a while.

Steven aimed Superman at the ground and thought, *Melt this with your heat vision.*

"What?" I said.

"I didn't say nothing," Steven said.

"Sorry," I said.

I'd learned to apologize when I mistakenly thought someone had said their thoughts out loud. People got angry when I didn't. They called me crazy.

Every night I prayed for God to make it go away, but it was always there, the noise inside other people's heads. I never listened on purpose. Never reached in and stole people's thoughts, like some believed. For me, it's like hearing a person's true voice, the things they really believe. It's a whisper from six feet, a scream at just inches. The more focused the thought, the louder it gets.

You know that silent awkwardness when someone is holding their tongue, stewing in anger after someone does something awful, because they don't want to cause a scene? Well, for me, it's like being face-to-face with a wailing psychopath. An endless scream of all the horrible things people really want to do to each other.

Back then I was still getting used to it. Part of me wanted to turn to Steven and see if his lips were moving. The other part was smart enough to know the things he was thinking weren't things anyone would say. He was pointing Superman at Corey, the kid who thought I smelled like a girl and that Steven was a fucking chink.

I started humming my ABC's, occupying my mind, blocking Steven out.

It wasn't long before Brenda's mom drove up. Then Darryl's. Then Jennie's. The next time I counted there were only five of us left.

Steven turned to me and held out Superman. Steven's eyes were so squinted I could barely see the black. He was thinking he should have stood up for me after I'd pissed my pants. "You can borrow him," he said.

I didn't know what to say. I almost asked if he could hear my thoughts, because I'd been watching him play with that toy and wanted it for myself. But I'd learned that was a good way to get laughed at. I just nodded and said thanks.

A shiny black Mercedes pulled up to the gate. Miss Parker called Steven by his real name, Hong, even though he'd asked her not to that morning.

That got Corey started. Bigger than most of us and blacker than all, he ran over and started doing his gorilla impression, pounding his chest, stomping snow everywhere. He shouted, "Hong Kong, Hong Kong."

Steven's face got red, but he didn't say a word about how he was going to jump in the car and have his father plow right into Corey. Then Corey slanted his eyes and unleashed his ching-chang-ching talk. Steven figured Corey was jealous of the car. He had no idea Corey was jealous of the stone-faced woman staring straight ahead in the backseat. Corey's mom had died of tuberculosis.

If I'd been bigger, braver, I would have said something to defend my very first friend, but I knew Corey would turn on me, ask me where's my diaper. Despite the cold, my feet freezing so bad they might crack, I had a warm feeling in my chest and didn't want to ruin it. Soon, Steven was out the gate, climbing in the front seat of the Mercedes.

In the next few minutes, Corey and the rest of the kids were picked up and gone. It was just me and Superman. The bone-aching cold. Miss Parker.

Miss Parker told me to stay where I was, that she'd be right back. I had nowhere to go and was used to waiting so that's what I did. She went into the classroom and came back out a few minutes later. Instead of heading back to the gate, she walked up to me, touched my puffy blue jacket and put her face real close.

Miss Parker had a face that made you pay attention. That's what Dad said to do. Pay attention to it. Miss Parker smoked cigarettes when she was a kid. She'd be a Miss forever.

Having anyone's face just inches away wasn't easy, but I didn't flinch. I just stood there, waited for her to talk. I've always been shy, have a hard time looking people in the eyes, but I looked Miss Parker in her murky blue ones because she'd been nice to me, gave me the corduroys and told all the kids that if anyone else laughed they'd be sent to the principal's office.

Miss Parker gave her half-smile, spoke out the right side of her mouth. "Your mom didn't answer, Joey. Is there another number I can call?"

I shook my head no. Mom had more important things to do than worry about me.

"Is there anyone else that can come get you? Maybe your dad?"

No one called Dad when he was at work. I wouldn't be first. I told Miss Parker no, held Superman tight and tried to stomp the cold right out of my boots.

This poor kid, Miss Parker thought. *I'm going to have to deal with this for the rest of the year.*

Miss Parker didn't know what to do. She'd never been stuck with a kid this long and never in the cold. The cold made her bones hurt, but she pretended it didn't.

I showed her Superman and pointed at his S. "He's made of steel."

Miss Parker walked me over to the gate. "That's nice."

I'd given up on Mom, but had an idea. It wasn't as cold when I was moving and it was just four blocks to my house.

A blue car passed by the gate, went through the intersection and pulled to the curb halfway up the block. Miss

Parker had her back to it so I pointed at the car and said, "There she is."

Miss Parker had no reason to doubt me and was already thinking about the space heater beneath her desk. "Tell your mom she needs to pick you up right here from now on. And tell her we can't wait so long."

I looked both ways and ran across the street. When I got to the other side I slowed down. I didn't want to get to the car too quick. It wasn't a Buick.

A fat man with humongous black boots pushed himself out of the car like it was a clown trick. Miss Parker didn't see because she was already heading inside.

The man walked in front of me and stopped all of a sudden. He pointed at the house we were in front of and said, "You the one fucking with my flowers?"

There weren't any flowers where he was pointing, just mounds of snow. I was smart enough not to argue and said, "No, sir."

The fat man thought I was a little fucking liar and walked to his house.

Turning around and running back to the classroom seemed like the smart thing to do. But it was just four blocks and I knew my address.

I kept walking, one boot after another, even though my toes felt ready to snap off. Then it started snowing sideways. I put my mittens out in front of my face, scrunched my eyes like Steven's. I crossed the street and kept on going, made it all the way to the next corner, where I was supposed to turn right. Or was it left?

I turned each way and tried to see the school, but everything was the same, just walls of white.

All I could do was guess so I went to the right, but that was really a left because I'd turned around in a half circle. The block was longer than I remembered.

I wasn't scared yet but I was getting close. I'd gone two or three more blocks when the snow finally stopped, the clouds parted, the sun shining, and that made me feel better, like maybe there was a God. Like He was actually looking out for me.

Still, I couldn't tell where I was. I kept walking and walking but never crying until this nice lady came up to me and knelt on the sidewalk.

I couldn't see her face because my eyes weren't really working, everything all blurry and bright. But I didn't have to see her eyes to know they were nice.

The lady put both her hands on my shoulders. "Honey," she said. "Are you lost?"

I didn't trust myself to speak.

She knew I was lost without me saying a word. Gave me the biggest hug, wrapping her arms so tight around me, tighter than I'd ever been held. "It's going to be alright," she said. "Don't you cry."

I hadn't even known I was, but the tears were there, coming down hard.

The lady didn't stop hugging me. She didn't think what a whiny baby, like the other kids. She just hugged me harder and held me until I was all done.

"Do you know where you live?"

I nodded, sniffed up the snot pouring out of my nose.

Her shiny green car was right there so she told me, "Go ahead and get in."

I went to the back door but she opened the front, the place I never sat with Mom.

The nice lady started the car and spoke real soft and called me Honey ten times trying to find out where I lived. But even though it took that long she never got mad. She said how smart I was to remember the address.

When we got to my house, the lady looked out the passenger window. "Is this where you live?"

I wanted to say no. I wanted her to drive forever. But I didn't want to lie so I said yes.

"Good," she said. "Let's get you inside. I'm sure your mother's worried."

I got out of the car, and the nice lady got out too. She put her hand around my shoulder and started down the path to the front porch. "I'll make sure she's home."

Mom's big old Buick that she was dying to trade in for something sexy was in the driveway. I didn't recognize the van parked behind it.

Even at five years old I knew what I was walking toward, that it wasn't something good.

The nice lady walked us up the three steps, her hand on me the whole way, even when she knocked on the door.

No one came so she knocked again. "Does your mom work?"

I said no and pointed to the doorbell. The nice lady pushed it and we heard a noise inside, fast footsteps.

The door opened halfway and there she was. Mom in that dark green towel that matched her eyes. She kept one arm pinched to her side to hold it up. Her hair was fire on that snow-white skin.

"Sorry, I was in the shower."

"I found him walking up and down our cul-de-sac on Cherry." The nice lady kept her hand on my shoulder, stopped me from running away. "That's over three miles from here."

"You've got to excuse him." Like I couldn't hear, Mom said, "He's a little special sometimes. What the hell were you thinking, Joey?"

The nice lady pointed at my eyes, the skin all around them. "He was out there a long time," she said. "It'd be a good idea to put something on him right away. Maybe get him to a doctor."

Mom grabbed my hand and pulled me past her, my face brushing against her towel that reeked of an over-ripe sweetness, something sour underneath.

The nice lady said, "Not butter, though. That'll make it worse."

Mom smiled, "I know what's best for my son." *Bitch.*

The nice lady started to say something. Mom slammed the door and walked me toward the kitchen. Her bedroom door was open and she was praying I wouldn't look that way. At the guy standing next to the dresser, buckling his pants, his chest all sweaty like he'd been doing pushups.

Mom saw me looking and said, "TV went out again. That's why I couldn't leave. He's fixing it." She opened the fridge, took out the tub of butter. That yellow tub was shaking, something Mom never did.

I wanted to back up, to get away from her.

She held me there and said, "Damn it, Joey, stay still."

Mom was really worried. Worried and ashamed. She couldn't care less about how she'd forgotten to pick me up. She was feeling bad about what she'd done in her room.

Mom stuck one hand into the tub, the same stuff that'd been good enough for her growing up. With a huge scoop of butter globbed in each hand, Mom said, "I need you to promise me something. Can you keep a secret?"

That was the one thing I was good at. Knowing people's secrets. Acting like I didn't.

Mom slabbed the cold butter on my tingling cheeks. "Not a word," she said. She spread the butter across my face, wasn't all that careful around my eyes. "Not about any of this. You can do that, can't you?"

I knew exactly what Mom was talking about. I said, "I won't tell."

Not like your father doesn't already know.

I hurried to my room and cried. Mom didn't know at the time I could listen to her thoughts, but she knew she couldn't trust me. After that, whenever she had a man over, she told me to go outside. When the weather was bad she locked me in my bedroom. I'd sit there and watch the rain leaking in through the tiny window.

I guess that's why I didn't freak out like the others when I first got to Brightside. I was used to captivity. The others weren't.

The first few nights I heard the screams, the uncontrollable sobbing. Sometimes the bootsteps would follow and the thuds and then silence. Other times they just let the people cry themselves to sleep. The apartment walls were too thick to hear anyone's thoughts, but we still knew what each other was thinking. You didn't have to be a telepath to know everyone was scared shitless.

　　We'd never leave Brightside.

CHAPTER THREE

A week before Brightside I was selling BMW's and drawing too much attention. It's amazing how easy it is to sell when you can hear people's thoughts. If a guy was worried about draining his kid's college tuition, I'd tell him driving a 5-Series was an investment in his career. I'd tell a woman she deserved it when I knew her husband was slamming his secretary.

Everyone came around. They didn't stand a chance.

One guy didn't like my tie, looked like one his father wore. I said my parents were coming for Christmas. Told him I might spike my dad's drink so we could make it through dinner without him reminding me that my brother was a doctor.

I didn't have a brother. The guy drove off in a convertible.

I shattered every salesman record across the country. In the last month, I sold more cars than the entire Beverly Hills dealership. My monthly commission check was going to be more than most people made in a year.

My dad called, asked if I'd heard about them taking ten more people to Brightside. I changed the subject, said I was thinking about buying a house with Michelle. He started lecturing so I hung up.

Two days before Brightside, Michelle was curled up on the couch. She was in her silky blue pajamas, both feet on my thigh, her head way down on the other end where I could barely hear her thoughts. She was drinking whiskey. She'd taken two pills. Her brain hardly making a sound.

Lily, my eight-year-old Lab whose sandy blonde hair matched Michelle's, was right below us on the soft white rug. All one hundred pounds wedged between the couch and coffee table, her warm breath on my feet.

It's exactly what I needed. Everyone at work had been talking about Brightside. How they were rounding up people all over the country. Thought Thieves were real.

Michelle just lay there watching her mind-numbing TV show. The one I couldn't watch with my last girlfriend because the doctor looked like her last boyfriend and she'd be thinking about how hard he used to fuck her, what she didn't get with me.

But not my Michelle. She was somewhere else, in that perfect little place, her thoughts a gentle sea.

I opened my computer, the article about the beautiful mountain town of telepaths, how it was in everyone's interest that they be isolated. Thought Thieves could destroy everything. Parents didn't want them in the schools or walking the streets. No one was safe.

Halfway through the article, Michelle started doing the thing with her toes, tugging my sweats and letting them go. Louder than anything she'd said all night, Michelle thought about making another drink. She tucked her toes beneath her and pushed herself up.

"Come here," I said.

I clicked on the Excel spreadsheet and pointed at the number in bold, left my hand there to block the tabs at the bottom of the screen. I waited for her to wonder why I had so many websites open, what I was trying to hide.

Michelle laid her head against my shoulder, ran her fingers on my stomach. She didn't realize I was showing her something. Sweet as ever, she asked, "You about done?"

"Yeah, just about." I pointed. "That's what I'll bring home next week."

Her mouth dropped open, stayed there. "No way!"

I wasn't trying to brag, just wanted to let her to know we could buy the house. "It's more than a down payment."

"Holy shit." Michelle's blue eyes dropped, lost what little shine they had. She was thinking about the crappy Christmas present she'd gotten me.

Her glass was empty except for some ice. I told her to make another while I finished up. Her thoughts were giving me a headache. Michelle got off the couch, was extra careful not to wake Lily.

I went back to my laptop, started closing out sites. Homeland Security. National Safety Council. Half a dozen others. Each called us domestic terrorists, all because one man said so. Our President was scared shitless when he found out what we could do. The possibility that one of us could sneak up beside him, learn his every word was a lie. The corporations, the corruption, all the money and the media. We never had a chance.

An executive order was issued to trample our rights. And the biggest irony of all, only two years before, Carl Pepper, a Thought Thief from Kansas, had single-handedly foiled the President's assassination. He'd been at a rally, heard the gunman's thoughts. There were celebrations, photos of Carl everywhere. But then someone realized there was no way Carl could've known the stuff that he knew. Thought Thieves were branded enemies. Carl showed up on the cover of *Time*. In big red letters: "Thought Thieves Among Us."

It didn't take long for laws to pop up all over the country. First, we were arrested, thrown in jail, but the regular prisoners petitioned to have us removed. That's when Brightside was created, an old mining town in California, more than a mile in the sky, high enough to make the normals feel safe.

I'd been surfing in private, but I still cleared the history before setting the laptop on the table. I didn't think Michelle would ever snoop, but there was no need to take the chance. There was no shortage of people who'd sell out friends and family for fifty thousand dollars.

Dad had taught me to trust no one.

Michelle knew I was a stickler when it came to my two-drink limit and put the bottle of Jack up in the cupboard. She came back so tall and graceful, my tipsy swan gliding across the floor, hardly a thought in her beautiful head.

I dimmed the lights and took her hand, brought her beside me on the couch. Getting so close wasn't always wise, but Michelle was different, especially on her meds.

I squeezed in behind her, the thinnest layer of clothes between us, her hair sweet vanilla, a home I never had. My right hand rested on the curve of her hip, my left arm under her neck, holding her closer, my hand on her chest, the thump of her heart. "This is perfect."

Michelle thought it was too, but bad thoughts started flying, ones about how I would eventually leave her, move on like every other guy.

I took her hand and got it scratching Lily behind the ear, knew there was no way to keep thinking bad things with that tongue licking the air, those two brown eyes so full of love.

Michelle recovered, kissed Lily's nose as a thank you. I massaged Michelle's shoulders and she sank back against me, let her mind go all dreamy. Then she thought something that tore open my heart.

She loved me.

And for the first time, I wondered if I could tell her the truth.

The next day I heard my boss, Saul, thinking I was making too many sales. Before BMW, I'd never stay at a job too long. Couple of months, tops. Just make some cash and quit. But I was so close to buying the house, I'd stayed there almost a year.

To ease Saul's suspicious mind, I tanked the next three customers.

"Boy Wonder having an off-day?" Saul laughed.

"I'm only human, Saul."

"Yeah..."

I knew my time there was up. I asked Saul if I could get my commission early, said I wanted to get something nice for Michelle. Saul said he'd think about it.

When I got home, Michelle thought I was acting strange. I'd been thinking about telling her the truth about me, but I didn't want to screw things up before I got my commission. Once the check cleared, we could take off, move anywhere, and I'd tell her everything. In public, Michelle spoke just like everyone else, saying Thought Thieves should be locked away, but I figured she'd change her mind if she knew I was one of them.

Still, I was too stressed. I just needed to clear my head and hers. I poured her a drink and took her to the bedroom.

Later, we were back in the living room, the lights off, a soft glow from Letterman because I was too comfortable to grab the remote off the coffee table next to our half-eaten dinner. Michelle and I curled up, our clothes back on. I felt calm, relaxed. And it wasn't just because Michelle took me to the place where all I can hear is myself saying Jesus, Jesus, Jesus, holy shit that feels good.

It was the closeness. The closeness to someone still awake, even if barely. Being able to lie with someone who wasn't constantly judging or whining or worrying. I wanted to live like this forever.

Lily was down below us, back from her banishment to the kitchen while Michelle and I had been busy. I was proud of her for not eating the leftover steak.

Then Lily's ears perked. She raised her head above the coffee table, looked toward the door.

I got up on my elbow and reached for the remote.

Lily got to her feet and I muted the TV, thought I heard a whisper by the window.

Michelle mumbled and I shushed her, said everything was okay. I concentrated hard, focused on the sides of my head, an inch above my ears.

A man outside the window. *This is gonna be a blast. Fuck yeah. Rock n' roll.*

Three.

Two.

One.

Then bam. The window shattered and the door boomed, flecks of wood flying through the air. Michelle's head jerked back, smacked my mouth. Lily barking.

I went for the steak knife, but Lily tipped over the table. The front door cracked open, a wall of yellow lights. I covered Michelle and looked at what just clanked off the floor, a metal canister rolling toward the couch.

The blast of light snuffed out my sight, an unbelievable pop and I couldn't hear. Everything was black, my shouts just whispers.

Michelle was flailing, not knowing anything, falling off the couch. Then came another pop and more whispers. A loud angry voice rushed toward me. He thought, *Take that.*

The blow to my back felt like a baseball bat at full speed, the pain immediate. I screamed but couldn't hear it, just the shrill ringing, piercing my brain.

I lost Michelle's thoughts, but felt her below me. Then fingers sunk into my arm, lifted me up, let me go. I bounced off the floor and weight came down on my neck, paralyzed my body.

The ringing continued. One hand then the other wrenched behind my back, metal pinching skin.

My vision came in, white and fuzzy, couldn't make out shit except someone had turned on the lights. It took me a second to see the puffy clouds were the carpet up close. Then Lily came into focus less than a foot away. Her eyes open, looking at me, the rug turning red around her. "My dog!" I shouted, "What the fuck did you do?"

The knee dug down on my neck and I pushed back because it felt like I was dying. The guy on top of me just put more pressure, made his forearm a lever between my arms and back, hoped I'd try something so he could fucking break me.

I closed my eyes and grit my teeth, said okay, okay, and gave up the fight. It got hard to breathe, even harder to think, my skull ready to crack.

His knee let off enough for me to open my eyes, the ringing beginning to fade. I watched Lily whine like never before, her back legs kicking slower and slower. From behind me, Michelle screamed, "Let me go! Lily!"

The ringing was gone, but I could only hear out my left ear. No more Michelle, just Lily and the sound of heavy footsteps shaking the floor.

Someone yelled, "Gomez, get him over here."

All the pressure left my neck as Gomez told Hendricks, "Yes, Sir." I got yanked up by my forearms, dragged three steps, screaming because that's all I could do. Gomez used his knee to knock my head the other way then dropped me down on the carpet, right next to the knife that would've got us killed if I'd been a little faster.

Gomez's knee came down on my neck, made it so I couldn't look away no matter how much I wanted.

Hendricks had Michelle bent over the edge of the couch, her head smashed on the cushion, eye shut and mouth open, somehow holding back a scream. Hendricks stood behind Michelle, wedged in tight between her trembling legs, his hand on her cranked back wrist. He wore all black, no letters anywhere, hid behind the helmet and face shield, ski mask beneath.

His eyes were the warning. Two black hollow points aiming at me.

Thanks to the mask, I couldn't see Hendrick's lips moving, but he asked if I could hear him.

Even then, all jacked up, I had the wits not to say shit.

There was no question Hendricks was talking out loud when he said, "Tear this place apart. He's got something somewhere. Everyone does. Grab his computer."

Michelle screamed, "Why are you doing this?"

He told me to go ahead and tell her. Tell her what I could do.

My vision was too clear, the biggest crack tearing through Michelle.

"Joe, what'd you do?"

Hendricks shut her up with a twist of her wrist. I didn't see the mask move when he thought, *Nine plus two.*

Say it, and it'll all stop.

I kept quiet, felt the puff of breath on my arm, Lily's nose on my elbow.

Gomez must've seen it because he thought it was some sad shit, didn't get why Hendricks lit her up in the first place. "Someone do something about this," he said.

Boots stomped across the floor, each one rattling my chest. All casual, like the guy was ordering a coffee, he said, "Friendly fire." Then two blasts, each a jolt through my body.

The whining was over, Michelle's face buried in the cushion, sobbing like Lily was her child.

Hendricks let go of Michelle's wrist, put his hand on her waist.

Nine plus two, fuckhead.

I said nothing and he said, "Fine. Get this piece of shit out of here."

The ski mask covered his smile, but I knew it was there. He thought about what kind of questioning he'd put Michelle through. How she'd do and say whatever he asked once she found out the prison term for harboring a terrorist.

Gomez jerked me to my feet and Hendricks asked, "What's it going to be?" All I had to do was say it. *Nine plus two.*

Michelle didn't deserve any of this. I told her I was sorry.

Then I said it.

"Eleven."

CHAPTER FOUR

I met with Sharon on Day 41, holding off as long as possible after the Rachel incident. I didn't want to hear her bullshit or talk about my feelings. Sharon invited me in, asked me to sit. I stared at the steady stream from her Zen waterfall. We didn't speak for at least a minute, Sharon smiling, her back nice and tall, perfect posture. I felt myself slouching, almost to the point I thought I'd slide right off the couch.

"What would you like to talk about today?" she asked.

"Nothing."

"Nothing?"

I hated how easily Sharon sifted through my thoughts. I tried not to think about Rachel, Lily, this whole fucked up place.

You don't have to say anything, Sharon thought. *We can just do this silently if it makes it easier.*

I backed into the couch. "Don't you have to want to share for therapy?"

"Therapy can work in many ways."

"Just stay out of my head."

Sharon smoothed out her white slacks, her short blonde hair plastered down. Sharon had the longest range of anyone in Brightside. She could hear your thoughts from fifty feet on a clear day. I never understood how she stayed so calm. She heard thoughts wherever she went. I guess the meditation helped. She said it did. I heard that soft humming mantra flowing from her skull.

Silent therapy made sense. Just cut through the crap and spill out every thought. Even with the waterfall's soothing sounds and these yellow walls to make us feel comfortable, people never say what's really on their mind. It's how society works. We glance off the truth, avoid conflict. We're trained to keep it pleasant, hold back. Silent therapy allowed Sharon to get past all that, but I didn't want her digging, not that I could do anything to block her.

"Where's Rachel?" I asked.

"Safe."

Right.

Sharon smiled, even as I imagined strangling her.

"It's perfectly natural to be angry, Joe. Brightside takes getting used to. We're all on different timelines. But if you're willing to open up, you'll see how wonderful it can be."

I pictured Rachel, catatonic, staring at nothing in The Cabin, the place rule-breakers were sent to drool.

"Carlos says you're doing well. Your sales are up."

Carlos was my boss. He wore American flag pins on his tie.

"How long do I have to be here?" I asked.

"Not long." Sharon studied me, staring, probing my head. "You know, I have a good feeling about you."

"You're going to be disappointed."

"I don't know. We'll see."

I'd only been forced to see Sharon twice. The first time was the hardest: Day 1 in Brightside.

There wasn't a trial after the raid. They held a group of us in a cell for the night. They woke us by yelling. My right ear was still out from the flashbang, my left muffled with a light ringing. They brought us to the helicopter outside and took us up into the sky. Some thought it was beautiful, the rising sun over the cute mountain town. I never saw it, kept my eyes shut, too afraid to look down, see the drop. Someone was telling us about Brightside, gave us a quick history. I only heard every fifth word, focused on my clenched fists cuffed behind my back, my pounding heart. Seemed like we'd been rising for hours, but it was probably only minutes. My eyelids didn't open until the helicopter landed. I took a deep breath. The air burned my lungs, so cold, thin. I thought I might pass out.

They finally unlocked the cuffs, told us we were going to be processed. Brightside loved paperwork. We had to sign forms stating we were here voluntarily. They told us we had no choice, that if we didn't sign, our stay would be unpleasant. If we just scratched our names down, things would get a lot easier. I don't remember signing, but I must have, because they took me to human resources, helped me land a job. They liked I had a background in sales. People were smiling, nodding. They said this was going to be fun. They loved that word.

"The ice cream parlor is fun."

"Karaoke nights are super fun."

"Summer is the most fun. We have intramural kick-ball games."

Next, I was sent to Sharon. All of us new residents were sitting in her pleasant waiting room. "Know Thyself, Love Thyself" painted in pink flowery sweeps across the yellow wall.

I recognized one of the guys, Phuc Li, the world famous poker player. He'd won every major tournament, collected eleven bracelets, racked up millions. He even had his own late night poker show on TV. Some called him "Lucky Li." Others used his first name. Turned out he wasn't lucky at all. I realized I'd been in the wrong business. He'd made more money playing poker in a single night than I made in the year at BMW.

Phuc stared at me from behind his sunglasses and smiled.

Everyone else stared at their laps or the floor. I heard one guy thinking about his wife, the bitch who'd turned him in. Another woman thought about her kids stuck with their alcoholic father.

Brightsiders weren't allowed to keep their kids. There were petitions, but they wouldn't change anything, normals couldn't stay on the mountain. After some time, we could have visitors, not that I expected anyone to ever show.

Someone mumbled, "Cut that shit out."

The guy beside me thought, *Yeah, who brought the retard?*

I wondered what I was doing and checked my feet to make sure I wasn't tapping.

Not you. My neighbor nudged his hand to the right, his last three fingers purple and swollen. *Einstein over there.*

The guy reading the comic book in the corner looked old enough for college, but his extra tight Donald Duck t-shirt and white name tag with big blocky letters said it was more likely he'd been hijacked from preschool. The tag was scrunched up and falling off, but his bright blue hat with red embroidered letters spelled out DANNY for everyone to see.

I turned my head so I could hear what was pissing people off. The rustle of paper and squeak of the comic book's battered cover as Danny rubbed it back and forth in his right hand.

Even though I hadn't met many Thought Thieves before Brightside, I'd assumed they were all masterminds, or at least intelligent, definitely brighter than me. There were two guys between us, but I did my best to block them out and focused on Danny. I listened to him silently sound out each word in his head.

It wasn't right to listen in, but I needed an escape from reality and I'd never heard GI Joe in slow motion. There were more "BOOMs!" and "BLAMs!" than I was expecting, but never any death. All that noise, all those bullets. I guessed there was no friendly fire.

The clack of heels stopped the story. Sharon stood in the doorway, cool and collected in her white pantsuit, hands folded in front of her. She was over fifty, but could have passed for thirty-five. All that age-defying meditation. Sharon retreated into her office, her short blonde hair sprayed into place. She called me by my first name like I was a friend and told me to step inside. She got behind her mahogany desk and waved me over like I was a puppy. "Come on."

She had me sit. Waited for me to speak first. When I wouldn't, she told me about Brightside, how it wasn't so bad, that I just had to settle in.

I later learned that things hadn't always been so cheery. The place had changed. In the beginning, people like us were kept in The Cabin or behind steel bars in the basements. Too many took their own lives.

Then the politicians and lawyers arrived. Phillip, the ex-Senator. Grace, the New York D.A. with her perfect conviction rate. Phillip and Grace formed the Brightside Council. They turned things around, got us more funding, lessened the security, even put a stop to the sterilization. Brightsiders could have babies and families. We could live normal lives.

"Things could be worse," Sharon said.

I didn't see how, even after I was shown my new apartment and taken on a tour of the town. We were given free meals for the first two days. After that, we had to pay for everything with the money we earned. Outside contact was forbidden the first week. No calls, no letters back home. Once Sharon and the Council deemed us safe, we could make contact. Monitored contact. We could also receive gifts. Not that I expected anything. After they dragged me from my place, Michelle thought I was a piece of shit. And my parents...right. They'd forgotten half of my birthdays as a kid.

The only gift I received was from the Council. A hundred dollar gift card I could use anywhere in Brightside. Day 7 I bought an iPod to block out all the thoughts. Danny bought comic books and a postcard to send to his sister, Sara. A bright blue pencil so he could sign his name.

Danny stood by the rack, the sharpened pencil clenched in his fist, his thumb sliding down then up to the eraser. He kept doing it as he stared at the comic books, his thumb going back and forth, his hat down low to hide most of his face.

Sara was there when they took him. Danny had been listening to a store clerk's thoughts. Two black guys were standing by the rack of CDs. Danny said he'd watch them to make sure they weren't stealing. Sara told him to be quiet, but the black guys had heard him, started shoving Danny. The clerk thought about going for his pistol. Danny told him no guns.

Suddenly, the guys and the clerk were on the same side. Sara begged for them to just let her and Danny go, but the Boots arrived. Danny was cuffed, taken.

I felt bad for listening and moved to the sketchpads. I used to sketch when I was a kid. Hadn't done it in years, but something about the pad and colored pencils made me want to pick it up. From the end of the aisle, Danny asked if I was a drawer. He sounded like a six-year-old cowboy with a speech impediment.

Thanks to the cowards too scared to knock, my right ear was still next to useless. I turned my head and Danny repeated the question. He used his finger to draw on the air because I was the one being slow.

I pulled down my sleeves to cover the purple bruises ringing both wrists and said, "I used to."

Danny tugged on his hat and walked over real slow, his custom-order Dino-shoes flashing red.

When Danny got to where the average person would stop, I said, "Cool shoes, man."

He surprised me and took another step, came in close enough for me to tell two of his favorite foods were peanut butter and pickles. Danny didn't say a word about my wrists, just pointed at his feet. "T-Rex is my favorite."

I nodded. "Mine, too."

He backed up a bit to give me some room, but stayed well within my six-foot range. Like he wasn't so sure he was saying it right, he said, "I'm Danny." His right hand was busy with the pencil so he stuck out his left with a rolled-up comic book in it. He raised his head and showed me his hazel eyes that were too close together.

Having someone look me in the eyes has never been easy, but Dad taught me to watch them when someone's talking.

He said if you want to know what people look like when they lie, just look them in the eyes and ask how they're doing.

Dad said the eyes show everything. They show the real you. And that was something I didn't want anyone seeing. Especially some stranger.

But Danny didn't have the eyes of a stranger. They were the kindest shade of hazel, the softest brown I'd ever seen. There was a whole lot of hurt filling those eyes, but the flecks of gold said he'd be alright.

I gave the comic book a shake like that's how everyone did it. "Nice to meet you, Danny."

Danny turned his neck like he was trying to get out the kink then pointed at the sketchpad and asked, "You a pro?"

"No, just for fun." That word "fun" making me want to puke.

Danny picked up the sketchpad and the box of colored pencils. He said, "You need these."

I still had money left on the gift card, but thought I should save it. I followed Danny to the register and told him, "I'm not sure I want to buy them."

Danny unzipped his blue fanny pack and paid with his own card. Then he handed over the pad and pencils and said, "Happy new home."

"Danny... I can't accept this."

"You have to. I want to see you draw."

"I haven't done it since I was a kid."

"Need practice. Come on."

Danny ran out the door, over to a bench, plopped down. Reluctantly, I sat and opened the pad to the very first page. "What would you like me to draw?"

Danny said he didn't know, but I knew he was being shy. I turned and listened for his thoughts.

I got nothing, the first time that'd ever happened to me.

I'd been around people who didn't think much or were always distracted, caught up in the moment. But this was different. With Danny there was nothing. Not one thought, just that smile.

Danny's kind eyes got worried.

I took out the charcoal pencil, finally heard Danny's thoughts. "You didn't ruin it." I gave him a smile and said, "It's cool. It'll be a surprise."

I turned off my mind and looked across the park. Rachel was sitting by a tree. I'd met her at work, but we'd barely spoken, both of us too scared, knowing we were being watched. My pencil got moving. In less than a minute, I had an outline.

* * *

It was a half-day, Mom another no-show. But this time I was six, old enough to use the under-the-mat key. I hoped I'd have the house to myself, even though that meant Mom would be at someone else's. But she was home, laughing so loud she didn't hear me open the back door.

I walked past the dryer's low rumble, my Ghostbusters backpack in one hand, my drawing in the other. I heard a man's voice, the aerobics instructor, the one with the big dick.

"My kid's a regular Picasso. Look at all the crap I've got on my fridge." Mom laughed.

I crumpled up the drawing and ran to my room. She came in later, heard me crying. She wished I wasn't such a whiny brat. She tried to console me, make me feel better, but her thoughts told the truth and made everything so much worse.

* * *

Danny couldn't stay still, kept shifting, tapping his legs like a drum, thumbing the paint off his pencil. I made him my helper and asked for colors, but he didn't know them all by name. I pointed. He figured it out. By the time I was done with the drawing I was ready to crumple it up like I did with Mom. Anyone who saw it would know I was no artist, I'd never been good with faces, but I'd sort of captured Rachel's insecurity, the way she adjusted, sucked in so her belly wouldn't spill over her skirt.

Danny asked if I was done. I tore it out and handed it to him.

He said it was perfect and I said it was nothing.

Danny held up the picture, his eyes all shiny. "It's everything."

He jumped to his feet and ran over to Rachel. Handed it to her. He pointed back to me and she smiled. I felt guilty and left, wandered out into the forest and carved Michelle's name in that tall pine tree. They hadn't told us we could venture into the woods, but I didn't care, just kept walking until I found that tree. Pulled out my apartment keys and dug into the bark. For a second, I thought the key might break, but I just kept carving, digging, needing to see her name, pretend I could make things right.

If only I'd told her the truth, hadn't been so greedy about the house, been smarter like Dad had told me to be. Maybe then I wouldn't have ended up here, trapped on this fucking mountain.

Fucking Saul.

I knew he was suspicious at BMW, knew he was thinking about turning me in, but I pressed, thought I had a few days.

When Michelle's name was finally carved, I fell against the tree and wept. I can't remember ever crying like that as an adult. My mind falling into the past. I thought about getting lost in the snow as a kid, that nice woman hugging me, taking me home.

The home I'd never see again.

The sun began to set, and the temperature dropped, the tears warm trails down my cheeks. I finally got up, walked back towards the apartment. That's when I heard the car. It rounded the curve way up the mountain. It was dark blue, definitely a Chrysler. The same kind Michelle drove.

I started running. She'd come to save me!

The car was half a block away. I still couldn't see the driver, but I knew it was Michelle. I wasn't a piece of shit. She'd forgiven me, probably knew about my ability all along.

I ran into the middle of the street, waving my arms like an idiot.

"Michelle! Michelle!"

The car was going fast and headed right for me. I closed my eyes, thought it couldn't stop, the screech of brakes louder than anything I've ever heard.

I opened my eyes, the car only a foot from me, its front door thrown open. It was the quickest I've gone from one feeling to another. First thinking I was free, saved, still loved, then straight to scared shitless, because the driver was out of the car, running right at me, screaming for me to get down, his big fucking pistol pointed right at my face.

It happened so quick I just saw flashes. Blue jeans, black windbreaker, angry brown eyes. And then he was on me, kicking my legs out, pushing my head, slamming me to the ground.

His black boot went on my cheek like he was squash-ing a bug. He shouted, "Stay the fuck down."

I yelled like a little girl. "Get off of me!" Then I grabbed his boot and pushed it off to prove I wasn't.

The boot went away, but metal came back. Hard. The barrel of the gun pushed at my temple, dug into the bone like it didn't need a bullet.

I could barely open my jaw. It sounded all screwed up when I said, "What'd I do?"

"You want to die?"

I didn't try to talk. Laid still. Focused on the cold gravel digging into my cheek, not on the gun twitching, pressing like all this guy wanted to do was pull the trigger and splatter my brain across the street.

He put more pressure on the gun, his breath straight caffeine. "You think it'd matter if I killed you?"

Two footsteps approached, cowboy boots. And then Melvin, Brightside's sheriff, asked, "Everything okay?"

I wanted to say no, it wasn't right at all, but the gun was still there, pinning me down.

Black boots said, "Yeah, it's fine. Go back inside where it's warm."

Melvin said, "I'm okay. Reminds me of home."

"I was just finishing up with this guy." The prick tapped the side of my head, letting me know where he wanted to put the bullet.

"I think he learned his lesson," Sheriff Melvin said.

Black boots pulled the gun off me and kicked my leg when he walked back to his car. "You get up before I'm gone and you'll be sorry."

The Boots called themselves agents, but I never would. Even the term "cop" was too good for them.

Face down on the ground, though, I'd never been so still, my eyes on the American flag rippling back and forth.

Melvin chuckled. When I didn't look at him, he said, "Know what I'm thinking right now?"

I turned just my face because I figured he wouldn't leave until I did. He stood there, a huge smile hanging underneath the darkest pair of sunglasses.

"I was thinking about what that guy asked you. I was thinking no one would care."

I got to my feet and stepped to the side. The Chrysler zipped by and for a split second I was staring into the eyes of the man who could have ended me. I wished he had.

Melvin asked, "You okay?"

I waited until the car made its way around the Circle and disappeared down Main Street. "Yeah, I'm alright."

Melvin put his hand on my shoulder and guided me to the curb. He had this bushy white mustache, which made him look like the guy from the Quaker Oats commercials on a bender.

"Have a seat a second."

I felt like I'd just been kicked in the balls, the body, the face, but I deserved it. I was the idiot who ran in front of a car. The idiot that thought Michelle would ever want to see me again. Even if she lived in the next city over, she wouldn't come. Not unless it was to demand an apology or watch me suffer.

Melvin used the side of his cowboy boot to sweep the bloody gravel at my feet. "You sure you're okay?" He pointed at The Cabin. "We can go in there."

I didn't know much about The Cabin at the time, but I knew enough to stay away.

I wiped off my hands, pretended like I didn't want to cry. I didn't have to ask Melvin to leave me alone or tell him I couldn't talk. All I did was look up and read the banner rippling above the Square, the big red letters on both sides:

"Welcome to Brightside. Welcome Home."

CHAPTER FIVE

Brightside was plastic. It was all just pretend. Everything. The jobs, the town, the Council, our freedom to shop. Each detail fabricated so we wouldn't jump off the edge of this damn mountain.

And the plastic rubbed off. It let me pretend Rachel and I were in love, that Michelle had come to rescue me, that I had options. It almost got me killed.

Day 8, I showed up to my job and pretended to work. Rachel kept sneaking glances. She was out of my range. The first few times I'd seen her, she wore thick pants, long-sleeved shirts. This time she was in that red leather skirt, her legs smooth and sexy all the way to the slit.

I wished I'd never drawn that stupid picture.

She said she was going to try out the diner. Heard they had good burgers. She asked if I'd like to go. She wanted to pretend this was all just fucking fine. I guess I needed that, too, because I said sure.

The first few dates were intense. Neither of us had been with a Thought Thief before Brightside. It amplified every quiet moment. No more pretense. No more lying.

Even the bad shit felt good, because it was true.

Our accelerated relationship let us believe we'd met our soul mates. I didn't even care when I received Michelle's letter, the one telling me how happy she was I'd been taken to Brightside, that I was out of her life. She said she felt raped by our relationship, that I'd lied, stolen every private thought. She wanted me to die a slow, painful death.

But to hell with her. I had Rachel, someone who loved me for me. It made me feel worthy. It made me better.

I did drawings for Danny, promised him one a week. Sometimes I gave him two. I wasn't a real artist, but Danny liked them. They brightened his day.

I'd spent my whole life hurting and disappointing other people, manipulating them. With Danny I just had to move my pencil. Vertical and horizontal lines flying across the paper. The images took shape, a massive brick wall filling the page, a hawk soaring through the sky.

My entire second week in Brightside, I'd sit on the bench sketching, put on my oversized headphones. I knew people laughed. I'd heard all their silent jokes, but I didn't give a shit.

I grabbed the eraser, put a giant hole in the middle of the wall, and then picked up the blue pencil. Brilliant blue skies and a luscious green meadow on the other side of the wall. A pile of broken bricks gathered under the hole, a young boy climbing up it. The boy had a lopsided grin on his face as he grasped the hand of an unseen man reaching through. Freedom.

It's not very often I looked at one of my drawings and smiled. They were never that good, but this one was and

Danny loved it. All he needed was a drawing to make him happy.

Rachel needed more, especially when she heard me dreaming of Michelle. Day 39 when I couldn't give her the answer, because pretending was so fucking exhausting. Then the Boots came to take her away.

* * *

Two nights later, after my session with Sharon on Day 41, I found myself walking. I couldn't sleep. It wasn't as cold as it'd been the day I burned my five-year-old face, but cold enough to snuggle into my jacket and zip it up all the way. Cold enough to remind me my low expectations for this place had been way too high.

The Cabin sat up on the hill, where Rachel was most likely sitting in some catatonic state, wondering why she ever trusted me. I could have visited, but I didn't want to see what I'd done.

I shoved both hands in my pockets and went to the railing overlooking the park. I leaned on it, but not too far because the weld looked weak and fifteen feet was only high enough to hurt. Still, it was too high. I stepped back.

Brightside spread out before me, our nothing of a town stuck on the side of a mountain. The cemetery was another two hundred feet up. Three hundred yards to the welcome center. The town of telepaths was hard at work, my thoughts all my own.

The statue of Jonas Stonebrook stood by the pond. Jonas was the founding father of this place. His son, William, had been branded a Thought Thief. Some guy shot him in his home. William bled out on his bathroom floor. Jonas was old, angry, thought there was a better way. He sold the land up here for a buck, thought he was giving the government a humane option.

The statue of the skinny old man with his gray hair and scraggly beard stood stoically by the frozen water, almost like he was lost in thought. I wondered if he regretted creating Brightside.

I stayed on the path until I hit the woods, the full and bright moon illuminating the way. I headed for the tallest tree, found the five long slashes buried in the bark. Michelle's name scratched out. Rachel's name in her place. I pulled out the knife I'd swiped from the diner, started scratching it out. I don't know why. I suppose I was simply crossing off another woman, another broken heart, bullshit love.

I'd told myself things could last with Michelle, even if she found out the truth. Then I tried to believe it was even better with Rachel.

Always pretending. Making shit up in my head to believe I had a chance, that happiness was possible, even for someone like me.

Sharon would say my expectations were the problem, that they were setting me up for failure. Reality can never live up to your imagination. Expectations imply a future, which doesn't exist. There's only the present.

The next day I met Krystal. I was at the deli and something smacked the tile behind me, made me jump. I spun around and bumped into this amazing ass, grabbed it for balance so neither of us fell.

Krystal was bent over, straight-legged, picking a small box up off the floor. I couldn't see her face, but the bright red hair gave Krystal away. That and her ass pointed right at me, her white bakery coat so short I could see the tiniest strand of her red thong.

I'd seen her a few times, but always thought she was too intimidating, her arms covered in tattoos, her pierced nipples on full display under that tight shirt.

I wasn't thinking about Rachel locked away in The Cabin. I also wasn't thinking about work because I was done for the day. I was only thinking about the present. Krystal's ass.

I let go of it and said, "I'm sorry." I left my hand on her hip to help her up. Kept it there because she was nice to touch.

Krystal didn't pull away. She backed up into me, gave me a little bump then turned around. I knew her name, but we'd never been this close.

Her eyes so green I never had a chance.

I let myself think every nasty thought, let her know it didn't bother me she was listening. Krystal was used to guys thinking these things. But they'd never say it out loud. I wasn't either, but thinking it like a roar.

In just about the sweetest voice I'd ever heard, Krystal said, "Hi there." Then she stuck out the tip of her tongue, slid it all the way around to wet her smile.

Aren't you different?

You have no idea.

Krystal did the thing with her tongue again. Real slow. She was sizing me up, taking in her latest catch. "You doing anything right now?"

I shook my head. Couldn't believe what was happening, but I was standing right there, letting my thoughts cascade. She loved it. Krystal wanted to fuck me. I couldn't wait to oblige. I pointed at her uniform. "Aren't you working?"

"I can do whatever I want." She took off her work coat and headed for the door. "You coming?"

My holy-shit-this-is-really-happening happiness shattered. Sheila, this nosey bitch from work, stood four feet away. She was friends with Rachel.

Krystal walked by Sheila, completely ignored her. Krystal wasn't ashamed she hadn't said a word about Charlie, the guy she was dating. I hadn't said a word about Rachel.

Sheila looked down at her watch, her long brunette hair hiding her face. She didn't want to see me. She hadn't meant to overhear. She wouldn't tell anyone else. She promised. My new attitude turned Sheila on.

Krystal pulled me out the door and paraded me back to her place. Neither of us giving a shit what anyone thought.

Lodge Two was the exact duplicate of my building. Walking to work in the morning, I could see right through every window.

Krystal's room was halfway down on the left side, right in the middle, overlooking the park. Right where she wanted it so everyone could see what she did.

I pinned her up against the wall, ripped her underwear off like she said to. We fell on the floor, did things to each other I've never even imagined.

I felt nothing but the moment.

I used to feel guilt. Women would look at me, their minds giving away secrets, a map into their pants. I'd take advantage, use their thoughts to get them in bed. They never knew what a dirtbag I was.

But Krystal knew and she fucking loved it.

Of course, I ruined it. It's what I do. We'd just finished, both of us sweaty, the sheets all bunched up. She thought about the last time she'd done something like this, back in Vegas, no holes barred at the Green Door.

I wondered if anyone could count the number of men who'd seen Krystal's tits. How many tourists had stuffed dollar bills into her G-string, let their hands linger, feel her soft skin? How many men had she gotten hard, whispered in their ears, telling them every dirty thing they wanted to hear?

Krystal rolled over and tugged up her panties. "Fuck. You."

"I'm sorry. I didn't mean it."

I'm always thinking about everything the wrong way.

The answers didn't matter. None of it did. Krystal used what she had to trick men into handing over fistfuls of cash. It wasn't any different than what I did at BMW. Krystal didn't judge me for how I made my money. I had no right to question her. But there I was, doing the same shit I always did.

Krystal threw my clothes at me. "Get the fuck out!"

With other women, I'd deluded myself into thinking it was okay to manipulate them. It made up for all the terrible things I had to hear. Krystal felt the same, but she didn't want to listen to my bullshit thoughts. She kicked me out, me hopping around with one pant leg on, trying to slip in the other.

Before she slammed the door I looked at Krystal. Really looked at her.

Krystal was her hair. Torch crimson. Fire red.

Krystal was her clothes. Bakery jacket a size too small, no bra underneath. Her sweatshirt Couture, proving she was worth every penny.

Krystal was her face. Beautiful. Molded. Injected.

Krystal was Mom.

That's what I thought about as I hopped out of the building. The way Mom loved to go to church to shake her ass for all the lonely men, just like Krystal.

* * *

I was five, two days after I'd been lost in the snow, my cheeks burnt and basted with butter. Mom took me to church wearing her tightest red dress, the one that pushed her boobs up, the thin black bra straps peeking out from the shoulders.

Dad never went to church with us. "No, I think I'm going to pass," he'd say. "Maybe I'll go later." But he never went anywhere with large groups. I didn't understand why.

Mom opened the church door super slow, loving the loud creak that made almost everyone turn around and look. Especially the men.

All I wanted was to not be noticed, embarrassed of my cheeks. Not Mom. She wasn't there to blend. She was there to be coveted so she got her hips swinging back and forth even further.

Teenage boys sat up straighter. Men pretended they were looking at the sorry little kid behind her. Women shook their heads.

When we got to the third row, Mom did something with her hand, touching her face once, her chest three times. The row was full. No one moved, just pretended they didn't see Mom standing there in her blood of Christ red dress, the black beneath.

Mom squeezed in, pulled me beside her, my shoulder rubbing her arm, the closest we'd been in a while. The bench was harder than anything I'd sat on, the reason I thought so many people were on their knees.

Mom saw me looking at the exit and pointed down by my feet. She whispered, "Pray for your sins."

I got down, glad to be further away from her perfume and thoughts. But I heard the others, all the scary shit they were thinking. I heard them pray for the dying, the dead, for a piece of my mom's ass, for forgiveness of sins, for winning the damn lottery, swearing they'd donate some. Some guys were thinking about sex or their fantasy football teams. A teenager thought I was lucky I got to suck on Mom's tits.

I blocked the voices by doing my own thinking, wondering what a sin was, figuring I probably had a bunch of them, way more than my share. I wasn't sure how to pray, but guessed it was like wishing, just another thing that wouldn't come true.

Mom said that was enough and pulled me back towards the people behind me, all their thoughts filling my head, making me want to smash it.

I pressed my hands to my eyes to help quiet the voices. Especially Mom who was thinking about the man in front of us, the one with two kids, but no wife.

My cheeks still stung when I pushed on them. Mom hit my arm. I put my hands back on my lap and there were huge flakes of skin sticking to my fingers.

I rubbed my hand on my pants then touched my face to see if there was more. Every time my hand came down, more pieces came with it, each one bigger than the one before. My cheeks were shedding skin. I prayed my whole body would do that. Just rub away. The whole thing.

I kept trying until Mom saw the mess covering my pants. She grabbed my hand, jerked it away from my face, and squeezed it, hard. She looked right at me, at the big patches under each eye. "I can't take you anywhere," she said.

"I'm sorry."

Mom didn't hear me. She was too busy pushing me out of the pew, saying excuse me as we stormed out, some people thinking what a terrible mother dragging her diseased son.

* * *

When I stepped out onto the Square, I kept thinking about Mom, Krystal, their tits and asses. That's what I was thinking when I almost bumped into Wayne King. His eyes smiling above all that beard, spilling over his orange jumpsuit.

Mommy and your girlfriend...fucking nice.

Wayne leaned on his snow shovel, his eyes never leaving me, not even when the guard took notice, started walking past the dozen other people in jumpsuits. The people who'd snapped long before Brightside. They'd killed people, robbed banks, tortured. Everyone's thoughts infected their brains, turned them into savages.

Most Brightsiders cheated. They scammed, got women into the sack, drained a guy's life savings. Some just used it to win at charades.

Nothing violent.

Not like the ones in orange. The only people here kept behind bars, allowed to work outside if they were good. Normal prisons couldn't hold them. They always found a way out.

Wayne knew the Brightside guard was coming, already telling him to get back to work.

At just four feet away, I heard Wayne's thoughts loud and clear. That I looked like his favorite victim. The one he gutted real good and scooped out the insides. Turned the belly into his outhouse. The one he filled up then left for the bears.

The victim had looked at him wrong. Thought he needed a bath. That's the kind of sick fuck Wayne was.

Wayne said, "We should find some time to talk more about your mom."

The guard ran up. "We have a problem, King?"

"No problem at all, sir." Wayne went back to shoveling snow. He whistled to the image of my mom and Krystal's naked bodies rolling around on the bed.

I tried not to run back to my place, tried to get Wayne's sick thoughts out of my head. Everything was spinning, my head, stomach. I couldn't breathe. I'd heard enough twisted shit in my life to fill a canyon. People weren't as innocent as we're led to believe. They think about horrifying acts. But they're just thoughts, fleeting desires. Wayne King followed through.

That image of Mom and Krystal knocking around my brain. I'd never thought of Mom that way. Other men had. So many others. Did I crave that attention? Is that why I chose the women I did?

My thoughts were interrupted by the strangest thing: a present at my door. A medium box wrapped so poorly I assumed it was from Danny. Then I noticed it'd been opened and rewrapped. Brightside inspected every gift from the outside.

This was from my dad.

CHAPTER SIX

Day 100 and I'm pouring bleach. I have no idea if it's covering the smell. I've been inhaling it too long, even with the shirt wrapped around my mouth. There's just so much blood, all the little hunks of flesh. On the ceiling, the floor. I just need this to buy us some time in case they come looking.

Two air fresheners are on that table. I plug the first one in beside the dresser. Can't even glance at the closet when I pass by on my way to the bathroom.

The closet. The fucking closet...

I take a deep breath, clear out the bad thoughts. I get in the shower. Scrub so hard I think I'm going to peel off my skin like that stupid kid in church. Soon, everything is wiped, as good as it's going to get. My watch says I have ten minutes to make it to work. The last day I'll ever step foot in that place.

My shirt's hanging on the chair. Blood-free. I put it on, ignore all the cracks overhead, and step in front of the full-length mirror. Need to make sure I don't look like someone who just stepped out of a slaughterhouse.

My shoes are beat up but have enough tread to make it through the snow, up the hillside. My wrinkle-free khakis aren't slacks, but they're ironed. My pearl-white button-down with its crisp collar the only thing making me feel like the salesman I used to be. The guy I'm really going to have to be today to pull this off.

I check the contents of my bag: sunglasses, iPod, my oversized headphones. Necessities for surviving Brightside.

I look back at the closet. If anyone comes in here, we're screwed. I've been running through the plan in my head, but every time it ends badly, so fucked up it makes me think I should just grab the shotgun now.

But I still have to come back.

I head for the door. The knob is cold. Nothing compared to the little world on the other side, but I'm going to face it. Day 100. Ready or not.

My beat up shoes crunch two pieces of broken gifts on the floor. So many pieces I had to puzzle together. What Dad really wanted. My chance to get out.

To think it all started with that fucking fish.

* * *

I don't remember how long I sat on my bed with Dad's gift on Day 44. Fingering the re-taped paper, that sad little bow mashed down and frayed. He'd never wrapped anything when I was a kid. Just handed me the Rite-Aid bag, the contents visible through the cheap, white plastic.

I'd been in Brightside a month and a half and my parents hadn't written, hadn't called, so seeing this gift filled me with dread. My father loved to lecture. I pictured some hand-carved sign that read, "Told You So!"

Finally, I unwrapped it. Tore off the paper. That stupid fish staring at me, head twisted to the left, that tiny red button telling me to press it. I did, and Billy Bass sang, "Take Me to the River." Tail flapping, mouth opening and closing to Al Green's words.

My father wasn't known for practical jokes. I'd only seen him laugh a few times as a kid. He never bought me anything fun to play with, unless it had to do with hunting or fishing, but even then, he lectured me on responsibility and sucked all the fun right out of it. We went on a few fishing trips to the Black River in Ohio. Father-son weekends because Mom said it'd be good for us. I knew it was just so she could have men sleep over.

* * *

I was seven the first time I saw a real fish. Dad dressed the part in full-length waders and a black vest with pockets so he could stay in the middle of the river all day. I wished he would have.

Dad had just reeled in a fish the size of my forearm, brought it to the bank. He pointed at the flopping flounder. "See that, Joe? Look at it."

"What's it doing?"

Dad took off his hat to wipe his forehead. He knelt down beside me and put his hand on my shoulder. "Its finale."

Even though Dad never got this close, all I could think about was the fish. I knew fish couldn't talk like Billy

Bass, but this one was screaming, trying to snap its spine. I told Dad, "Put it back."

"No."

"PUT IT BACK IN THE WATER!"

The fish flailed and Dad caught it in mid-air. He put its wriggling belly a few inches from my face. "You see that hook? Look, son, I want you to see this."

"I don't wanna."

"Open your eyes," Dad said.

Goddamnit, look!

Dad turned my chin back to the fish, down its mouth. Pink goo pushing around both sides of the shiny red metal. It was impossible to see anything else.

"See how it went right through? Even if I could free the hook, I'd tear up his insides getting it out. I can't put this guy back." The fish kept fighting. Dad's hand squeezing so tight the eyes were going to pop.

The part of the hook poking out wasn't that big. I figured the fish would be okay if it got back in the water. I said, "Try it."

"No." He set the slowing fish against the ground. His other hand reached to his side, brought out the knife I'd never seen unfolded. "It's over."

The knife ripped through the air. Ripped through the fish. Its severed head tilted onto its side, one big eye staring, accusing, saying, Remember this.

Dad wiped the blade on the grass, acted like it was no big deal. Then he got up and walked back into the river, sang some stupid song about rolly, polly fish heads.

Maybe he did have a twisted sense of humor after all.

* * *

Billy Bass's song ended on my lap, the batteries almost drained. There were two more giant D-Cell batteries inside the package, but I saw no reason to continue Dad's joke. Billy Bass would sit in my closet until Day 74 when everything finally made sense.

I didn't know my father was trying to help.

* * *

I was in fourth grade playing football in the field behind the school. Corey and Gilbert versus Steven and me. They were bigger, faster, stronger. They won every time. I never cheated because at least they let us play, and it stopped them from picking on us during class. They'd beat us up and taunt us on the field, but basically leave us alone afterwards.

This day we were tied. It was their ball, fourth down, five feet from the goal line that ran between the two baseball backstops. I stayed away from their huddle, but had a good idea what they were going to run. Something tricky.

At that point, I was prepared for the loss, Corey's hooting and hollering. That stupid dance he did. Plus, it was hot and I was sweaty.

They broke huddle. Corey went to the ball, Gilbert all the way to the left.

The bell rang and Steven started walking for the blacktop, acting brave in my old Star Wars shirt I'd given him because he kept staring at it when he'd come over.

Then Steven actually talked smack. "Guess you don't win this time, Corey."

Corey held out his arm, kept Steven back without touching him. "No way, Hong Kong. One more play."

Steven pointed at the classroom way on the other side of the school. "The bell rang."

Corey kept his arm out. "No shit, Sherlock."

"Come on, Corey, let him go," I said. "It's either a tie or we'll finish next week."

"Stop being such a muff, Joe" Corey said. He walked to the line of scrimmage and backed Steven up behind the ball.

Gilbert, in his Columbus Conquerors' t-shirt and matching shorts, got in the special stance he'd learned at camp. "Yeah. Mr. Mosley's always late."

The blacktop was covered with kids, only a teacher or two. "We still got time," I said. "Come on, Steven. It'll be quick."

Steven pulled at his baggy shirt, the Luke Skywalker iron-on so faded it almost wasn't there. It sounded like he might cry, something a fourth grader should never do. "I have to change."

"Change later, chinker-dinker." Corey squatted down and grabbed the ball. "Last play."

Steven finally shut up, his thoughts shouting into my head:

Fucking Pecker! If you get near me I'm going to kick you in the balls. Make it so Corey could never make fun of him again.

But I knew if Steven tried it, he'd miss. He was the most uncoordinated kid in class, his belly round and jiggly because his mom made him pork dumpling nearly every night. I knew Corey would beat the piss out of him.

Corey squished up his face so his eyes were almost closed. "Ohhhh, me so a scared."

Steven made a noise, almost sounded like a growl. Corey laughed and I knew what Steven was going to do. That's what made me do it. What made me become the cheat Dad always warned me not to. I asked Gilbert, "Whatcha' running?"

Gilbert smiled, thought there was no way I'd be ready for the flea flicker.

Corey hut, hut, hutted and hiked the ball. Gilbert pretended to run forward, put on his best fakeout face. He was supposed to come back behind the line, catch the lateral, throw it back to Corey.

So clear. So goddamn easy. I jumped in front of the pass, picked it off and hauled ass for the blacktop.

Corey shouted a super loud, "Fuck!"

The race was on.

The other goal line was between the swings and monkey bars, still half the field away. Gilbert and Corey were both faster than me, but I had a lead, pumping my arms as fast as I could.

I didn't need to look back to know Gilbert was just a few feet away, thinking about diving for my legs. Corey was next to him, wanting to teach me no one beat him. Especially some little white pussy.

I zigged to the left. Gilbert dropped, face-planted. I zagged and Corey tripped over Gilbert. The goal line was less than twenty feet away, Corey stumbling to grab my shirt. I spun. Corey fell. And I backpedaled into the end zone.

That spike was the biggest Fuck You I'd ever delivered. I slammed it hard, yelled, "Touchdown!" loud enough that even the kids sick at home would hear.

Corey popped off the grass and ran over. "No way. It doesn't count."

Steven slapped me a high five. "Yeah, it does," he said. "We win." He did this ridiculous robot dance, the one he'd been perfecting at home in front of the mirror. He looked like a spaz, but I'd never seen him happier.

The kids were filing into the school. I told Steven we needed to go. He finally stopped dancing, bent over to pick up his notepad and school clothes.

Corey charged and pushed him to his knees.

Steven got up and brushed off the grass, saw the stain he wouldn't be able to explain to his parents.

"What the hell, Corey? Why'd you push him?" I said.

"Cause he's a crybaby and a cheater. You both are. The touchdown didn't count."

"It counted and we won. End of story." I told Steven, "Come on."

Steven held up his perfectly folded shirt that almost matched his cheeks. "I have to change."

"What's wrong?" Corey asked. "Hong Kong don't want to show off his chee-chees?"

None of us liked changing in public, but the thought crippled Steven, left him standing there holding the shirt, waiting to be told what to do.

"Come on, dude, everyone's already in line," I said. "The second bell's gonna ring any second. I'll stand right here. No one's even looking."

Gilbert pointed at the principal's office way at the other end of school. "There's Mosley."

Mr. Mosley was talking to Miss Shannon. She was leaning against the wall, their bodies pretty close. They could've been talking about anything but it was probably about his divorce, why he didn't get one yet. I'd heard disgusting things when they stared at each other in the cafeteria.

"Hurry up, Steven," I said. "I don't want to be late."

Corey kept pushing Steven, who was losing it.

He shrieked, "Go away, Corey."

"I've got all day. Bitch Hudson gave me detention this morning. What's Mosley going to do?" Corey showed how white his teeth were with a giant smile. "Come on, Hong Kong, let me see those titties."

Steven silently whispered my name to help.

We didn't have many options. I told him to just change. "Mosley's saying goodbye."

Steven slipped the shirt off his head and started to put on his nice one, but Corey ran past me, grabbed hold of each shirt, and ripped them free. I turned but Corey was already running. Steven took off after him, his toothpick arms flying back and forth.

Corey ran around the jungle gym, jumped over the sand pit, hit the blacktop full stride. He was an athlete and an asshole.

Steven gave up, kicked at the sand, arms folded over his chest. It was probably for the best. I don't know what he could have done if he caught Corey.

When Corey got halfway to the classroom, he glanced over his shoulder, gave a big smile. Then he had to go and raise both hands, the shirts flying behind him, making sure everyone saw him coming.

The other fourth graders were already in two lines leading to the classroom. Corey ran through the middle of them and yelled, "Here come the cheaters!"

Everyone turned to see who he was talking about.

Corey stood at the front of the class. "You just gonna stand there?" He wasn't talking to Steven. His brown eyes were on me. "Or are you gonna come help your rice-jammer butt-buddy?"

It was hard to talk with everyone watching, but I managed. "Give him back his stuff."

Corey held up the Star Wars shirt. "Hong Kong even wears your clothes. What else you two doing?"

The kids laughed, mostly the guys. But Gina, the girl I had a crush on, was right there, a few feet away at the end of the line. She didn't think it was funny. She thought Corey was a jerk.

I said, "You mean besides beating you at football?"

A bunch of people oohed. Someone said Corey got burned. Corey just got mad and made his nostrils get even bigger.

"If we played tackle, you pussies would never score."

"Guess we'll never know. Can he have his shirt now?"

Corey acted like he didn't hear me and wrapped the Star Wars shirt around his fist. "Tell everyone why you won't play tackle. Is it because your mommy and daddy won't let you or because you're chickenshit?"

From behind, the place he always seemed to be, Steven said, "Forget it, Joe. Mr. Mosley will be here in a minute."

Corey came closer. The lines moved, formed into a circle. Corey pounded his shirt hand onto his palm. "Shut up, you stupid chink," he said. "Go run home to your momma-san."

I was glad I couldn't see Steven's face turn red, his eyes tear up. The others could, though, and almost all of them thought it was funny. But not Gina. She told Corey to shut up.

Corey smiled. He thought no one was going to say anything. "Aw, does a girl have to fight your battles?"

Everything got kind of blurry, except Corey and his big fucking mouth. Something had to be said. No one else was going to say it so I did. "At least he has a mom."

Corey started to shake, his eyes got all big. "Your mom's a WHORE!" Spit flew off his lips. "And you're a little-dick honky, just like your dad."

It was the first punch I ever threw. He never saw it coming. Connected full on, knocked Corey's head back. He tried to swing, but couldn't land anything, didn't look like such a great athlete with me rushing him through the circle, throwing him into the wall.

Corey's eyes were closed when his head smacked against the brick. His lip split on the next punch, shot blood everywhere. The third punch dropped him hard.

Kids screamed for me to stop, a couple said, "Fuck him up."

I obliged. Got on top of Corey's chest and kept punching his face. Made it so he wouldn't ever say anything about anyone's mom again. Then I grabbed his head and slammed it into the ground so he wouldn't even think it.

A giant hand flung me off and I smacked into the wall. Mr. Mosley got on his knees, wiped the blood off Corey's face. He told Gina to get the nurse.

My father was called.

I was suspended. We drove home in silence. I'd rarely heard his thoughts. He'd always kept his distance, seemed to move when I got in range.

I was afraid to listen in the car, already knew he was pissed. He told Mr. Mosley the suspension wasn't nearly as bad as what I had coming at home.

As we passed by the high school's football field, I thought back to our game, spiking the ball. Steven's robot dance.

Dad was so pissed he could barely speak. "I told you never to cheat."

"What?"

"I told you *never* to cheat!"

I hadn't mentioned the game to Mr. Mosley or my dad.

"So I'm going to make this real goddamn clear. If you ever pull that shit again at school, with your friends, with anyone..."

I could hear his guilty thoughts, the ones about whipping me with his belt.

"Dad?"

I'm sorry. I should have told you.

And right there I learned I wasn't alone.

Dad pulled the car over and told me the truth. Some of it was out loud. The rest was just between us. He said Mom didn't need to know. She knew enough. About him. But not about me. It'd be too much to handle. I had to keep it in check, had to learn to control myself, hide what I could do to keep us safe.

They'd split us up, send me to live in an orphanage. My father would lose his job, the one he hated, but it put food on the table, a roof over our heads.

I asked if there were others. He told me there were, but that we should never associate, never seek them out. The world was already starting to learn the truth. Soon they'd start coming for us. Brightside didn't exist yet. But there'd be repercussions.

Dad said people were being institutionalized. Thrown in nuthouses. Like my grandmother.

"I thought she lived in Florida?" I said.

"She does. Just not in a condo."

My entire life, I thought Dad hated me. Turns out, he was just scared, trying to protect me.

After that, things changed. We went on more trips. He helped me be a better son, giving me silent instructions to help Mom in the kitchen with the dishes.

He showed me how to hunt. Taught me to field-strip a shotgun. Bolt always rounded-side up. Center the hook in the receiver. The slide should drop right in.

Dad learned all this in the War. He said it was the last time he'd abused his ability. It saved his life, but got his platoon killed.

The shotgun was my grandfather's. A Mossberg 12-gauge. American metal. Dad took me to the range, let me fire it. The kick nearly ripped off my shoulder. I never wanted to shoot it again. Dad said, "Never let fear take control."

He loved to lecture. I was young enough to listen, just couldn't put it into action. I didn't tell anyone what I could do, but I couldn't stop hearing others' thoughts. I'd hear answers for tests. When I discovered Lacy liked me in seventh grade, I got my first kiss. I couldn't turn off the thoughts, no matter how many times Dad told me I could. He said I just had to focus my mind. We got into fights. I ran away twice. Came back only to fight some more.

When I moved out for good at seventeen, Dad begged me to reconsider. He didn't want to be left alone with Mom. He grew paranoid. Refused to leave the house. He'd call me at odd hours once he heard about Brightside. He sent me articles about the town, but always hidden on the back of an article about something else: fishing, a new vodka, the risks of smoking. He didn't want to draw suspicions, said I couldn't either. I didn't want to hear it. I told him I was smart, I wasn't going to get caught. But that was before Saul, before BMW, before Michelle.

* * *

Dad's Brightside gifts didn't stop with Billy Bass. He sent a fishing pole. More D-Cell batteries. He sent a tuning fork, even though I'd never played an instrument. His letter said I should learn new hobbies. He wrote he'd been learning to kayak.

None of it made sense. I worried he'd developed dementia. It explained the last few years, the paranoia. There were studies linking telepathy to brain damage.

I shoved all the gifts in the closet. Some I didn't even unwrap. I didn't want to think about him, that if I'd just listened to his advice, I'd be in the real world, not staring at Rachel's empty desk every day or hiding from Krystal in the Square.

The darkness was closing in. I didn't want to leave my room. I just wanted to stay in bed, stare at nothing, but I didn't have a choice. Isolation got you sent to The Cabin so I looked for reasons to go outside and act like everything was fine. I took walks, hung out with Danny, bought him some new comic books. He reminded me of Steven. But as bad as it was for Steven and me as kids, it was nothing compared to how Danny had it. The out loud taunts hurt, but not nearly as much as the silent ones, the kind even bullies kept to themselves.

Danny had heard them all, but somehow he was still happy. I envied Danny and tried to learn from him. I even stopped feeling sorry for myself about Rachel, Michelle, Krystal...

But still I felt awful for how things ended with Steven.

By eighth grade we'd stopped hanging out, rarely spoke. I'd been listening to other people's thoughts, started hanging out with the jocks, the pretty girls. I knew what they wanted to hear. Said all the right things to make them think I was cool. Steven wasn't, never would be, so I cut him off.

Then he got sick. Real sick. His parents pulled him out of school. I knew I should visit, but I couldn't face him.

Dad found out, heard me thinking one night at dinner when Mom asked how Steven was doing.

Dad drove me to Steven's house to make me apologize. He sat in the car, while everything was yelling at me to run. I breathed in, breathed out, told myself I'd be okay. I didn't use the doorbell because I didn't want to wake Steven's parents if they were sleeping. I'd asked Dad to just let me do this over the phone, but he refused, said I needed to look Steven in the face, hear what Steven was really feeling.

I knocked on the door, prayed his parents would tell me to go home.

I didn't know his parents well, even though I'd been over there a hundred times. They kept to themselves and never said a whole lot, hardly ever more than hello. Steven said they didn't really speak English, but I knew he just didn't want them doing it around me, embarrassed of how they sounded.

Steven's mom opened the door, her straight black hair now frosted gray, her eyes tired black holes above pursed lips.

I bowed my head to show respect. "Hello, Mrs. Chang. Can I see Hong?"

Calling Steven by his real name reminded me why I'd cut him off in the first place.

Mrs. Chang gave the slightest nod and stepped to the side, revealing the path of clear plastic protecting the bright white carpet.

I slipped off my shoes and set them next to the other two pairs. His mom was waiting, not saying a word, glad I was there.

The plastic crinkled under my feet, the sweet smell of rice mixed with incense. I couldn't turn back so I went down the hall. Steven's room was the last one on the left.

The door was closed, nothing on it, his sign gone. HONG'S ROOM, nice and neat block letters, the most rebellious thing I ever convinced him to do, no way he'd ever write Steven.

I opened his door. His room used to be blue. Now it was brilliant white, every single inch. No more Star Wars posters. No superhero cardboard cut-outs below them. All of it was gone, Steven was done with childhood.

Everything else was just as white. The carpet, the walls, the ceiling. The candles in the corners. Everything gone except the giant silk screen that hung in front of the window, the soft white fabric with its border so green, a blue river and a big white bird floating down the middle of it.

I stepped forward. Steven, whiter than he'd ever been. So pale. So weak. So small.

Steven's head was propped three pillows high. All his hair was gone, all that was left was his skull and some skin, his thin slits for eyes staring straight ahead at the picture. He was thinking about death and what it would be like.

Steven winced and let out a long sigh that sounded painful to say. "Unnhhhh." Keeping his hand under the sheet, he grabbed hold of his hip. His bones hurt. All the time, even with the meds.

I stepped closer so my legs touched the bed. Seeing him like this made it hard to think. I didn't know if I should call him by his real name. I cleared my throat so I wouldn't scare him and said, "Hey, man."

Steven slowly turned his head and blinked twice. His thoughts trying to figure out how he felt about me. If he hated me for making fun of him at school because he still played Dungeons and Dragons or if he was too embarrassed to be seen like this, bald, deteriorating, naked under the sheet. Or if he was just glad someone had finally cared enough to come.

I had no idea what to do. No one had ever told me what to say to someone dying. Someone who had less than ten days, two weeks at the most according to our teacher, Mrs. Kauffman. She'd made us make this giant card. We all signed our names, some words of encouragement. I only wrote, "Feel better."

I nodded at the picture covering the window. "Cool goose."

Steven spoke so low, I had to lean forward. "Swan," he said. "That's what Hong means."

I'd never thought his name actually translated into anything. "That's what it means?"

"Not gorilla," Steven said through a cough. Then smiled.

For a second it was like old times. Then his smile twisted into a grimace because he realized that even the shittiest, loneliest, most humiliating times would be better than no times at all. He'd sit through Corey's little dance all day every day if it meant getting better.

I pointed at the swan. "I'll take it down. You want me to?"

"They know best." He paused to catch his breath. "They say I'm just a child."

I didn't know what to say, so my lips stayed still. I thought, *I'm so sorry.*

Steven's eyes grew wide. I'd never spoken to someone in thought. He looked frightened, and I took off running, ran all the way to the car. Dad knew what I'd done, but this time he didn't lecture.

Two days later, Steven was gone, taking my secret to the grave.

CHAPTER SEVEN

Night 58, lightning flashed on the other side of the mountain, a loud boom less than a second behind it. The freezing rain fell in sheets.

I was out walking and got caught in the storm. I took off for the Square, ended up at Riley's, the tiny, dark tavern at the edge of town. Cheap vinyl booths lined the walls. The door to the storage room was propped open with a brick. A woman with a brown braided ponytail was dragging a keg. The way she moved said she'd been doing this her whole life. She was covered in tattoos, her strangely hypnotic eyes pulling me to the bar.

She wiped her hands on the back of her low-cut jeans. She was definitely new to Brightside. Still, there was something familiar.

She smiled and leaned over the counter, her voice rougher than expected. "You okay?"

"Yeah. Maybe, I don't know."

"Well, that's no good. What are you having?"

"Beer."

She said that wouldn't do, not in my condition. She offered to make me something special. I shrugged. I hadn't had a drop of anything since Day 39, the day they dragged Rachel from my room.

The bartender said her name was Lexi. She asked mine and I told her. Then she wanted to know my last name and said, "I've heard of you." I had a hard time believing that with her acting so nice. She told me to stop being ridiculous and have a seat.

I pulled out a stool, sat down, and reached for my wallet.

"Put that away," she said. "First one's on the house."

"I'm probably going to only have one, so I should just..."

She told me to stop being silly, but I did way more than that, my thoughts drifting to Steven's funeral.

"You're a dark one, aren't you?"

I shifted back on the stool, considered leaving.

"Just give me a smile and I promise to make it better."

Lexi was too pretty not to smile at. She walked to the back wall, the rows of bottles three stacks high. She asked where I was from.

"Outside Columbus." Saying that made me feel like a tourist, like this was simply a business trip. Tomorrow, I'd be home sitting with my dog curled up at my feet.

Lily...filled with bullets on my carpet.

"Hey, stop that. There's no bad thoughts when you get a free drink."

"Sorry." I tried to play the part, returning the favor, asked where they nabbed her.

"L.A." She poured the Jack, gave it two quick stirs. A drink in each hand, both full to the top. We clinked glasses, somehow managed not to spill.

The whiskey was so strong I couldn't taste the mixer. I said, "Just what I need."

Lexi put her glass to her lips, finished it in one long swallow. She closed her eyes, rolled her head around her shoulders, the liquid medicine kicking in. "Thought you'd like it."

"L.A., huh? How was that?"

"Just like anywhere else."

I knocked back my drink, tried not to think about all the places I could've been.

"Another?"

"Sure."

"Thata boy."

"You haven't been here long, have you? I haven't seen—"

"Five days."

"You should go to the diner. They have a decent turkey sandwich."

"I'll check it out."

"The banana split isn't bad either."

This inane conversation was heaven, especially with the next drink, a bit sweeter, but also tart. I asked about her tattoos. She told me the guy who did them was a magician. I thought she meant he was an incredible artist, but she said no, he pulled rabbits out of a fucking hat. The tattoo thing was just a side gig.

Lexi tossed the washrag into the sink and walked with a swagger that hadn't been there before. I tried not to stare at her ass.

She flashed a grin, held up her hands. "Easy, Tiger."

"Sorry. But...do I know you?"

Lexi's eyes rolled. Was this really my line?

"No, I mean it. You look familiar. You sure you were never in Columbus?"

She shook her head. "Nope."

Something about her smile kept me going. I said, "We've met before. I know it."

Lexi washed out her glass. "You probably know my girlfriend. People get us confused. She's been here almost a year." Lexi kept talking, but the clinking glasses and people walking in made it hard to hear. The buzz didn't help either. It was strange, tingly. I didn't feel that drunk, just loose and confident.

Lexi said, "She'll be here soon."

I nodded, having no idea what she was talking about. I held up my drink, tried to guess what it was.

Lexi headed to the other end of the bar to serve the new customers. "It's good, right?" she called back.

I took another sip and said, "Yeah." I couldn't place the contents, but it was delicious and I wanted another one. Lexi was making one of the girl's a drink. Lexi kept glancing over at me, but not in a friendly way. It was like she was pissed. But I hadn't done anything.

I set the glass on the bar, promised myself to hold off on another one. There was a little bit of liquid at the bottom of my drink. I finished it and set the glass down harder than I meant to. Faces of the people I'd hurt flashing before me.

Rachel, Steven, Michelle...

The door opened and rain smacked off the sidewalk. One of the women from accounting stepped inside and shook the rain from her coat, her bulldog cheeks flapping.

The woman saw me, pretended not to, and took a seat in a booth.

I could feel my heart beating, felt it even in my thumbs. I needed to get home, but Lexi was no longer behind the bar.

My knee was bouncing, made my foot slip off the bottom rung of the stool.

Lexi walked out of the storage room looking like it was normal to disappear for ten minutes. At least it felt like that long. She greeted another customer, went to the tap, never once looked my direction.

I considered heading over to order another drink when the front door opened. Two guys from the deli entered, nodding hello when they slid in the booth.

My thumbs were beating a rhythm on the glass, who knows for how long. The door opened again, the rain blowing in. I didn't check to see who it was. I kept my eyes on Lexi so I could motion for another round. I was feeling good, alive.

Lexi poured a glass of wine without once looking up. The front door opened and closed, but Lexi was busy, wiping down the damn tap.

A girl said, "Sorry I'm late."

I knew that voice. I turned toward the front door. Krystal.

She took the last stool at the bar, just out of my reach. She smiled at Lexi, and Lexi set two drinks in front of her.

Krystal said, "Two? You trying to get me drunk?"

Looking like she really wanted to hear the answer, Lexi said, "Do I need to?"

Krystal reached over and put her hand on top of Lexi's. "What are they?"

"They're good." Lexi pointed at me. "Ask your friend. He'll tell you."

Krystal turned, her glare carved right through me. "What are you doing here?"

I pointed at the roof. "Just trying to stay dry."

She bit the side of her lip. She looked at Lexi over at the other end of the bar then back at me. "What'd you tell her?"

"What do you mean? We barely talked."

Krystal leaned forward close enough to see the concealer packed into her pockmarks. Krystal's tongue pushed out her cheek, her huntress eyes never leaving me. "So?"

"I didn't say anything."

It suddenly felt like everyone was staring. I started to get up, but saw another drink in front of me. Lexi was walking away. She'd finally given me another.

I picked up the drink and finished half of it, tried to get my thoughts together. The front door opened, the rain louder than before. I must have looked startled because Krystal leaned over and said, "That bother you?"

I took another drink, looked over at Lexi bending over. "No."

"You going to tell her what a slut she is?"

"What? No."

"She is though, just so you know."

I took another drink, wondered why my mind was racing, why I couldn't understand what we were talking about.

"These drinks are good, huh?" Krystal said.

My skin felt hot, like I was sitting inside an oven.

"I thought you didn't drink."

"I drink."

"Right, two. That's the limit." She pushed out her bottom lip, mocking me. "Rachel said you love your rules. Only two drinks." She wagged her finger. "And no caffeine."

I wrapped both hands around my glass, looked at the ice. "I didn't realize you two were friends.

"We're not. It's a small town."

Lexi walked up and put an arm around Krystal's shoulder. "So? Do you like them?"

Krystal kissed her cheek. "Absolutely perfect."

Lexi squeezed Krystal tight then stepped back. "What about you, Joe? Want another?"

I kept quiet while my mind yelled at me, shouted what the hell was going on. My thoughts were jumping everywhere. The jukebox, my first kiss, the day Steven caught a frog. I thought of the rollercoaster rides with my first girlfriend, the morning I woke up in the cell after the Boots took me from my home, the ringing in my ear...

Lexi and Krystal started laughing. Crazed, cackling laughter.

Lexi turned toward me and smiled. "They're good, right?"

I nodded, bit my tongue, which was moving around my mouth like a wild snake.

Lexi pointed at Krystal's glass. "Another?"

"No way, I need to sleep at some point."

"No you don't. I'll keep you company." Lexi kissed Krystal.

Then both of them stared at me, waiting for me to realize they were behind this scheme. I looked at my empty glass then at the bar. Next to the wine bottles and the wobbling tower of glasses, two cans of Red Bull.

I looked down at the drink, not sure how long I'd been back thumbing a drum beat on it. I thought a stream of "oh fucks."

Lexi said she was going to have a smoke and walked off, disappeared into the storage room.

Krystal looked at me like a little kid. "You'll be fine. Go get yourself a water."

Four drinks didn't seem too much until I stood, everything off. I held onto the back of the stool for balance. Every booth had a body in it. The place suddenly packed.

I made my way down the bar, towards the storage room. The busboy waved his rag to get my attention. "Hey man, what are you looking for?"

Louder than she needed to, same as she always talked, Gloria from Human Resources said, "Gimme a gin and tonic, a bottled water."

I said, "Me too, about the water."

The busboy pulled two waters from the cooler. One for me and one for Gloria who wouldn't stop thinking about her two kids at home.

I took the water, headed back to my stool where Alex, the perfectly dressed schoolboy with his bulging muscles, was now sitting.

"Excuse me," I said.

Alex kept talking to Krystal, acting like he didn't hear me. If he didn't move out of my way in two seconds I was going to pick up my almost empty glass and slam it into his head.

My thoughts always give everything away.

Alex whipped around, his right hand smacking my forearm, sending the water bottle flying. Not about to apologize, Alex said, "I didn't know you were there."

"That's my seat."

"No need to get upset, bro." Alex got off the stool and looked down on me. "Just saying hi."

I knew I was acting like an idiot, but couldn't control it. "Well, goodbye."

Alex stood there, his mouth set like he had something important to say. I clenched my fist, ready to take my best shot.

"Why don't you find another seat," Krystal said to me. "Or another bar."

Alex tried to sound tough, his eyes never leaving my hands. "You heard her."

Krystal finished the rest of her drink and slid it next to the empties.

I glanced over my shoulder. Everyone in the place was looking at me or pretending not to. Except Krystal. She was too busy looking at Alex, her shoulders back, chest out.

Without looking at me, Krystal said, "Go home, Joe."

It wasn't even eleven. Twelve. Twenty-four. Forty-eight. I gave it up, my foot pumping up and down, knee bumping the stool Alex was sitting on. My fucking stool.

"Do you like making a fool of yourself in front of everyone?" Krystal said.

I thought everybody else could go fuck themselves. "What do I care?"

"You should watch yourself," Alex said.

I looked around, no one next to us. Just Alex, Krystal, and myself.

"It's not good to think like that. People might not like you." Alex smiled.

"Who? Edward, Frances? Sheila, Gloria? They're like eight, ten feet away."

The truth was there was no real way of knowing when someone else was hearing my thoughts. Not in Brightside, not unless they started thinking about the same exact shit or said something about it.

Thunder crashed down the street, rattled the whole building. Krystal liked it, enjoyed the driving rain on the roof.

My brain was on hyperdrive, thoughts racing around the slippery track. My problems, my options, the possible solutions.

Krystal was past irritated. "Just leave. We're obviously not good enough for you. You're *sooo* much better than everyone, right?"

I said no, but couldn't stop the names flashing. Krystal's list.

Krystal grabbed one of the glasses and threw the ice at me. "Fuck you, Joe."

I took a napkin, wiped my face. I told her, "Don't be mad. You're a doll." I nodded at the purse some guy bought. "You even come with all the right accessories." I thought of everyone I knew she'd been with, the hundreds of faceless figures from her past. "Packaged for mass consumption."

Alex couldn't believe all the men I was thinking about, all the horrible acts of depravity on Krystal's body. It was turning him on.

"We're all just whores, right, Joe? Like Rachel?" Krystal looked at me with disgust. "You put her there. Just admit it. You made her feel like a piece of shit and she broke. You broke her."

I forgot everything, but the dirty no good stupid bitch in front of me.

Krystal licked her lips, tasted victory. Knowing exactly how much it would hurt, knowing it was something I couldn't hear, she said, "Rachel loved you, but that wasn't enough. You had to grind her down into nothing. You're just a pathetic coward."

I started walking towards the door, held up my middle finger because Krystal was too far away to know how much I hated her right then.

She yelled, "Why don't you tell everybody what you think of them?"

Wendell was squeezed into the booth to my right, minding his own business, thinking he didn't want to hear it. Stephanie slipped off her stool and hurried away, bumping my shoulder.

"Go ahead, tell them!" Krystal screamed.

I needed to head for the door. My mind no longer my own. Each face firing off judgments.

Tommy and his ridiculous Mohawk, a kid who needed his ass kicked. He slunk into his seat.

Krystal said, "See, Tommy. I'm not lying."

Tommy felt everyone looking at him. He got up from the bar and looked right at me, forced himself to sound strong, even with his cracking voice. "You planning on doing it or hoping someone else will?"

"I don't think...I mean that's not really—"

"Or what about Erica?" Krystal said.

Erica, with those sad eyes, so tired because she couldn't stop playing with herself at night, wishing she had more fingers.

Erica's face turned red. Her hands slipped under the table, not wanting anyone to look at them. She wouldn't look at me, just thought about me getting sent to The Cabin.

"You're close enough, Wendell," Krystal said. "Does Joe think you should either stop feeling sorry for yourself or cut out the donut holes?"

I thought no over and over and over again.

Everyone's thoughts slamming into me, just like kindergarten. Everyone hating me, wishing I'd just die.

I saw the door, took off running. Got out before I hurt someone else. The rain pummeled me as I stepped onto the Square. I headed for Main Street, splashing across the sidewalk. My life was over, a sorry joke.

I looked back across the street sure I'd see everyone pointing, laughing their ass off, but I was alone. Here in this mountain town filled with people just like me, I was the goddamn freak.

A strong wind nearly knocked me over when I turned the corner and left the Square behind. Down the street and over the park, the clouds were beginning to break. The giant moon hung in front of me, casting a dull white light, a spotlight on the world's biggest asshole.

The one who judged everyone: Krystal, Erica, Wendell, Rachel, Mom, Dad, and even poor Steven, my first real friend.

I kept walking, tried to stay away from the spotlight. I could see the cemetery, the place I'd never been because I knew I'd see it soon enough.

It was my own fault for drinking, for being in the bar in the first place. The sidewalk was one answer. I could bash my head into it until the voices stopped, my skull cracking on the concrete.

I slapped myself harder than I'd ever done before and started for my apartment. That's what everyone wanted. Sight unseen so I couldn't hurt anyone.

I entered the park and kept to the path. I heard Dad yelling at me to stop acting like a child. All I had to do was rationalize what I was feeling. It was my brain, I could think about what I wanted, feel whatever I told myself to. I would control my emotions, not the other way around.

When I crossed by the pond, I saw The Cabin on the hill. I thought of checking myself in, taking a seat, swallowing whatever they gave me. At least I'd be with Rachel.

Rachel...

It'd been two weeks since they'd taken her from my room. Just like Steven, I'd avoided her, but it was time I looked her in the eyes, to apologize.

The Cabin never closed. I went inside, found Rachel just sitting in the front room. Her mouth so dry, there wasn't any drool. I asked if I could give her some water. The nurse handed me a cup and I tried to pour it in, but it just spilled out of her lips.

Drink.

Rachel's eyes gained a little focus, then closed. Her throat began to swallow.

I'm so sorry, I thought.

Rachel's eyes turned towards me, but there was nothing inside her head. So quiet it made me want to scream. She turned towards the window, the big moon hidden behind the clouds.

"I understand if you hate me. You actually have some company." I forced a laugh, hoping she'd join in, that it'd be like old times, but she just kept staring out the window. Silent, broken.

The nurse came over and said, "It's time for her bath."

"Right..."

The orderly lifted Rachel to her feet and she took the tiniest steps down the hall. The nurse said I could wait, spend more time with her after the bath, but I'd seen enough, which is what they wanted. That's why they allowed visitors. They wanted everyone in Brightside to know what would happen if we broke the rules.

Back at my apartment I found another package. My father had sent me a picture of us fishing. He'd put it in this strange homemade frame cobbled together with pieces of metal. I put it in the closet with the rest of his gifts. There was hardly any room with all the boxes. I thought about taking most of it down to the garbage.

The fishing pole clanged to the floor. I picked it up. The rod was jet black, heavier than I'd ever felt before, like it was meant to catch some huge monster of the sea.

I started to place it back in the closet, but remembered my father's words after Steven died.

"When someone dies, you have to remember there's still so many people that need your love."

I remembered I did have one friend in Brightside. Even if everyone else hated me, wanted to see me thrown off the edge, I still had Danny.

CHAPTER EIGHT

On Day 61, the sun was out and it was kind of warm, so I asked Danny if he'd like to go fishing. He started jumping up and down, clapping his hand against the fist that held the faded blue pencil. I took that as a yes. We cut a small hole in the ice. The pond didn't have any fish, but I kept it to myself. We just sat quietly on the bank, Danny's mind as calm as Michelle's on the pills and whiskey. I guess that's the other reason why I liked hanging out with Danny. The silence.

But two days later Danny became the loudest thing in Brightside. He ran up to me on the street, nearly knocked me over.

"I need a drawing!"

I hated to spoil his fun, but he couldn't hold still. "Okay, Danny. Just calm down."

"No, I need it now!"

"I have to go to work."

"Please, you gotta!"

"What's going on?"

"My sister... She's coming!"

The next day, Rachel's desk was no longer empty. Danny's sister, Sara, sat there, everything neat and organized. Nothing personal to distinguish her workspace from anyone else's, except for one of my drawings Danny had wanted her to have.

Rachel had been the opposite, papers scattered, pens everywhere, pictures of her father, mother, dog, and cat spread along the edge, a proud collage of her past.

It was stupid to date Rachel. First time I saw where I was going to be sitting, I should've told Carlos I needed a new desk. I should've said I needed somewhere I could be by myself. Somewhere I couldn't hurt anyone.

My whole life's been one big should've. Should've known better. Should've listened. Should've paid attention. Should've stopped worrying about everyone. Should've realized I'm only as dumb as I let myself be.

Sara dialed another number, some lady in Kentucky about an island getaway. She followed the script, but made it her own, telling each person how she'd always dreamed of living by the ocean. It sounded believable, but her thoughts told me she didn't want to be anywhere but Brightside.

It was creepy. I mean, there were some who believed Brightside wasn't so bad. People like Sharon and her puppet, Vanessa, women so positive it made you sick. But Sara was the first I'd heard of that really wanted to be here.

She'd turned herself in on purpose, demanded to be reunited with Danny. They kept her in a cell for a month. No one turned themselves in. She must have had a plan, a scheme. They interrogated her, deprived her of sleep, but Sara never cracked, just kept whispering her brother's name.

The picture I'd drawn for Danny, the one with the boy escaping through the brick wall, sat on her desk. For me, the picture was about escaping Brightside. For Sara, it was about breaking in.

Sara was twenty when their parents had died, Danny away at a special needs school. She took him in, cared for him, made sure he wore clean shirts, combed his hair, fell asleep in bed, not in the chair watching cartoons.

All morning, Sara and I hadn't shared a single word. She was already working the phones when I'd come in. She wanted to make a good first impression. After what she'd been through to get here, I didn't blame her.

Finally, on our break, Sara caught me staring at the drawing. She tucked a long strand of brown hair behind her ear. Her nose had this cute little bump, like she'd broken it as a kid. She pointed at the drawing and said, "It's really good."

"Oh, I just..."

"I'm Sara."

"Yeah, Danny told me you were coming. Showed me a picture. I've never seen him so excited."

"Yeah... Look, I wanted to thank you. You know, for taking care of him."

"It's not a big deal. I didn't do anything."

Yes, you did.

I suddenly felt uncomfortable. People's thoughts about me were rarely this nice.

Sara said, "Danny wants to go to the diner tonight. He'd like you to come if you're not busy."

"Sure."

Sara and I each had sandwiches. Danny ordered pancakes with a whipped cream smile. He got some on his face and Sara wiped it off while Danny talked about us fishing.

"You need to get those worms out of our apartment," Sara said. "It's gross."

Danny's special hat shook back and forth. "But we need them."

My thoughts slipped out, how there weren't any fish in the pond.

Danny dropped his fork.

"I'm sorry," I said.

He picked up the fork and started thumbing it "You lied?"

"Danny, cut it out," Sara said. "He was being nice."

He lowered his head so all I could see was DANNY in bright red letters. He was pissed when he said, "But you lied!"

"I know, but I still like going with you." I thought about my apartment, about Dad's first gift.

Danny raised his head, his eyes big and shiny.

After we paid the tab, we went back to my place and I dug around in the closet. Danny was hopping around and Sara told him to stop it, that he was shaking the floor.

He'd probably already heard my thoughts, but I still said, "Alright, close your eyes."

Danny squeezed his lids so tight I thought he might squish his eyeballs. I put Billy Bass into his open palms. Danny smiled. I pushed the button and it still had a little juice. Billy turned his head and sang. Danny's laughter filled the room until the batteries died.

"Hold on, there are extras." I pulled out the D-Cells from the closet. Only they didn't fit. It was strange.

Danny said, "It's okay." He opened his backpack, pulled out two C batteries. They popped right in and Billy came back to life.

I couldn't believe my father had given me the wrong size. It said C right on the box. I set the unusable batteries on the counter. They felt strange, a little light.

Sara was annoyed she was going to have to hear this damn song every night. "Okay, I think that's enough, Danny."

Danny started hopping again, but this time it wasn't out of joy.

Sara told him to put down the fish and hurry to the bathroom.

Danny had to hit the button one last time before handing it to Sara and scurrying out of the room.

Sara was looking at Billy Bass.

I said, "Sorry."

She said it was okay and cracked a smile. "He loves it."

We stood there awkwardly, neither of us really knowing what to say. She was tired, thinking of her bed. I saw how beautiful she looked, even that little bump in her nose. She turned, embarrassed. I was picturing her lips on mine, and she didn't feel the same way. I was destroying her opinion of me, and for the first time realized how hard it was for women in Brightside, having to hear all the nasty thoughts men carried.

Danny came bounding back in, breaking the tension.

"I think you should get a dog, Joe!"

I tried saying I wasn't a pet person. Lily's breath on my feet, the puff on my arm. Fucking cowards.

Sara felt awful for hearing my thoughts. "We should probably go. It's getting late."

"Yeah...I'll see you both tomorrow," I said.

Danny collected his things, and they walked out, leaving me alone with my thoughts of my dog and those fuckers firing into her whimpering body.

* * *

I was ten years old in Mom's new car holding my yellow Lab. Sunny wasn't a puppy anymore, but just barely. I'd had her for six months and she wouldn't leave my side. For the last week, I hadn't left hers.

I had one hand holding her tiny head to keep it from quivering. The other picked all the yellow hairs off the leather. No need to give Mom another reason to freak out. She'd found Sunny throwing up in her room, fur falling off in clumps. Dad had carried her to the car.

I was in the back seat, leaning into the corner furthest from Mom. The safest spot.

Mom pulled over to the curb. "Okay, you two get out. Go do whatever you have to."

Dad was in the seat right front of me, his head three feet away. When he said Mom's name, he stretched it out, let her know it wasn't right for her to talk like that.

Mom pulled down the sun visor, checked her fire red hair in the lighted mirror, poofed up the sides. "What? I didn't say anything."

She hadn't. But she was thinking she hoped they'd put Sunny to sleep.

Dad opened the passenger door, put one foot on the sidewalk. "Are you going to park? We might be a while."

"And I'll be here," Mom said.

Dad got out and opened the back door, helped with Sunny. She was shaking real bad in Dad's hands so he gave her back to me once I got on the sidewalk. I held her against my belly and cradled her with both arms. She looked up with eyes that'd lost all their shine.

The sliding doors opened and a blast of cold air blew down from the vent. Sunny shuddered real hard, needed to be held tighter, have a hand on her bony back to keep her warm.

There were two people at the counter and nearly every seat in the waiting room had someone in it. A dog or cat by their feet. Most of the animals didn't look sick. Not like Sunny.

Dad got in line, looked down and saw me shaking. "Why don't you have a seat, Joe? There's one right there."

Sunny liked it better sitting down. I gave her a quick peck on her head when no one was looking. She didn't react, just closed her eyes. I put my finger in front of her nose and couldn't feel a thing. Finally a small puff. Then, keeping her eyes closed, Sunny stuck out her tongue, licked me once to say she was still there.

The girl with braces smiled at Dad. "I'll let the doctor know. Go ahead and have a seat."

Before Dad even got to me, Dr. Gentry stuck his fat face out of the back and waved us over. "Hank, I've been waiting for you."

"Thank you for getting us in," Dad said.

Everyone stared at us walking past the receptionist's desk. They'd been waiting all morning, and now they were pissed. None of them knew Dr. Gentry and Dad shared a secret.

Dr. Gentry showed us into his office that was half the size of a real doctor's. He sat behind his desk, his fat finger pushing up the eyeglasses that didn't hide his beady pig eyes. Then he took Sunny to the examination room and ran tests.

I need you to keep your mind calm, Dad thought.

"Okay."

Dr. Gentry is like us.

My eyes must have looked like they were going to pop out of my head, because Dad told me to get a hold of myself.

"But you said we should never seek—"

"I know what I said. But we can't afford this."

Mom's new car had pretty much cleaned us out.

Thirty minutes later, Dr. Gentry came back with Sunny and sat at his desk. I was standing in the doorway because even right there I could hear that creepy bastard's thoughts.

I didn't think I could get closer; then Dad lowered his voice and said, "Sit. Right now."

Dr. Gentry waited until I was sitting next to Dad before he said, "Sunny's not doing so good."

You didn't need test results to figure that out. She could barely move.

All matter of fact, Dr. Gentry said, "If she doesn't have help, she'll die."

I nodded again and again and again. It was the only way for me to not cry, to not yell shut up.

Gentry twisted an old ruby ring he wore on the finger next to his shiny wedding one. "The treatment and operation she needs costs a lot."

You owe me, Dad thought.

Dr. Gentry kept twisting that ruby ring, never the wedding band. "Your dad's a good man." He looked right at Dad. *But what I owe you is far less than this.*

Sunny shuddered, almost made me start crying. Dad reached over and put his hand on Sunny's head. He told me everything would be alright then kept thinking that, like maybe if he thought it enough times it would make it true.

"I'll work here after school," I blurted.

Dr. Gentry's face twisted a smile. "He's got it too?"

Dad's thoughts told me to shut up.

Gentry snapped his fingers and pointed at his big puffy face. "Up here," he said to me. "I want you to listen because this means you won't be able to play football or basketball after school. You won't be able to be on any teams."

That was fine. Sports were no big deal. It just meant there'd be less coaches, refs, and fathers for Mom to meet.

Dad kept patting Sunny's head, his wedding ring dull as ever. "Joe, you don't have—"

"I want to."

Dr. Gentry cleared his throat, this awful hacking. "So let's say I'll take care of your dog as best I can and in exchange you work every day after school, plus Saturdays."

I said okay, but Dr. Gentry held up his pointer finger and took a drink from his cup.

Sunny's heartbeat was weak, one every other second. This was just wasting time.

Gentry wiped his mouth with the back of his hand and said, "For two months." He dragged out the next word. "And...whatever your dad has on him. To help cover costs."

Dad swallowed hard, but Dr. Gentry didn't see because his eyes were glued to Dad's hands pulling out his wallet, digging out all the bills inside. The hands that would hand over everything he had.

Dad said, "Hold on a sec." Dad held out the bills, to me not Gentry. "It's your choice."

It would have been nice to yell, "Put the money back. We don't need this fat bastard and his goddamn rings." But Dr. Gentry was needed. Sunny's chest barely rose with each shallow breath. "Give it to him," I said. "Please."

Dad pushed the bills over. "This was for the art class you wanted. I'd been saving up for your birthday."

It was a lot of money. Too much.

"Take it, Joe. I'll tell your mom I lost my wallet."

Dr. Gentry held out his hand and pretended to look sad.

I gave it to him and said, "The class is stupid anyway."

"It's not polite to lie," Dr. Gentry said. He stuffed the money in his pocket and reached for Sunny with those fat fingers.

I gave Sunny one last squeeze, a kiss on her head before she went in his hands, those fingers I hoped were full of miracles.

Gentry headed for the door. "Let me get this guy taken care of and I'll see you three o'clock Monday."

A real doctor would know Sunny wasn't a guy, but nothing was said on the way out, all five operating tables right there, so hard not to look at. It was easier to stare straight ahead, follow Dad past the receptionist's counter, through the front door. Sunny was going to be okay and that's all that mattered.

Dad stepped to the edge of the sidewalk, looked up and down the street, Mom's car nowhere in sight. He came back and knelt close. "I'm proud of you, dealing with this so well."

Dad's thoughts let out his little secret. Dr. Gentry had slept with Mom.

I nodded, but couldn't speak. I pictured Dr. Gentry kissing Mom.

Dad's face got hard, the way it did when he had something serious to say. "Don't think about that." He took my hand. "Look, sometimes the things we love will die. Sometimes they won't. But it's always important to fight. Life's worth fighting for. Don't give up. Sunny's not going to. You've given her a chance. I'm proud of you."

I said thanks, but still couldn't look him in the eyes. "And for the money."

Dad got up and brushed off his knee. "I'm sorry about the class."

I looked in the parking lot. "Think Mom will be back?"

"Probably, but what do you say we start walking?"

I said fine, but with an attitude.

"I know you don't like him," Dad said. "I don't either. But Sunny's in good hands."

Dad had a point but it didn't make anything any better. It didn't make it any easier to follow him, not sure how he could hold his shoulders back, head high as if there was nothing to be embarrassed about, like there wasn't a care in the world.

* * *

Day 65, I was at work talking to a guy in New Mexico about a condo in Vail, I told him he could ski right to his front door.

"Yeah, I don't know," he said.

"You just have to picture it. Fresh powder. A warm fire." I was drawing a picture of Sunny, only had the eyes, those sad eyes as we left her there with Dr. Gentry. "And you'll never beat the price. You even qualify for—"

"I'll call you back. I have to go."

"Okay, well, let me just give the best number to reach—"

He'd already hung up.

I set down my pencil, stared at Sunny's eyes that took up half the page. No mouth. No nose. No face. Just those eyes.

The irises were so brown I colored them black, red squiggles stretched across all the white. The eyes were terrified, the eyebrows angled up because she just wanted me to stay.

Sara said, "Can I see?"

I banged my knee on the desk, had no idea Sara was at hers. "When'd you get in?"

Sara took off her black peacoat and put it on the back of her chair. "Just a few minutes ago. I said hi."

Sara had on a silver turtleneck. Sleeveless. I'd never seen her arms. The scars crisscrossing her flesh. Permanent reminders of how she used to deal with her gift.

She nodded at my notepad. "Anything good?"

I flipped to a fresh page and said, "No, just scribbles."

Sara put on her headset and turned to her screen. "How are the calls?"

There was no point in lying, but that didn't stop me. "Good."

"It'll turn around. You just have to stick with it."

Sara and her optimism. It's what got her here, that belief that things would get better, she'd eventually be reunited with her brother.

"I, uh, had a good time with you and Danny," I said.

Sara was on another call. I looked down at the desk, wondering why I had to be such a creep, picturing her lips on mine.

Sara spun in her chair, mouthed, "Me too."

It made me smile. Sara spun back, telling a woman how there were only three units left. I started to pick up the phone, but one more hang up, one more stop calling, and I was going to lose it.

Carlos's door was closed. I picked up the pencil, not sure what I'd draw. Something I could share, not be ashamed of, like Sunny.

My hand got moving, etched the outline of Sara's desk. She was looking at her screen, a perfect model with her hair pulled back, her gentle face no longer hidden.

I did her hair quick, a bundled brown ponytail. Her eye was six o'clock sky blue, her nose with that small bump. I

shaded her lips the lightest red, even though I'd never seen
her with anything on them.

Two soft lines for her chin, the side of the pencil to
color the turtleneck. Her shoulders and arms were next. I
hesitated, not sure what to do. Her scars were a dull pink
under the fluorescent, none looking newer than a decade. I
thought of leaving them off because that part of her life was
behind her. But that seemed dishonest, fake, too much like a
half-truth. It'd be like drawing Mom holding Dad's hand.

I carefully nicked a few lines on Sara's arm, made it
so they were barely there. The picture wasn't complete so I
filled in some shadows, added the tinge of red to her cheeks.
I had to make her smile a bit bigger too, like the moment she
saw Danny after processing.

I took my time tearing it out of the pad, folding it in
half. I felt like a first grader on Valentine's when I got up and
handed it to her. "Sorry about...sorry." I quickly walked back
to my desk.

Sara tried to keep the woman on the line, but lost
her. She took the paper, opened it up, and didn't say a word.
She couldn't pretend it wasn't her with all the tiny scars.

Sara sounded so young when she said, "I can put on
my coat if it bothers you too much."

"Oh, God no. No. Please. I'm sorry. You look great. I
was just...I didn't..."

She leaned back in her chair, but we were still in
range, no reason to lie. "Some people prefer I cover up. I
don't blame them."

"Sara, they're idiots. If they don't like the way you
look, they're blind. You're beautiful."

She kept looking at her arms. "Oh yes, gorgeous."

"Your scars just show you survived." I took my time looking at her, letting her know everything I said was true. "They show you've been through some bad shit." That wasn't what I meant to say. I wanted to make her feel good, to let her know I loved that she was showing them to me.

She must have heard me because Sara's cheeks got a bit more colorful. "Thanks."

"I mean it. I'm just telling you... I don't know. It's just a drawing."

"And I like it." Sara taped it to the wall where we could both see it.

"You don't have to put it up."

Sara smiled and swiveled toward me. "It's mine, right?"

I said it was, heard Sara thinking maybe I was a nice guy. Then she hoped I wasn't going to start thinking.

It was too late, my pad turned back to Sunny.

Five days of injections hadn't made a difference so Dr. Gentry started her on an IV, strapping Sunny down so she didn't pull it out. She wanted to fight, to run. She wanted to go hiking. She wanted to pull my dirty socks out of the hamper and play tug of war until they were reduced to rags. She wanted to wait until Mom turned off the lights and locked my door so she could jump on my bed and snuggle into the warm spot beneath my arm, little snores all night long.

Demarius, this huge black telepath, who worked security for the building, was suddenly standing beside my desk. His wrap-around sunglasses and crisp uniform said he had power, but this was Brightside. No one had any control over anything.

"Damn, Joe," Demarius said. "You cool?"

I had no idea how long he'd been standing there or what he'd heard. Lying was pointless so I just shrugged.

Demarius took a step back and sat down on the edge of Sara's desk like he was planning on having a deep conversation. "You need someone to talk to?"

I knew he meant Sharon, but felt like testing him. I turned my pad so he could see the drawing. "Let's talk about how I wouldn't let her die."

"You need to clear your head, Homie."

Demarius shook his head and left the room. He didn't want to hear how Dr. Gentry had to operate on my birthday.

* * *

Both of Dr. Gentry's receptionists looked down, saw who it was, and looked away. Mary Ann, the one with braces, picked up the phone that hadn't rung. Jessica, the freckled redhead, got up, went into the back. I hoped they were being nice, trying not to stare at my sweat circles. I'd jogged all the way from school to have an extra five minutes with Sunny, to tell her she'd be okay.

Someone thought they were being funny with the time cards. The pink one Dr. Gentry made special for me was up on the top slot, way out of reach.

But that was nothing next to Dr. Gentry. He'd pass me in the waiting room and let his thoughts fill my head. Images of Mom's sweaty body underneath him. He knew I wanted to punch him, knew every violent thought flowing through my mind. He'd just smile, because there was nothing I could do. He held Sunny's life in his hands. I just had to grit my teeth and take it.

Pamela was at the end of the hall looking like a Q-tip with her rail-thin body and puffy blonde perm. Even if she wasn't busy moving stuff around in the cupboard, she wasn't the person to ask for help. Pamela was one of those people that smiled real big all the time. The kind of smile people give when they're really just holding back a scream.

After a few minutes, the exam room's door swung open. Nancy headed down the hall looking at her clipboard.

Nancy was the only one who could weigh the big dogs. She knew others laughed behind her back because she looked like a man, but that didn't stop her from always smiling, real ones nothing like Pamela's.

I was so glad to see her. I wanted her to be the one to give the good news about Sunny, that she was all better like a miracle. Nancy would have loved to say that. She didn't think I was just a stupid kid who got in the way. She didn't think Sunny wasn't important. She thought Sunny would be okay.

I waved Nancy down and pointed at the pink card. "Can you help me?"

She tried to smile, but it crumpled. It took her a moment to start talking, then all she said was follow her. She walked past all the tables, the place quieter than ever, everyone's eyes trained on their patient or tool or each other.

Nancy turned around in front of the door to the last operating room. She put both arms around me and pulled me close. She didn't say a word.

It was hard to breathe with my mouth smushed against her chest, but Nancy kept hugging. She wanted to take the pain away. She knew it wasn't fair.

Nancy couldn't say she was sorry, but she was, her eyes wet when she stood and walked away.

Everything got super quiet, the occasional beep and buzz too loud. The door was wood with a big window too high to look through.

The door pushed in, squealed the whole way back. Everything was dark. Then I flipped on the switch and it was way too bright, Sunny curled up on the table like she did in that space below my arm. The place that'd be empty forever.

I lowered the lights so they were just barely on. I stepped to the table. Sunny smelled like she did the first day I got her. Her fur was soft except for all the parts shaved off. They'd given her a bath and closed her eyes. The eyes that'd showed so much love no matter what.

This was the last time to see Sunny. Last time to pick her up, hug her tight, let her know she'd be missed every day.

My tears fell on Sunny's face, bounced off the bright collar that never got a chance to get old. From the other room, Nancy said, "He's in here, Mr. Nolan"

The door opened then closed. Dad didn't get off work before five but he was stepping up right behind me. "I'm sorry, Joe," he said. "I really am."

Crying made it too hard to talk. There were no words to say. Everything hurt and it always would. Nothing would make that better.

Dad put his hands on my shoulders to keep them from shrugging up and down. In a way he hadn't said it before, Dad said, "Control it, Joe."

I was trying to, but Dr. Gentry had killed Sunny. I knew it.

"I know this hurts. It hurts me too," Dad said. He walked around so I could see the sadness behind his glasses. "But it'll pass and you'll get over it."

Not this. Not Sunny.

"Stop shaking your head and listen to me." He held my chin because I didn't. "You're feeling a lot of things right now, but you need to relax." He bent down, got eye to eye. "You're sad. Scared. Alone. Pissed off. At God. At Dr. Gentry. Your mom. Me."

I couldn't stop sobbing. Sunny was dead. "Look at her."

Dad raised his voice to cover my crying, not because he was mad. "Understanding what you're feeling is the first step, but naming it's not enough. Then you got to think about it. Rationalize it. Use logic."

Logic said Sunny was dead. Always would be. Just a piece of meat.

"Stop it, Joe." Dad went back to holding my shoulders. "You're feeling an emotion that you're in control of. It's your brain. If you want to be happy, you can choose to be happy." Dad's brown eyes were getting shiny behind his glasses. "If you decide to be angry, that's how you'll be. It works in degrees and won't always get rid of what you're feeling. Lots of times it's just postponing it, but that's alright."

Dad put his hand on Sunny's head, the other on my hand. "There'll be plenty of times where you can think about Sunny and miss her. Way too many times. Then you can cry all you want." Dad checked over his shoulder and turned back, his face all hard. "But don't ever do it in front of that prick."

Dad stood and pointed at the table.

The table was cold, too cold to put Sunny on. The whole room was cold and smelled funny. She couldn't just lie there by herself.

Dad said my name real slow. "Knock it off and put her down."

Sunny went down all relaxed, legs going out each way. Her nose was cold, not wet, no more snores.

"One more kiss and that's it. It's better that way," Dad said. He knew it was true, thinking of holding his first dog, Brutus, while the shivering pooch threw up its insides trying to get rid of the poison.

I gave Sunny one final kiss on top of her head and turned my back on her.

Dad took off his glasses just long enough to wipe his eyes. "I'm proud of you. That's what it means to be a man. It's easier to be controlled by sadness and fear, hatred and jealousy, and all that other bullshit than it is to control them."

The man talking right then wasn't the same man that came home after work every day. This one was someone to look up to.

There were no more goodbyes, we just went right through the door, into the main room, right past Donny who thought it was pretty queer for me to be holding hands with my dad. Past Felicia who said she was sorry, thought poor kid, that dog never had a chance.

At the counter, Jessica said sorry, too, like it could make it all better. And maybe it did a little because she really meant it, her bottom lip shaking because Sunny looked like her Princess.

I tried to say thanks, but it came out all mumbled.

Jessica understood. She said to take care. Then Dr. Gentry came out of the consultation room. He said he was sorry but didn't sound it. "Go ahead and take tomorrow off, too."

Instead of running out the front door like my after-work dad, Dad stood right there and put his hand on my shoulder. "Joe won't be finishing up."

Gentry went red, used his I'm-not-mad voice. "It'll be good for your boy to learn the value of hard work and fulfilling promises."

"He already knows both of those."

"You have any idea how much that dog cost us?"

"Well, it wasn't enough so we're leaving." Dad turned for the door. "And if you have a problem with that why don't you take it up with my wife? I'm sure you'll be talking to her."

Dr. Gentry thought of Mom bent over his desk.

I don't think Dr. Gentry even saw my dad's fist before it sent him crashing to the floor.

We left. The door swooshed shut, Dad's rusty red Tercel parked at the curb. Dad opened the passenger door for me. "And just so we're clear, I said try to control your emotions. I didn't say it always works."

Sharon nodded. "I understand."

"Is that something you have to say? That's what they teach you?"

"I don't say it unless it's true."

Sharon had seen me at my lowest, heard my darkest thoughts. I knew it wasn't her fault, but I couldn't stop myself. "This is a fucking joke. You love it here."

"Not all the time."

"Well, you act like you do. Is it better in Brightside because you didn't leave anyone behind? No one back home gives a shit about you?"

You prick.

I felt like crawling into the chair.

Sharon opened her mouth to speak, then closed it and cleared her throat. After a second, she regained her composure and said, "I left everyone."

Neither of us said a word. There were no pictures up. I'd figured her a lonely workaholic.

"Six years Tom and I were married," she said. "Abby just turned one."

I looked away from those eyes, down to her wedding finger, the white circle of skin.

"Don't feel bad," Sharon said. "No one here knows."

I couldn't get over how she could keep that from everyone.

"I don't think about them during the day," she said. "And no one's ever asked. No one asks me anything."

I said I was sorry. "Look, it was just a thought. Are you saying you've never even had the thought?"

"We're not here about me."

Again Sharon slipped. Thought about the first time she'd swallowed that bottle of pills, before she found meditation, inner peace.

For the first time, Sharon showed she was just as broken as the rest of us. I felt sorry for her, especially as that stupid mantra hummed in her head.

She sat up straight. "Let's talk about your parents, about your mom."

"There's nothing to talk about."

"But you hold so much anger."

"Pretty sure every kid does."

"You're not a kid."

"You know what I mean."

"I think it's time you give them a call."

"Why?"

"To get closure."

"Closure?"

"You need to let go."

"Fine. Sure. Whatever. I'll call my parents. Can I go now?"

Sharon bit her lip. She'd let me into her mind, all those sad moments. She wanted me out of the room. She said, "Go down to the first floor to pick up a prepaid cell." She filled out a form, gave it to me.

On my way out, I turned back. "I'm sorry about your family."

She gave me a sad smile.

The clerk downstairs handed over the phone. He said it was monitored, that if I called anyone but the people on Sharon's list, I'd be sent to The Cabin.

Outside the wind was whipping the trees, turning them into curled fingers, looking like they were ready to break. Snow falling in clumps from those towering pines.

I jogged into my building, headed down the hallway, walked soft on the creaky carpet. Vanessa, Sharon's flunky, had the first room on the right. She probably had her ear to the door, waiting for me to walk by so she could get me one-on-one, smother me with good thoughts, try her hand at making me happy. Vanessa said all I had to do was listen, give her a chance. If she could see the bright side, anyone could.

Harry and his shitty toupee had six pairs of shoes lining the hallway, a proud display for everyone to see. His attempt to make people think he had friends, but the guy was a hermit who loved Lysol, the whoosh whoosh whoosh of that can always going.

It smelled like nothing outside Ivan's bedroom, but that's because he'd been taken to The Cabin for trying to steal a car, as if he could actually get through the gate. Alex, the first anorexic man I'd come across, was taking bets on if we'd see Ivan again.

The worst was Erica, the girl who doused herself in perfume to cover her lactose intolerance. She kept her stereo all the way up to hide the awfulness she poured into her toilet.

Every day was the same, the smells never changing. No guests staying over long enough to add their own scent. Everyone on this floor usually alone.

Some of my neighbors had been married, and some still were, probably the loneliest people I'd ever met. Brightsiders still went out, hung out, fucked their brains out.

They just went about their business when they were done, something always keeping people apart. Things better left unsaid turning us into what we'd become, not trusting others enough to let them close. Not allowing ourselves to become vulnerable.

When I finally got to my door, I found another present. I threw it in the closet with the rest of the crap.

Crap just like the rest of my apartment. It came with the room, what Belinda left behind. The Ikea dresser with the 27-inch TV taking up the top of it. The light blue armchair with sweat stained armrests stuffed in the corner. The tiny table beside it, a place to put my drinks.

The cracks shooting out from the ceiling fan, which hadn't worked since Belinda's first suicide attempt.

Erica's stereo was shaking the walls.

I sat on the bed, flipped open the phone, and powered it up.

* * *

I was eight, sitting Indian-style on our living room couch, just me and my Rubik's Cube. The TV was off because Mom figured watching all that crap was part of my problem. She was in the kitchen waiting for Dad. He'd just pulled into the driveway.

The Rubik's Cube wasn't mine. Steven said I could borrow it until I figured it out. I'd had it over a year.

There were a bunch of people who couldn't figure out the puzzle, but most of them said it was because they weren't trying. If they wanted to waste a few minutes of their life, they could do it.

I'd been trying, failing. Steven even let me watch him solve it real slow. Five times.

I was staring at that stupid block, the center square a smudgy white, eight bright yellow ones circled around it. It was the closest I ever got, just two squares in the wrong place. The white one on one side, yellow on the other. No matter how many twists and turns, it was always those two squares.

The back door opened then slammed shut. Dad's feet stomping into the kitchen. I held onto that cube and waited for him to toss his keys onto the table then say goddamn it when they slid right off. Like they always did.

Dad stayed in the kitchen where I couldn't see, him and Mom talking too low to hear. Ice clinked, the fridge opened and closed. A soda fizzed.

They were way too far for their thoughts to be heard, but I knew they were talking about me. That I was such a disappointment.

Mom had her proof. My IQ test from school. Knowing Mom, she was gloating, shoving that paper in Dad's face, saying I told you so. It made me keep trying with that cube. If I concentrated, I just knew I could get it right. I wasn't an idiot.

She left the kitchen and stopped next to the dining room table in her green and white checkered sundress like she was a good housewife. She gave me one of her quick smiles and said, "That's enough of that, Joey."

I turned to the TV, saw my sad face staring back at me in all that black. I wiped off the tears and looked back at Mom. Mom was done with me, already to the hallway, closing the door behind her. A few seconds later, the shower started. There was no noise from the kitchen.

Up until then I was never a cheater. Partly because I thought I'd never get away with it. Partly because I just knew it was wrong. That's what Dad always said.

A soft clink of ice cubes came every few seconds. Dad was still in there, drinking his drink, most likely figuring out what to say.

What I did next wasn't hard. Corey did it all the time. He'd bet five dollars that he could solve it in under five minutes. He didn't always get paid, but he never lost.

I put my fingernail under the corner of that white square and raised it up slow, careful not to scrape off the sticky stuff. I did the same thing with the yellow square on the other side.

The fridge opened again and Dad poured another drink. I concentrated real hard and laid down the white square, made sure it was lined up. The fridge closed. Dad headed for the dining room and I placed the yellow square, rubbed it smooth with my thumb and turned it over so the red, white, and blue sides showed.

Dad stepped into the dining room and stopped at the table, his wrinkled white shirt, his tired blue slacks. He set his wallet and keys down so quietly I barely heard them over the shower.

He took a drink and turned toward me. From his spot at the table, Dad spoke way softer than normal, like he might have to come close. "So, you want to tell me what's wrong?"

"Nothing."

Dad took off his glasses. He needed the top of them for the TV, the bottom part for reading. I'd only seen them off when he was in bed. He set them next to his wallet.

He said, "You've been crying."

I couldn't look at Dad so I stared at the TV. "I'm not crying."

Dad came closer and stood in the way, his white button-down my new screen. "Don't do that, Joey. Look at me."

What I liked about Dad was how he usually stayed on point, only speaking his thoughts. "It's okay to cry once in a while," he said.

I said okay because I wished he'd just leave me alone, forget all about me. But another part of me wanted him to sit down and see the cube, understand that maybe the numbers lied. I wasn't as dumb as they thought.

Dad stepped right up to me. "Can I sit?"

I wasn't used to Dad asking permission or him being close so I just sat there, didn't say a word.

Dad picked up the Rubik's Cube and sat down beside me, the hair on his arm touching mine. The cube was in his far hand but Dad didn't even glance at it, those naked brown eyes of his really looking deep. "So what's going on with you?"

I wasn't used to Dad's smell. It was too clean, like he hadn't done anything at work. Mom smelled more like a man than Dad did. Underneath all that sweet, a light touch of cologne always there, always different.

The water stopped but neither of us asked why Mom needed to wash up before her tennis lesson. I didn't say it was her second shower of the day.

"So what is it?" he said. "Why were you crying?"

"It's dumb."

I pictured the test lady, the one who wanted to do things to me. Awful things. Naked and alone in her office.

Dad jerked back. I didn't know he was like me at the time, but I suddenly wondered if I wasn't alone.

He was picturing the test lady, the one he'd never seen.

When my eyes widened, I just heard a hum, Dad's way of pushing out the thoughts, the things he didn't want me to hear.

He kept his eyes on me, but started playing with the cube, turning it over in his hand. "Those tests aren't all they're made out to be. We shouldn't have had you take it in the first place."

"Cuz you know I wouldn't do good."

"That's not true." Dad turned the cube even slower. "And don't say cuz unless you want everyone to think you're stupid."

"Everyone's gonna anyways."

"No one will know about your score unless you tell them. You're smart and I don't want you to ever think different."

"No, I'm not."

"Don't you think I'm smart? You're just like me."

That almost made the tears come back.

Dad gripped the cube, had it so the yellow side was up. "But being book smart isn't what's important and you need to understand that. Scores on tests and grades in school don't mean squat. Your mom thinks they do, but, between you and me, what you have is more important."

I thought he meant hearing thoughts and I couldn't breathe. How much had he heard, what things had I thought about him?

"You're kind," he said. "You have a big heart. You're going to be a good man. You're special."

I relaxed a bit, but it was hard to listen. I looked him in the eyes. "You think so?"

"You know it's true."

He finished his drink, set it down on the coffee table and wiped his lips. "You got to be careful, though. You have a real gift, but you have to remember who you are. You can't always tell people what they want to hear."

"I won't."

"You do it all the time," he said. "And I totally understand it. It feels good for everyone to love you, but sometimes the right thing isn't going to make people happy. But it's what you have to do."

Nodding seemed like the only thing I was capable of.

Dad turned to the cube, acted like it was the first time he saw it. "You solved it?"

I started to say yes, wanted to make him proud, but after what he'd just said, I told him the truth. "I switched the last two stickers."

Dad laughed, told me I was learning, that he was proud. Mom walked by in her towel and rolled her eyes. She thought Dad was coddling me.

* * *

Day 66. The sun was setting and I suddenly had this urge to call Mom. When Sharon suggested I give her a ring, I had no intention of following through, but here, in this room with a closet of weird gifts, I wanted to yell at someone. I punched in the numbers faster than I could think about it.

The phone rang and I tried to remember what she sounded like, if I'd ever had a real conversation with her. Once I'd moved out, I basically only heard from my father. It rang again and I almost hung up.

Mom used the same greeting she used whenever a guy would call and Dad was around. "Who's this?"

"Uh..."

"Joey?" she whispered. "Is that you?"

The setting red sun filled my window, everything beyond it. I brought the phone back to my ear. "Yeah."

Like she was sorry to hear it, she said, "Oh my God."

I realized it was late in Ohio. "Did I wake you?"

"No, not at all. Are you alright?"

"I'm okay."

She sounded genuine when she said she missed me. "So much, I really do."

Suddenly, I was three years old again, just happy to hear her voice.

"I hate this," she said. "I've tried to call, but they won't put me through. I was scared. Have they hurt you?"

"No, I'm fine."

"You don't sound it."

If anyone had been listening to the call, they probably would've believed her, the way she sounded so sweet. "You know you can call me anytime, right? I'm so glad you called."

"Yeah..."

"So how you been, Joey? What's it like?"

I rubbed my temple, tried to quiet the voice telling me to hang up. "It's different."

"It seems loud."

"It's my neighbor."

"Oh, what's his name?"

"Her."

"Oh. Are they nice?"

I knew someone was listening in, waiting for me to slip up. I suddenly felt trapped, felt the anger building.

"I'm sure you're meeting other people. Like you. That must be exciting? Just be yourself."

"What's that mean?"

"Nothing. You're always smart, sometimes too smart—"

"I thought I was an idiot."

Mom sounded a lot more like the woman I remembered, when she said, "I never once called you that."

"You thought I was stupid."

"Joey..."

"You did. I was there. I got a ninety-one on my IQ test. And you thought I was an idiot."

I opened my eyes, looked out the window, everything red.

Suddenly, I was five years old coming home from the snowstorm, hating my mother. I said, "It wasn't my fault. The stuff she was thinking made it so I couldn't think."

"Who?"

"The test lady. She wanted to hold me, feel my skin on hers. She wanted to breathe in my hair."

"You didn't tell us."

"And say what? I'd been hearing thoughts my whole life, knew damn well you hated me?"

"Don't you ever say that!"

"Why? Should I just think it? Does that make it better? Does it make it any less true?"

"Stop it, Joey. Stop it right now."

I did. But only because I was done. I heard the hurt in her voice, even if it was barely there. That would have to be enough.

"Is that why you called? To accuse me? Point fingers?"

I thought about it a minute, loved not having to hear what she was thinking. Imagining her heart being crushed. "Closure." Sharon's word flying out of my mouth.

"How do you think I feel?" Mom said, "You don't think you owe me an apology? Listening in to whatever you wanted."

I took my time to answer, chose to speak the truth. "I guess I do owe you an apology. For the time when I was six and you were fucking Brian's stepdad."

"Don't talk that way."

"When all you could think about all day long was how much you loved him. How you wanted to fly away, how it'd be so much better." I looked at the sky, wishing I could turn back time, put her on that plane. "How he was going to send you to New York, you'd only have to see me when you wanted to."

"Joey, I always loved you."

"I'm sorry for giving you the guilt trip. I should have let you abandon us. Maybe things wouldn't have gotten so screwed up."

"You make it seem like I thought bad things all the time," Mom said. "What about all the good thoughts I had? Don't those count for something?"

"Should they?"

"Don't you dare tell me there weren't times you hated me. I listened to you scream you wished I was dead."

I kept quiet.

"It's natural to have bad thoughts every once in a while. It's natural to be upset and tired and cranky. It's natural to not be satisfied, to want something more." She paused like she had something important to say, then I heard the sobs. "You think it was easy living in that house with you and your father, leaving nothing inside my head. Ripping it out whenever you wanted. I could have left. I thought about it. And yeah, I took comfort in the arms of other men. But I deserved some time to myself, away from you and your dad."

"Poor you."

"You have no idea what it was like."

"Just put Dad on the phone."

"He's not here."

"Then I have to go. I only have a certain amount of minutes."

"Joey, please. I don't want you to hate me."

"Well, I do."

"How can you say that?"

"You know, it wouldn't even surprise me if you were the one who turned me in."

I pictured Saul, that douchebag making the call. I pictured his fat fingers and that shit-eating grin.

Then everything changed.

"I would never turn you in, Joey. Never. And when I found out your father did, I felt like I was going to die."

My stomach churned acid. "You're sick in the head."

"I don't know why he did it. I'm so sorry..."

I don't remember letting go of the phone, but I heard it crack against the floor, my mother sounding like she was screaming from the bottom of a well.

My foot stomped down on the phone, cracking it, shattering her goddamn voice.

Dad turned me in. Just handed me over.

I saw the closet. Opened it. All those fucking gifts. I flung them from the closet. Ripped them open. The little swan figurine, I smashed it against the wall. The fishing pole, I snapped in two. Everything obliterated. Tiny pieces flying across the room, sliding under my bed, cracking against the window. I destroyed it all and collapsed. My own father. The man who would never give up on me, told me he'd always be there. No matter what.

Through my tear-bubbled eyes, I saw a tiny piece of metal. Curved, shiny. Resting right in front of my face on the floor. My hand reached out. I held it under the light. So small and hard and silver, and it wasn't the first time I'd seen it. Felt it pressed against my finger as a kid.

No...

Frantically, I crawled across the floor, sifting through all the broken bits, the tuning fork that wasn't really a tuning fork. The fishing pole snapped in two, the bottom part hollowed out. The metal picture frame with the strange spring.

Everything coming into focus.

My hands putting it together. Dropping the bolt slide into place like Dad showed me. Screwing the barrel.

In ten minutes, there it was.

Eight pounds of power. American metal. The shotgun Dad got when Grandpa decided a mouthful of buckshot beat cancer hands down.

Dad was an only kid, just like me.

The stock's been rubbed smooth, the last bit of sun shining on the wood, bouncing off the steel.

Dad used to say an empty gun was useless.

I searched under the bed, gathered everything, but they weren't here. I wondered if Dad had forgotten. Or if I'd have to wait until his next gift.

But there on the shelf, I had my answer. I walked over and picked up the D-Cell batteries, the ones that didn't fit Billy Bass, the ones too light in my hands. I began peeling the label, saw the plastic red shell. Under an inch. Thirty-eight grams. Eight tiny balls to cause so much damage.

The shell slipped into the receiver with a soft click like it was meant to be. It was the first time I loaded this thing without Dad over my shoulder.

I heard his voice in my head:

Never be afraid when you pull the trigger.

Is this what he wanted? All these stupid gifts to give me a way out?

My hand ran over the stock, smoothed shiny from years of handling. It was a piece of history to be passed on, the history of my grandfather's final shot.

I pushed in the shotgun's safety then popped it back. The little circle was so red. Red like the sun. Like the rage eating at my mind, making me want to scream.

I raised the shotgun, liked how it felt. Something real. Something solid.

Dad's voice still in my head:

Be a man and deal with it.

I looked back at the sun, my eyes hurting, chest hurting, everything fucking hurting. I wanted it to end.

I racked the shotgun, couldn't hear Dad's voice anymore. The man who was supposed to take care of me. The man that was supposed to be there, to love me no matter what.

I guided the barrel into place, the metal cool under my skin. I put my thumb on the trigger guard. The barrel pressed against my chin, keeping it up like Mom always said.

Head high. Eyes straight ahead. My last sunset. Seeing only red.

Everything yelling at me to just fucking do it. Like Belinda. Like Grandpa. Like all the other Brightsiders. The ones smart enough to escape.

But then I pictured Paul breathing into that tube to make his electric chair roll. I pictured my mangled face, some nurse cleaning the shit out of my pants.

I pictured Danny pushing me through the Square, everyone thinking, *What a fucking dumbshit. Couldn't even kill himself.*

The shotgun fell against my lap.

My father's one simple request and I couldn't even do it.

I just ran.

CHAPTER TEN

Day 100 and I'm just trying to get to work. Walking down the sidewalk, the morning air so cold. The helicopter is still circling, which means they haven't found Wayne. That's good, means the Boots are busy. Busy means they won't be checking my apartment, the closet.

I'm running the plan over in my head when I see a group of people outside Lodge Two. They're watching guys in white coats wheeling someone out on a gurney. There's no hurry, because whoever it is isn't moving under the black plastic bag. I know I should keep moving, get to work, look like everything's normal, but I find myself getting closer.

I see Tommy, the nineteen-year-old punk with his bright orange Mohawk, and ask him what's going on.

"Another one bites the dust," he says.

I think about my closet, knowing it's just getting started.

Palmer, the only Boot I know by name, is taking statements. He's got his aviator sunglasses and fuck you attitude. He catches me staring and I don't blink. Palmer's the Boot who almost put a bullet in my head, the day I thought Michelle was coming to save me, when I ran out in the street waving my arms like an idiot.

Someone grabs my arm. Sheriff Melvin and that bushy white mustache.

"You're supposed to be at work, aren't you, Joe?" The way he says it, I know he's telling me to move along, but I ask who died.

"Sheila Clark."

Sheila, the one who saw me with Krystal, the one who swore she'd never tell Rachel. Swore she'd never say a goddamn word.

Melvin wipes crumbs off his shirt. "You know anything about it?"

"No."

"Where were you last night?"

"Home."

"People saw you running all over town. What were you doing?"

"Couldn't sleep."

"You do some laundry?"

"Huh?"

Sheriff Melvin steps in, sniffs. "A lot of bleach."

"Yeah, like I said, I couldn't sleep."

Melvin takes off his sunglasses. I hadn't really seen his eyes before, how they were so open, trying to look like hey, remember, I'm on your team.

Palmer's staring at me, smiling all smug, wanting me to know when this is over he might finish the job. I give him a nod to say my schedule's wide open.

Melvin thinks about reaching for his gun, shoving it in my face, yelling I'm one dumb son of a bitch. The sort of thing he used to do back in the real world.

"I should get to work," I say.

Melvin says that's a good idea. He waits until I'm crossing the street before he heads back into the crowd.

So I keep walking, not running like Day 66, after I found out my father was the one who turned me in.

* * *

I can't tell you where I was running after I'd hung up on Mom. I just kept going, through the dark and desolate park and into the woods. I'd made it three steps when my foot sank into the snow, cold rising over my shoe, seeping through my sock. I yanked my foot right out of my shoe, bent over and pulled it out with a loud *shhhlopp*. There wasn't any grass nearby so I took off my sock and wiped down my shoe, cleaned it out as best I could.

With both shoes back on, I continued up the trail and looked for signs of someone else, kept an eye out for deep snow. The sweet smell took me back to a time I had hope. Back to all the hikes I'd taken with Dad. The hikes Mom couldn't go on because her knees were acting up. How we all pretended it had nothing to do with how much time she spent on them.

Then I pictured Dad on the phone, telling someone to arrest his son.

It took me a few minutes to get to the thick pine where it looked like the trail ended but really just whipped around to the right. I was back at the tree. A rough heart carved into the bark with my name on top, a small heart beneath it, Michelle's name ex'd out at the bottom. Rachel's name, too.

The women I'd hurt, the pain I'd caused.

I kept walking for hours, paying just enough attention to stay away from the fence line. The wind doing its best to knock me over.

Suddenly, a huge cracking sound filled the air.

I spun and watched as a huge tree slowly toppled to the earth. It landed with a thud and bounced right past me, knocked over two small trees before coming to a stop.

One boulder, then two, rolled down the mountain and nestled up against the fallen pine. Several other large rocks were scattered up above. I made my way to them and stood in front of a half-covered cave someone had been hiding.

The fence line was up another couple hundred feet, but sometimes Rangers roamed. I looked around. The woods were silent, no one in sight.

Danny had given me a flashlight keychain and I flicked it on. Wood beams braced the rough walls carved out with a pick. Little metal tracks snaked into the darkness. I followed them, my feet crunching over the dirt. The tunnel seemed to go on forever, and I started to fear another tree toppling, crashing into the cave, trapping me in there forever. But I pressed on, continued down the steep slope, needing to know where this led.

I must have gone half a mile before I finally saw light, that full moon shining at the end of the shaft. My heart pumped and I thought about all those island getaways I'd been selling, pictured myself on the beach drinking something cold as the waves crashed and spread up to my toes.

But then I got to the end of the shaft, a tiny outcrop on the edge of the cliff. My heart stopped. The bridge that had once connected Brightside to the next peak had been destroyed. Two hundred feet down. I threw myself against the ground, shut my eyes. My stomach flopping around. Every inch of me pouring sweat.

But two hundred feet wasn't a mile.

With a lot of rope I could make it. Just not with this wind.

I hadn't thought I'd been up there that long, but my watch showed I had two hours to get to work. As quick as I could I made my way back up the shaft. There was no way I was leaving my new secret exposed so I gathered rocks and piled them in front of the entrance. I swept huge mounds of snow over it as the sun peeked over the horizon. It wasn't perfect, but it'd have to do. I only had ten minutes to be at my desk.

My pants were in decent shape and I'd clean off my shoes better at the office. My jacket was a mess so I stripped it off and wadded it into a ball, walked over to the wall of rocks. Real quick and quiet, I moved a boulder near the top and tossed the jacket into the darkness.

When I stepped out of the woods, it was light enough for me to put on my sunglasses. I cut across the wet grass and headed for the southern archway. That last part of the park was always the hardest for me. The Cabin up the pebbled path on the left. The dog park to my right. The one that'd make me start thinking about Sunny and Lily.

I got on the sidewalk, Super Pawn directly ahead, a name too big for the one tiny window. It'd been a while since I'd looked inside. I usually avoided the store because Robert was always hanging out front, playing with his voice box, trying to get someone to talk to him, make him feel like a person.

The display had a little of everything, mostly rings. The tennis bracelet was on its own, center stage. I couldn't see the inside of it, but I knew Belinda's initials were engraved there.

I was wondering how Robert got the diamonds so sparkly when I walked right into the payphone. My shoulder smacked the glass dome hard enough to turn me toward the beauty salon and dry cleaners across the street, no one in either place to see what an idiot I was.

That's when I saw the orange jumpsuits coming with their shovels. I thought about heading the other way, but I needed to get to my desk. Needed to look like everything was normal.

I tried to control my thoughts, tried to think about anything but the mineshaft, my escape. But I couldn't help it. I finally had a way out, just not the way Dad wanted.

An arm swung out and grabbed my shirt.

Wayne King and that nasty beard.

"Momma's boy has a secret."

I threw his hand off, kept moving.

Wayne called out, "Don't go leaving without me!"

"King!" the guard yelled. "Shut your damn mouth or I'll do it for you."

When the office elevator doors opened, I had to squint my eyes. The sixth floor was always too bright and my head felt ready to split. Nearly every inch of every wall was covered with ridiculous posters of exotic locales.

Until this moment, I hadn't been able to look at them. The bungalow sitting a foot above the Tahitian clear blue waters. The massive Swiss Alps, the sun shining off the snow-covered ski slopes. The promise of the pyramids, the adventure of an African Safari.

Before this moment they had been brutal reminders of all the exciting places I'd never see. But now, with the mineshaft, I just might.

Changing out of my shirt was a priority, but first I had to sit down. I had to get my shit together.

I squeezed between the desk and the wall and dropped into my chair.

My body was already feeling like one big bruise from lifting those rocks. I'd scraped up my arm.

My Extra-Strength Excedrin was on the desk, always in reach. I popped two like they could actually take away my pain. I'd need the whole bottle for that, but with my luck it'd just make me sick.

I pulled out the shirt from my desk. Carlos suggested I have a spare after I'd spilled toner in the copy room, had an accident with the coffee machine. As I buttoned with one hand, I powered the computer and waited for it to warm up. The dinosaur was two years old, plenty of time to get out my yellow pad and two pens, and try not to stare at the wooden picture frame and the fading Polaroid, edges crumpled and black. But I didn't need the photo to remember just how blue the Mad River had been, the number of brown trout I was holding, the way I was smiling at Dad because there was never anyone else around to take the picture.

That stupid kid. That stupid smile. I pushed the frame off the edge, right into the trashcan.

I was letting things get to me so I took a deep breath and leaned back in the chair, rubbed my temples to clear my head. It worked better than a slap in the face and so much quieter.

I reached into the brown bag I'd gotten from the cafeteria and pulled out the cherry-filled donut. It miraculously remained intact except for the blob of red oozing down the side. With no more shirts, I threw it in the trash, gave the frame some company.

Then came the distant drone of a helicopter.

Panic.

To most people the helicopter was no big deal, and maybe I was overreacting, but I just knew they'd found my escape. The escape someone else had tried to cover.

The helicopter sounded like it was coming from the front of the building. I hurried down the hallway.

Grace, Yung, and Trevor had their offices on the left side of the hall, but I was only interested in the ones facing the street. Wendell's was first, the door closed, probably locked, a sad attempt at keeping the donut holes a secret. Sheila's office was next to his, her door closed as well. Always locked.

Nathan, Brightside's resident artist, had the office before the bathrooms and emergency stairwell. His door was wide open. He never closed it, said he didn't see the point because he wanted everyone to know he was so fucking cool.

The bit of morning light coming through Nathan's window let me see without flipping the switch. I entered the office. Five miniature figures stood sentinel around the room and watched me head behind Nathan's desk, the Exacto knife right there, ready to create, remove. The figure sitting on the monitor looked bored, jealous of the one by the phone, both hands on his ears.

I looked out the window and saw all of the Square, but no helicopter. It sounded further to the left so I hurried out of Nathan's and turned down the south hallway. The noise was coming from straight ahead. Past the conference room on the left, Gloria and Edward's office to my right. It was loudest behind Carlos's door, the only one I couldn't see through.

Entering the boss's office was never a good idea, but I did it anyway. From his window, I could see the dull black helicopter was much further than I'd thought, well out of the mounted gun's shooting range. Where it was flying was what bothered me. Hovering halfway up the mountain between the park and the peak, not too far from my carvings, real close to the cemetery.

I closed Carlos's door behind me, started for the elevator and tripped. If I hadn't Demarius would have heard about my plan, not just me thinking about my ankle. Demarius leaned against the wall to my office, his eyes hidden behind the sunglasses.

Demarius was first to speak. "Damn, son, whatchu rushing for?"

"Just trying to..."

"You crack the safe?"

"What?"

He pointed at Carlos's office. "Why you snooping?" Demarius took a step away from the wall, his usual grin nowhere to be found. He called me over with his finger. "Let me holler at you."

I focused on my ankle, not the rocks I'd lifted to hide the cave. "I'm really busy."

"Look, I just wanted to tell you I'm sorry. You know, for telling Sharon about your thoughts."

"Oh...no big deal." I headed for my office, hopped so my ankle was all I could think of.

You one skittish motherfucker.

I threw myself into the chair. My mind back in the forest. The helicopter would see everything. I was fucked. Everything fucked.

Sara was back at her desk. I hadn't even seen her on the way in. She was staring at me. Her eyes looking ready to pop.

"Joe, you need to stop."

"Stop what?"

"Just stop." I knew she'd heard every thought, but I couldn't control it.

She stood and grabbed me by the arm. She was stronger than she looked.

"Get up."

"Why?"

Get. Up. Thinking like a drill sergeant, just like Dad.

I had no choice and hopped on one foot, trying to save my ankle. Sara peeked out the door, checked to make sure the coast was clear. Then she dragged me out of our office, me jumping like an idiot. We made it to the stairwell. There wasn't a camera, but Sara still wouldn't open her lips.

Are you fucking crazy?

"It was our chance to—"

Sara smashed her hand over my mouth and thought, *You're going to get yourself killed.*

I don't care.

Joe, if you go running out there, trying to find whatever you found, they're going to send you to The Cabin. And then they're going to ask who else knows. They're going to ask Danny.

Danny doesn't know.

But I do.

I hated everything coming out of her head, but she was right. If I went out there, I'd never make it to the cave. Even if they didn't know about the mineshaft, I'd lead them right to it.

Sara took my arm. "Let's just go back to work."

I clicked my teeth, knowing it was my only option. I spent the rest of the day at my desk, trying not to think. I couldn't help it though, which was why Sara never let me leave, even for lunch. I stayed tethered to that computer, away from everyone else.

After work, Sara invited me over for dinner with Danny. My mind on the helicopter. There'd been no reports of the cave, no mention of anything, except for a few new Brightsiders delivered into the fold. I prayed that was it.

Danny popped up from the take-out we'd gotten, started spinning around, his mouth motorboating, spit flying like a disgusting sprinkler.

"Danny, sit down," Sara said.

"I'm a helicopter!"

"Danny, go wash up. NOW!"

Danny kept twirling to the bathroom, almost toppling over into the kitchen.

"Maybe I should try that." I tapped my skull and said, "Might turn off this stupid thing."

Sara gave a sad smile, a small shake of her head.

I felt awful and said I was sorry. "And thank you for earlier."

"You're welcome." Sara took a bite of her cold fries. "Although, you would've had plenty of time to spin in The Cabin."

I smiled, but my mind went to Rachel, to the Boots taking her away, to the forest, the cave, the long, winding shaft, and that terrifying drop. Sara flinging over the ropes. Both of us rappelling.

Sara looked at me, her eyes hard and cold. "No."

"But we could get out of here."

"And I told you no. Now, you need to stop—"

"Why? Don't you want to be..." I trailed off, suddenly afraid there were cameras. The Council said they'd had them all removed from the apartments, but there was no way of knowing.

We can be free, I thought.

And if we get caught? Sara shook her head. *Then everything I've done to be here will be for nothing.*

The awkward tension physically hunched my back. Thankfully, Danny broke it by walking in with toothpaste caked around his lips.

I stood and said my goodbyes, said it was late. Sara walked me to the door.

Joe?

I turned, saw the sadness swirling in her eyes.

I care about you, and I can't thank you enough for looking after Danny. But if you're going to put us in danger, then you can't see us anymore.

My lip started to split between my teeth. I nodded and left before Sara felt sorry for me.

Staying away from Sara was impossible. Her desk was eight feet away. But it might as well have been a mile. She focused all her energy into her calls, and when she did look at me, she only told herself I was a co-worker, nothing more. She had to do this for Danny, because she knew I'd made up my mind.

CHAPTER ELEVEN

Day 100 and I'm alone in my office. I keep staring at Sara's desk, wondering when she's going to get back. I need to talk sense into her. That's what I was trying to do when Carlos came in, said the Council needed to see her. She asked for what, but he didn't know.

Now, her desk is empty, except for the single red rose, which isn't for Sara. It's for Rachel. Alex, the little kiss-ass put it there when I went to the bathroom, just to let me know he wanted her. I'm lucky I wasn't there because I would've cracked, let him know the truth about Rachel. Alex with his short brown hair perfectly combed like an innocent schoolboy. Don't worry about all those muscles, the smirk that said anything he wanted was his. Like Rachel.

Poor Alex has no idea it's never going to happen.

I put my headphones on, trying to block out the thoughts, but I keep falling back to when Rachel re-entered my life. The biggest mistake she'd ever make.

* * *

By Day 70 I'd made up my mind, so I stayed away from Danny like Sara had asked. I bought an audio book, "Learning Spanish 1 and 2" to keep my mind busy, keep me focused on something other than the mineshaft as I passed Brightsiders in the Square or the halls of work. I looked like a weirdo, repeating "Cuánto cuesta la carne," "Me encantaría un vaso de agua," and "Puede que me señale el bar más cercano?" Weirdo was better than everyone knowing the truth.

I stayed away from the woods. Had no idea if the cave had been discovered, boarded up, filled with cement, like the one on the Eastern edge, but I couldn't risk going up there to look. Not right away. I had to appear like everything was normal.

At work, I'd pull up maps of California to chart a course to Mexico, memorize names of cities, the closest airports, the distance to island getaways. I learned all I could about the best places to go and every time Carlos came around he was thrilled to see I was taking my job seriously.

In Brightside, everyone had to find a purpose, a reason to stay alive. That's what Sharon would always say. And Grace. And Phillip. Carlos, too.

Well, I definitely had my purpose: To get the fuck off this mountain.

Every night, I'd train. Started jogging. Did push-ups, sit-ups. Needed to get my body ready for long trek to Mexico and beyond.

I even practiced the hum Dad taught me to clear my head. I realized it was just another version of Sharon's mantra.

Dad used to say, "Sometimes you have to make noise to make everything quiet."

I hated him for what he'd done, for turning me in, but I finally had a purpose here in Brightside and no one, especially my father, was going to screw it up.

I only allowed my fantasies of beaches and bikinis at night, holed up in my apartment when I knew everyone was asleep. I actually felt sorry for the others, the ones who'd never breathe free air again. I felt awful about Sara, too, but I'd given her a chance. She just refused.

Still, I knew she was right, that Danny wouldn't survive on the outside. He'd end up getting us caught. He was better off here. When I would remember, I'd make him drawings. I'd been putting the good ones into a book and was planning on leaving it by his door on my way out.

Finally, after two weeks, on Day 85, I decided to visit the cave. Snuck out in the middle of the night. Looked like I was just taking a jog, my normal routine, running around the mountain repeating, "Gracias por el bridis."

There wasn't a soul in the Square. I ran a few laps to make sure then took off into the trees. Even the calm Spanish woman's voice couldn't tamp my anxiety. My heart thumped against my ribs as I climbed up the hill, passing the tree with Rachel and Michelle's names scratched out, stepping around the huge tree that had fallen and cracked open the cave.

And there it was. Perfectly untouched, just the way I left it, every stone in place. Not a single crack to see into the cave. Part of me wanted to rip them away, just take off down the shaft, but I didn't have my supplies. If the cave had been demolished, I didn't want to get caught with rope, bottles of water and cans of soup. I ran my finger along one of the rocks, knowing it wouldn't be long.

Day 86 would be my last.

The next morning I tried to stay vigilant, focused, but the excitement made everything fizz. I felt like a kid going to school on his birthday, waiting, watching the clock, needing it to move faster so I could go home. Only this time home was everywhere. Anywhere but Brightside.

I put on my headphones and opened the door. "War Inside My Head" was playing, just the right song for the number of people on the sidewalks, everyone heading to work.

I cranked the iPod as loud as it went and kept walking, not worried about someone stopping me. A question not heard, a question not answered.

The music shut everything out. Dad used to hate it.

* * *

I was thirteen and we were in the car when Dad ripped off my headphones and chucked them into the back seat. "You think I want to listen to that crap?"

"It's not crap."

"You're going to blow out your ears. And mine."

I forgot he could hear my quiet rage, the screaming, blasting thoughts.

He blew out a long breath of decaf and was much calmer when he said, "You really think you need to listen to that stuff?"

I hit Stop so I didn't waste the batteries. "I like them."

Dad grabbed my Walkman, slid out the tape, held it up so he could read it. *"Fear is the Mindkiller.* Funny."

It wasn't funny. It was power. It blocked out the rest of the world. Three men punishing their instruments, their fans, themselves. Saying the stuff I wanted to, but didn't know how. I didn't bother telling Dad any of that because he wouldn't get it. I held out my hand and said, "Maybe I like noise. Maybe it's better than most of the crap I hear in your head."

Dad took the tape, dropped it into his shirt pocket. "Real nice."

I sounded like a baby when I told him to give it to me, said it was mine.

Dad pulled the tape out and looked at me like he wanted to know the truth, not what I thought he wanted me to say. "Let me ask you something," he said. "You do know what people think of other people who listen to this music?"

I couldn't lie. Not when Dad looked at me like that. I said, "People are gonna think what they're gonna think. I'd rather not hear it."

Dad shook his head. "Who cares what others think of you. Let them think what they want. That's your answer?"

"For now."

Dad handed me the tape and headed down the street. "You're a better man than me."

And I was. I never would've turned someone in, especially my own son.

* * *

Day 86. I tried to keep busy at work. Made calls. I even sounded enthusiastic for the first time, because I wasn't selling the customer. I was selling myself. On the island bungalows, the desert resorts. But time wasn't moving fast enough. I kept thinking it was time for lunch, halfway there, but it wasn't even ten. I decided to get something to drink, headed for the door.

Sara said, "Joe..."

"I'm fine." I put on my headphones. "See?"

The break room was to my right, a good chance it was empty. This wasn't a place where people hung out by the water cooler so I opened the door, stepped inside.

Carlos finished digging in the fridge and headed toward me, a water bottle in each hand. He was talking so I had to take off my headphones and ask him what he said.

"I've been going over numbers with Sara. I think we can crack Canada."

"Cool." I pictured myself walking the streets of Montreal.

Carlos cocked his eyebrow.

Quickly, I said, "I can put together a list of territories."

"Great."

I went over to the cupboard, tempted to grab the dusty can of regular coffee, but I started a fresh batch of decaf. The last thing I needed was having my mind race. There was just no telling how far it would go, what I'd give away.

Carlos asked when I could have it ready.

"End of day."

"Great."

Thankfully, he left. I felt bad for Sara, knowing she had to sit in his office every day listening to Carlos wearing out the word "Great!" and yet somehow keeping my secret.

I poured my cup, walked out, and nearly spilled it at the sight of Rachel. Her hair was dried out and frizzy. She wore this baggy wool sweater that reminded me of my grandmother's before she was sent to the psych ward. Rachel's eyes were wide and jittery like she'd been electrocuted. Her skin pale, almost gray.

Those wide eyes grew even wider when she saw me.

"Joe!"

She hurried over and threw her arms around me. More life than when I saw her in The Cabin, but still not Rachel.

"Thank you for visiting me. The nurse said you were really sweet."

"Oh..." I noticed everyone in the office coming to gawk at the girl formerly known as Rachel. This shattered creature standing there in that disgusting wool sweater. I brought her to my office, the one that used to be hers.

It was a mistake. Rachel started crying, sobbing, then suddenly pulled it together because she knew people were still watching.

"Why don't you give us a second, Sara?"

Sara said sure thing and closed the door behind her.

Rachel just stood there staring at her old desk. She wasn't blinking.

I asked her, "When did you get out?"

"Um...this morning. Yeah..."

"Well, that's great."

We stood there for a few seconds. I couldn't believe how old she looked. Rachel messed with her hair. "I'm getting a new apartment. They're painting it now so I haven't had a chance to shower."

"You look great."

Rachel knew I was lying, but she appreciated it.

"So," she said, "I was thinking maybe we could have dinner tonight?"

"Tonight?" I pushed the thought of the cave out of my head. "I'm buried in work. I don't really know how long..."

The tears spread across her eyes again. She had the image of the cave rattling around her damaged brain. It confused her. She shook her head like she was mad at it.

"Screw work," I said. "Dinner sounds perfect. Where do you want to go?"

"I was thinking Oscar's. You know, like old times."

"Oscar's it is."

Rachel smiled and it looked like it hurt.

"Well, let me get back to work. I'll meet you at eight."

She sounded a little more like her old self when she said, "Okay."

I couldn't have her near anymore. As calmly as I could, I opened the door and smiled, told her, "I'll see you tonight."

Rachel leaned in and put those dry, cracking lips on mine.

Sara came back in after being subjected to Rachel's scowl. I couldn't look at Sara, not with what was going through her head.

She was telling me to look at Rachel, to really take a good look, because that's how I was going to end up.

* * *

I shouldn't have gone out with Rachel that night. I should've just blown her off and made my escape. But Rachel deserved better than that. I wasn't the only reason she got sent to The Cabin, but I could've stopped it. Could've told her what she needed to hear. I knew the Boots were coming and I just sat there like a coward. If I didn't have the balls to face Rachel and tell her how sorry I was, how would I ever step off the two hundred foot drop, stay one step ahead of the dogs and the bullets?

Plus, I needed an alibi. I wanted everyone to see me out on a date. My weird late night jogs were causing people to talk. Some thought I was overcompensating, trying not to lose it. Others thought I already had.

Rachel was waiting for me on the bench under the flapping American flag, just like Night 38, only this time she wasn't in her fancy green dress. She wore a long skirt, a big puffy coat. When she saw me she wished she'd worn something nicer. I was in the only suit I had in Brightside.

"You look nice," Rachel said.

"You too."

Rachel fidgeted in her coat, looked down at her big, ugly snow boots.

"Come on, let's eat," I said.

I hadn't meant to take her hand, but there it was. Rachel blushed, she had hope we might actually work out. I hummed in my head to keep out the truth.

"What song is that?" she asked.

"Just something my dad used to sing."

Rachel heard what I wanted to do to him for turning me in, but she didn't say anything, just rubbed my arm as we walked through the Square. It felt good.

We sat in the back, even though the hostess wanted us up front to make it seem not so empty.

"I've never seen it like this," Rachel said.

The hostess told us that they'd been bringing in so many new people everyone's wages had been cut. I worked on commission so I hadn't thought about it before. But it made sense. There was only so much money to be made on a mountaintop.

Rachel looked over the menu, but I knew what she was going to ask before she even said it.

She wanted to sound normal, not broken inside, the girl trapped in The Cabin, swallowing pills to sedate her mind. "Tell me about Sara."

"She's Danny's sister. She came here to be with him. Actually turned herself—"

"You like her."

"We're just friends."

Rachel studied me, her eyes peering over the menu.

"Nothing happened."

Rachel ducked down behind her menu. "I know."

How easy it was to remember all the reasons Rachel and I should never have been together in the first place.

She took a drink, steeled herself. "Okay, I just want you to listen."

I pulled on my sleeves, wished I'd worn something more comfortable. "Alright."

"I need to apologize," she said. "For what happened. For us."

"No, I'm the one who—"

"I said listen. Just...listen."

"Yeah, okay. Sorry."

"I thought about you a lot. I mean, when I could think. And I understand that I have way too much stuff going on inside. And I know you didn't always find me attractive."

"Rachel..."

"And it's okay. I'm not perfect. And I didn't want to accept that. It's why I did a lot of the stuff in the past."

The list of men spinning in my head like a Rolodex.

"And...you have a lot of stuff, too, which is okay. We have this thing, whatever it is, and it makes life so much more complicated. Sometimes we feel hurt because we know what other people are thinking. Other times we feel superior because no one can ever lie to us."

The cave flashed in my mind before I could catch it.

"Joe, what's going on?"

"Nothing. Keep going." I thought loud and clear, *I want to hear about The Cabin.*

She focused and said, "It was really hard at first. Like you were strapped to something, only you didn't really care. But it taught me things. To be accepting. Open. To realize that Brightside offers us a place to be with our own kind. In the real world, relationships are always one-sided with us. Here, for the first time, we're on equal footing."

Sharon's words spewing out of her mouth. I focused on the fork, the starting lineup for the Cleveland Indians. It was teenage sex. Thinking of anything to push it back, delay.

"Joe, I need you to hear me."

Jim Thome on first base.

JOE!

"I'm here."

"We rushed things and that's my fault. We really don't know each other, but I'd like to try. I mean, we have all the time in the world."

Time. In five hours I was supposed to be tying the rope.

Rachel's first thought was I was going to hang myself.

"I've been drawing," I blurted. "Like a lot. For Danny. And I think I'm, uh, getting pretty good. Even faces, which are impossible."

Rachel thought about my first drawing, the one of her under the tree. Her nose so Jewish.

The waitress arrived and I took a breath, happy to have something new to focus on. But when the waitress left, the thoughts started coming in waves. I ate breadsticks. Savored every bite. Focused on the crunch, the crumbs melting on my tongue. I'd never taken such pleasure in a breadstick, never focused my entire being on a bite.

Suddenly, Rachel's foot was rubbing against mine. She'd taken it out of the boot. I felt her stockings sliding up my pant leg. Nylon on flesh.

Rachel slowly took a bite of her breadstick, like she was going to make it explode in her mouth. It was weird and a little sexy. Sexy was just fine. Meant I didn't have to think about the cave, my escape. I put my hand on her foot, brought it up between my legs.

The waitress came back, pretended like she forgot something and left. Her thoughts calling out: *Why do the perverts always sit in my section?*

At some point during dinner it started to sleet, and by the time we hit the sidewalk, we could barely keep our balance, the wind howling in the night. I wasn't drunk, but I'd had a glass of wine at Rachel's insistence. I figured it'd give me courage for the long night ahead. But with the ground covered in ice, my escape would have to wait. Climbing down a dry rope was treacherous enough.

"Joe, what are you thinking?"

Shit. "We should get inside."

"Yeah."

The wind was so loud I couldn't hear Rachel's thoughts. Prayed she hadn't heard mine.

The sex was odd. First, we're tearing off each other's clothes, the next, I'm underneath her and Sara pops into my head.

Rachel touched my cheek.

"I'm sorry," I said.

"There's nothing to be sorry about. It's natural. Let's just focus on us."

The Cabin had broken the old Rachel, left this kind-hearted creature behind. I wondered if some time in The Cabin was just what I needed.

In between licks on my chest, Rachel said, "You. Really. Don't."

Afterwards we stretched out, caught our breath. Then Rachel got up to pee. Two steps later she cried out. "What the hell's all over the floor?"

Rachel navigated through the jagged pieces of broken gifts I hadn't fully swept. The pieces to Dad's puzzle. I thought Rachel was out of range, but when she came back, her body haloed by the bathroom light, she said, "I want to see it."

"Rachel, I don't think—"

"Yes, you do. You want to show me."

Fucking telepaths.

I got up, threw on some underwear because my dick had shriveled like a snail, and there's something not right about holding a shotgun buck naked. I stepped into the closet, reached up to the top shelf, where it was hidden behind a bunch of Dad's boxes.

All shiny and ready for action.

"Can I hold it?"

I knew there weren't any cameras in my room. The Boots would have come the night I'd assembled it.

"Be careful."

"It's heavy." Rachel pretended like she was going to drop it, but caught it and laughed.

"Don't mess around."

"Why? Scared?"

Rachel pointed the gun at my chest. I couldn't re-member if I'd taken out the shells.

"That's not funny."

"Kinda is." She aimed at my dick.

So kind-hearted, so fucking crazy.

"Just give it to me," I said.

Rachel backed me up and I fell onto the bed. She grinned like a child who'd found her Christmas presents. "Tell me about the mine," she said.

Rachel, shut up.

Tell me about the cave.

Rachel knew I wasn't going to say shit, not with her pointing the shotgun at me, so she handed it over. I thought about hitting her with it like a baseball bat.

In this little girl voice, she said, "Please don't hit me, Mister."

The tension broke into laughter.

Truth was I wanted to tell her. Sara was the only person who knew and she thought it was the dumbest thing that had ever clanged around my head. So I silently told Rachel everything. How I'd found it, traveled down the shaft in the dark, seen the drop-off, covered it back up with rocks. We both figured the Boots and the Council never knew it was even there, it'd probably been covered up before we arrived.

Rachel sat next to me, and I realized I wanted her to come along. Didn't want to do it alone. I needed someone to help me down the two hundred feet and Rachel used to rock climb. Before I could even ask, Rachel said:

"Yes."

CHAPTER TWELVE

Our accelerated relationship took off again. Rachel and I were already gone in our heads, already free, lying on some beach, our sweat glistening in the sun. But she had to meet with Sharon every day. Had a daily check-in to make sure she was still on the mend. I worried Rachel would slip, our plans landing right in Sharon's head. We'd both end up in The Cabin, this time forever.

"You don't have to worry," Rachel said. "Listen." She closed her eyes. "What am I thinking?"

I zeroed in, but heard nothing. No mantra, no hum, just silence, like Danny.

"You're too far," I said.

Rachel pressed herself against me. I listened. Still nothing.

She stepped back, curtseyed. "I learned it in The Cabin. That's why they let me out. Nothing but a blank slate."

"How?"

"Something about the pills. I can just shut it off now."

I thought back to the howling wind outside Oscar's, how I couldn't hear her thoughts, but it wasn't the noise. She just wasn't letting me in.

I asked if she could get me some of the pills to see if they might work for me. She said she'd try, but it probably wouldn't happen. The medicine was locked up in The Cabin. Always a guard posted.

We focused on the plan, focused on training. Rachel said if I was going to do this I had to get more comfortable with heights. We started with a few thirty-foot drops near the pond. Then we moved on to her building, had me lean out her window on the fifth floor. When a Brightsider passed underneath, I sprayed Windex on the window, pretended to clean. All of it made my heart feel like it was going to pop. My lungs closed. Everything tunneled. But I had to keep pressing, pushing myself higher.

By Day 99, I was ready for a rooftop. My office stood seven stories high. The final test before our escape.

I woke early, already sweating, picturing the fall, my face splattering. Rachel asked if I was afraid of falling or landing.

"What's the difference?"

Rachel said, "Landing means you don't want to die. Falling means you're a pussy."

I didn't answer, but we both knew which category I fit into.

Rachel asked if I wanted her to go up there with me for moral support. I told her no, this was something I had to do alone. Plus, rooftops were completely off-limits to anyone not in maintenance, which was why after Rachel left for her meeting with Sharon, I had to see Danny, even though Sara warned me if I ever came around, she'd turn me in, tell Sharon, the Council, anyone who would listen. She'd tell them I'd found a way out.

Danny was technically a janitor, but all the maintenance men wore the same uniform. I watched from down below, hiding behind a tree, hiding from the rain, as Sara handed Danny his lunch. He'd done the buttons wrong again on his coveralls and Sara quickly fixed them. They came out of their building. Danny waved that pencil-clenched fist at her and headed to work.

I cut him off.

"Joe!"

"Hey, Danny."

"Where you been, Joe?"

"Sorry, I've been busy. But I brought you something." I pulled out another drawing. Billy Bass, Danny, and Sara singing.

"Joe!"

Seeing how excited Danny was almost made me smile. "You like it?"

Danny sounded like he was going to burst. "Best one."

"Good, that's good," I said. "Now, I was wondering if I could ask you a favor?"

"Anything, Joe."

"I need one of your uniforms."

"You're too big."

"Doesn't matter. It's for a...game."

"Can I play?"

"Eventually, but I'm still working out the rules."

Danny's eyes got all wide and weird. I was trying to control my thoughts, but something slipped.

"Why are you going to the roof, Joe?"

I pulled him close, whispered, "I'm trying to challenge myself. Some personal improvement."

"Like your jogging?"

"Just like that. Now can you help me out?"

Danny thought about it for a second, pictured his boss, Larry, yelling at him, but when he looked down at the drawing, his head started bobbing.

"Okay."

Danny started taking off his coveralls right there in the open.

"No, no, one of your spares."

He said okay and we walked back to his place. My drawings covered the walls. He'd kept every one, tacked them up like a museum.

Danny went to the closet, pulled out his spare uniform. He started to give it to me, but pulled it back. He was thinking about how I'd been avoiding him, angry at me for being such a crappy friend.

I told him I'd make it up to him.

"Can we have a party?" Danny asked.

"Sure."

"What's your favorite cake?"

"I don't know, whatever you like."

He handed me the uniform. "No, what you like."

"Okay, Angel Food."

"It's spongy, right?"

"Yeah, it's spongy. But now I have to go."

Danny sounded pretty sad when he said, "Okay."

I got to the door and Danny stared at me.

Be safe, Joe.

I told him I would.

* * *

Break was to be taken at ten o'clock, but it had stopped raining and I didn't want to risk waiting another twenty minutes. Sara was meeting with Carlos. I couldn't let her know.

The stairwell was silent, not a noise above or below. It was for emergencies only, definitely not breaks, something Carlos loved reminding everyone.

I peeked over the railing, made sure I was alone, then headed up the stairs. There was a padlock on the roof access door, but I'd also borrowed one of Danny's keys.

Quickly, I slipped on Danny's spare coveralls and matching hat, both two sizes too small.

The Council had ruled the roof off-limits after Paul's plunge. It was stupid to argue something could be completely fine one day, a liability the next. The roof was a roof. It wasn't safe or unsafe. It just was. Just like a rope. A knife.

Puddles covered the rooftop. It'd been warmer these last few days. I wondered if it'd stay this way.

I told myself to stop thinking, time was running out. I needed to get back to my desk. There was a folding chair leaning against the wall where they kept the air conditioners. I took my first step, and even though I was nowhere near the ledge, I was already soaking Danny's coveralls with my sweat.

Baby steps.

I moved over to the folding chair. Stepping up, even against the wall, made me dizzy. I looked out at the mountains toward the cemetery, couldn't see a thing with the sun peeking over the top, my eyes useless without my sunglasses.

It wasn't a great feeling knowing the Rangers could see me, but not so bad I'd be a good little citizen and go back downstairs. I needed to do this. I kept my hand on the wall at first then slowly peeled it away, just me standing on the chair, high above it all.

It wasn't enough. I didn't come here for the view so I got down, moved my chair a bit further. Closer to the tiny concrete ledge that spanned the front of the building. Closer to the ledge Paul said he tripped on.

If I couldn't beat my fear of heights, Day 100 would become 200 then 300. I'd never leave.

I focused on the piece of duct tape on the pipe eight feet from the ledge. I wiped my hand on my pants. As brave as I could, I took the chair across to the strip of silver. My next goal.

I'd like to say it was easy, that I walked right up to that line and put down my chair, but that'd be a lie. It took a minute, maybe two, to get the chair there, only a second to sit my ass down, get closer to the solid roof.

The map Rachel had made crinkled in my back pocket. I took it out, held it tight as a gust of wind blew across the roof. I opened the map, looked at it until my heart stopped thumping, until I knew every line, could see every squiggle. Every road within five miles.

I folded the paper in half two times. Then I ripped it again and again until there was no piece bigger than a stamp. I threw my hand in the air, let the wind carry most of the pieces away, the rest floating down onto the roof, soaking up the water.

I was doing pretty good right then, didn't feel nervous at all. Without a second thought, I scooped up the chair and duck-walked two feet, stopped about six from the ledge. My safe spot.

The move didn't do much to me, I was doing okay, my breaths still rapid, but not out of control. Still, I had to go all the way. Today wasn't the day to do anything half-ass. Not when it could mean getting my head blown off because I couldn't climb out of the mineshaft.

I wasn't scared. My father's voice in my head, *Be a man!*

The ledge was right there, close enough to touch. The building was less than a year old, but the foot-high hunk of concrete looked like it'd been slapped on as an afterthought.

I told myself not to freak out, that I was fine. Nothing was going to come along and push me off the chair, send me over the ledge. I was safe. I was doing it. I was being a man.

Somehow I got my right foot on the ledge, pressed on it a little to check for some give. I didn't feel any.

I looked to the sky, figured this should be the part I got rained on. Maybe a thunderstorm, the world's biggest flashflood, something to come and fling me off the roof, sending me to oblivion or a fancy wheelchair.

A long time ago, I learned God doesn't answer prayers.

If I wanted something done, I was going to have to do it. Before I could chicken out, I reached forward, put my hand on the ledge, the wet concrete, a rough slickness.

My heart was thumping like I'd run a mile, but I was holding onto the ledge. I straightened my legs, got my ass out of the chair. I took a step closer.

I was shivering, clutching that ledge like it was the only thing stopping me from going over. Scared shitless like a little kid. Scared of the American flag, snapping in the air.

Every day since my first one, I'd given myself two options; leave Brightside or else. But I couldn't do either one stuck on my knees.

I squeezed the ledge tighter, holding my breath without even knowing it. I blew out and took three quick ones, made my heart slow down. I was twenty-eight years old. I could let go of the ledge. I could lean over and look down. Look down eighty feet, the wet sidewalk below, the exact spot Paul landed.

The wind kept on coming, the red, white, and blue firing *whack, whack, whack.* I was getting up. One way or another, I was getting on that ledge. If I couldn't, I couldn't do anything.

I kept both hands on the concrete, my eyes on the flag, forced one foot up. I brought my other foot underneath me, had both on the ledge. I put my hand on my chest, felt my heart trying to break through.

There was no one around that could hear me, but I said, "I pledge allegiance to the flag of the United States of America. And to the Republic for which it stands."

And I was. I was standing so high above it all!

I squinted my eyes as the wind whipped at my face. "One nation. Under God. Indivisible. With liberty and justice for all."

From somewhere in my head, my father's voice, *Do it!*

I'm not sure what happened, but I wasn't scared. Of Dad. Of falling. Of anything. Dad couldn't hear me, but I said, "Sorry. Not today."

Then I heard Mom's voice, *Come on, Superman. Let's see you fly.*

I flipped them off with both hands, middle fingers to them and the world.

Fuck them. Fuck Brightside. I was tired of getting picked on, told what to do. I'd stand on the ledge all goddamn night.

A few Brightsiders took notice from across the Square.

I remained perfectly still, wondered who else was watching me openly oppose a Council sanction. The seconds ticked and the wind whipped, threatened to tip me over the edge. The longer I stood, the more ridiculous it got. I was being childish and irresponsible. I had a job to get back to, at least for a while, and I had the plan.

And then all of a sudden a woman shrieked from behind. "Joe! Don't!"

I turned to see who it was and my right shoe went back too far, the heel hanging off the ledge taking my weight with it. Sara screamed my name again and ran toward me from the doorway. I began to fall.

Everything switched to slow motion. My arms wheeling, Sara running, no way she'd make it in time.

I lowered my center of gravity and leaned forward, but my right shoe slipped off, took my left foot and the rest of me with it. I threw my arms out and they slammed onto the ledge, my chin bouncing off the concrete with a loud crunch. Blood filled my mouth.

I thought I might make it then my weight pulled me down, nothing for my hands to grab on. Sara kept running, about ten feet away, the sharp corner digging into my fingertips.

Like I wasn't trying to with everything I had, Sara shouted, "Hold on, Joe! Hold on!"

I blocked the pain and scissored the air trying to find the wall in front of me. My grip was almost gone, fingers bleeding, feet coming up short.

Sara skidded to a stop and grabbed hold of my hands just as my fingers gave way. My right hand slipped through hers, but she held onto my left, her nails sinking into my forearm.

She yanked on my arm with both hands, but I was dropping inch by inch. I threw up my right hand and gripped the outside of the ledge. It stopped my descent, but it wouldn't last long. My weight had already pulled Sara to the ledge and if I didn't do something, I'd be taking her with me.

I kicked my legs one more time and my right foot struck the smooth brick. There was a loud snap like concrete cracking and gravity kept pulling me down, but I held on, the tips of both shoes now pressed against the wall.

I was about to push off and up the wall, my one final shot, when Sara gasped and fell forward, losing her grip. Her shin smashed into the ledge an inch from my nose, a split second before my straining neck lost the battle and my head was pulled over the edge, my cheek dragged across the rough concrete.

I couldn't see anything but the wall in front of me. I flung my hand where I'd last seen Sara and clutched at the air. My fingers touched fabric and grabbed. "Pull, Sara! Pull!"

Sara grunted and took off some of the pressure. I dug the tips of my shoes into the wall and kicked off and up.

My head popped over the ledge and I slammed my face against the concrete, used it to pry myself forward. There was a loud rip and my hand fell against the ledge, Sara's sleeve beneath it.

I heaved up with everything I had as Sara pulled and grunted and pulled again. Finally, I was on my back, the wet roof feeling so good. Safe.

Neither of us said a word, our ragged breathing saying it all. I tried to catch my breath and stared at the gray skies. When I was able to sit, I put my back against the ledge. Sara sat beside me.

I was too embarrassed to look at her and I hated myself for ripping her blouse and hurting her leg. I grabbed hold of my pants to stop shaking. Everything was numb, no pain anywhere, but I'd feel it later. All the blood and scraped skin promised that.

Once I could speak, I said, "I'm sorry."

"It's okay."

"How'd you...?"

"Danny called me. He said you were..."

"I wasn't going to jump."

"I get that now."

Sara felt stupid, knowing she almost got me killed. She'd run right up after Danny's call, terrified I was going to take the plunge like Paul.

She'd come to Brightside thinking that Danny was all that mattered, but then she had to go and meet me, the only person who'd ever been nice to her brother.

"I'm sorry for pushing you away," she said.

I tried to lighten the mood. "I'm just glad you didn't push me up here."

We sat there awkwardly. I knew there were people down below who must have seen what just happened. I knew there were people down there that were probably laughing their asses off. I wondered if Krystal was down there laughing, too. And Wayne.

Sara said, "You're an idiot."

"I know."

"Which makes you a bigger idiot."

"Yeah..."

I'd thrown up my middle fingers to get caught.

"I hate that I met you, Joe. I really do. I don't want my life to be complicated. I just want things to be normal. For once in my stupid life. But..."

I took Sara's face, turned it ever so slightly, that cute little bump in her nose, those eyes. My lips pressed against hers.

Some kisses are just the prelude to sex. Others are simply a kind gesture, a more intimate thank you. But every so often, a kiss silences everything. The universe just collapses and obliterates your silly existence. You realize everything you'd been holding onto was plastic, stupid, just a distraction. Like Rachel. I didn't love her, never did. I just wanted someone to hold, press against. She never felt like this. Not like Sara.

Die or escape weren't my only two options. There was a third. Stay here in Brightside. With Sara and Danny.

I thanked her for the kiss, for putting up with me, for saving my life. I figured I might not see them for a while. My stunt would be a ticket straight to The Cabin.

Sara squeezed my hand and assured me everything would be alright.

Sara's entire arm was bare without her sleeve.

"Sorry about the shirt. I'll get you a new one," I said.

"Don't worry about it. We should get back."

It took me a second to get to my feet, the pain finally settling in. I wanted to thank Sara for being so calm, but all I could think of was how I couldn't even afford to buy her a blouse.

Sara stood, her shin all bloody. "I'll be okay."

We made our way down the stairs, my legs shaky. Not just from almost falling. But from the kiss.

"What the hell were you thinking?"

That voice. Not Sara's. Hardly human. Crazed, deadly.

Rachel's.

She stood at the bottom of the stairwell. Sara's eyes glanced at me, scared. I told her to go and she went.

Rachel pinned me up against the wall. "What the fuck were you doing? Everyone saw you!"

"I know. I'm an idiot."

Rachel's eyes narrowed. She raised her hand. I thought she was going to hit me, but she just wiped my lip with her thumb. Pink. Little flecks of glitter. Sara's lipstick.

Rachel's mind bubbled with rage. Sara's sweet neck in her hands.

"It's not what you think." The dumbest thing I'd ever said, because it was exactly that and so much more.

"I see..." Rachel trailed off, tiny steps back. She bumped into the wall, jerked forward.

"Rachel, calm down."

She started pulling at her hair. Spinning round and round. I tried to touch her, but she threw off my hand. Her frantic thoughts came in flashes. Us making love. The Boots dragging her away. Krystal underneath me. Sheila telling her everything, the stupid bitch who promised she wouldn't. I was pouring water in her mouth at The Cabin. I was telling her we could escape together, that I loved her.

Everything closing in. The darkness. Hurt. Anger. Everything but hope. That was gone. Nothing but the vile truth.

Rachel threw open the door, ran. I chased, but I couldn't catch her. Then Carlos grabbed my arm. Demarius grabbed my other. Rachel kept running, crying, broken once again because of me.

"Let go of me!" I shouted.

"Naw, bro," Demarius said. "You're gonna see Sharon."

CHAPTER THIRTEEN

After sitting in the waiting room for an hour, Demarius brought me in and threw me in the chair. He asked Sharon if she wanted him to stick around. Sharon said no, it was fine. Demarius closed the door and I sat there staring at her stupid Zen waterfall.

Sharon's mantra ran at full volume, caused my fists to clench. Unable to listen another second, I said, "Why don't you just send me to The Cabin?"

"Is that what you want?"

"Since when do I have a choice?"

"You chose to go up to the roof, showing everyone what you were capable of. A big F.U. to all of this."

I didn't understand why Demarius had taken me and not the Boots. I didn't see one of those assholes the entire walk over. They never missed a chance to crack down on an infraction.

"Would you like me to call them?"

The Boots.

I just kept chewing on the inside of my cheek.

"Getting caught makes things easier, doesn't it? Takes away any responsibility?"

I didn't know what she was talking about, but I figured she was trying to probe. I focused on Rachel and Sara, even Krystal. I thought about every dirty thing I'd done and thought.

Sharon looked disappointed. Not disgusted. Not angry. Just sad.

Something was different about her. She wasn't spewing her New Age bullshit, just sat there waiting for me to speak. My mind started to drift to the cave, but I refocused. Thought about Danny, my drawings, the non-existent fish in the pond. I forced thoughts of Steven, bald and frail in his white room. The picture of the swan.

"Joe."

"What?"

You can trust me.

I hadn't even been thinking about the escape, but it seemed she already knew, that she'd known for a while.

"Why do you think your father turned you in?"

"I don't know."

"Take a guess."

"Because I'm a coward."

Sharon's face squinched up, like she was mulling it over. "Seems strange, doesn't it? Your father turning you in for that. I mean, if he thought you were a coward, why would he send you here, where you could easily tell us about him?"

It didn't make sense, but nothing ever did with him.

"Everything I touch turns to shit," I said. "He probably figured it was only a matter of time before I fucked up and he didn't want me to get hurt. So he took the necessary steps to make sure..."

"So your father loves you?"

"What?"

"He risked exposing himself, didn't he? Drawing attention to you, put the spotlight on him. Seems pretty selfless. He must care about you an awful lot."

I didn't want to let Sharon see me cry. I ran my fingers over the dried blood on my chin.

"Why am I even here? I broke the rules. I should be in The Cabin, right?"

Sharon sighed. "That's correct." Then she leaned forward. "But you wanted to get caught, didn't you?"

I honestly didn't know why I'd stood up there like a maniac.

"You didn't think it was fair to get out by yourself, did you?"

How did she know about the escape? Her range was beyond mine, sure. But I'd been careful.

"You also didn't want to get Rachel hurt, right?"

Rachel... She must have said something in one of their little check-ins.

Sharon shook her head. *She never shared a single thought.* "You were afraid you'd freeze at the edge and they'd find you, putting Rachel in even more danger. She would've been shot for attempting to escape."

"You have the wrong opinion of me." *I'm a coward. I only think of myself.*

Sharon cocked her head, smiled. "I don't think so." Her perfect posture returned. "Do you remember the first time you came to see me? I said I had a good feeling about you."

"And I said you were going to be disappointed." Just like every other woman dumb enough to get near me.

I turned. The distant sound of the helicopter grew louder and louder, even shook the window. I saw the metal bird racing across the sky, figured it was bringing in more pathetic fuck-ups like me. But then it started hovering, like it was looking for someone.

"Joe, I need you to look at me," Sharon said. "Joe!"

I'd never heard Sharon's voice above a librarian's. My neck swiveled.

"Do you really want to go to The Cabin?"

I pictured myself in the chair, sitting there catatonic, not a care in the world.

Sharon's jaw clenched. Her mantra was failing her. "You know what? Why don't we take a break?" Sharon stood, threw some stuff in her purse. "I'll be back in five minutes and you can tell me your decision."

She was really leaving me alone in her office. The door closed and I sat there confounded, almost going out of my head. Was this some sort of ploy, some psychological mind game?

The helicopter was still hovering. I got up, watched it circling around the Square, where the Boots were patrolling. Something bad was going down.

I turned, saw Sharon's desk, her stupid calendar of daily affirmations. Next to it was a letter. From my father. It was addressed to Dr. Sharon Appleton.

I'm writing to you on behalf of my son, Joe. He's a good boy, might not seem like it at first, but if you have patience, I have no doubt he can be everything you need him to be.

Turning him in was the hardest decision I've ever made as a parent, and I will probably always wonder if I made the biggest mistake of my life. I will carry this guilt to my grave, because I can't undo it, so I only ask that you look out for him. I'm trusting you here. He's smart and has a good heart. He might not always act like it, but he knows right from wrong. And he'll make the tough decision when called. He's a soldier, just like his old man.

The only other thing I ask is you don't tell him right away that I'm the reason he's there. He'll need time to adjust first. But when you feel he's ready, just let him know that I love him.

Sharon closed the door. "Your father's a good man."

I tossed the letter on her desk. "For turning me in? That's your definition—"

"He's *always* been a good man."

I stepped back. "You know my father?"

"I do. But I'm not going to say another word about it until I know your decision."

The way she said it, I realized The Cabin wasn't just a physical location. Sharon wanted to know if I'd rather bury

my head, sit there drugged up, my mind a gentle sea, or if I
was ready to hear the truth.

You can't just dangle something like that. I didn't
move, stood there waiting. Sharon pointed to the seat. After
a few seconds, I sat, knowing this was going to hurt.

Sharon walked over to the window, stared out at the
whirring helicopter. Just stood there and I started to shift
uncomfortably, suddenly afraid.

It's okay, she thought.

Then she silently began the tale, never once turning
back, knowing if she looked me in the eyes, she'd never
finish.

According to her account, Sharon met my father
twenty years ago at a small underground rally for people like
us. Hardly anyone knew telepaths existed, but there were
rumors, speculation. Some of us had been locked in loony
bins. People like my grandmother. It's why Dad showed up
in the first place. He was angry and alone. He sat in the back
and listened to unspeakable stories of violence and fear. And
everyone knew it was only going to get worse.

After the meeting, Sharon went up to Dad and they
shared their experiences. She asked if he wanted to be more
involved. Dad said he couldn't, told her he had a family, a
son with the same gift. He didn't want to draw attention, see
anything happen to me. So he left, but every so often, like
once or twice a year, he'd seek her out, wanted to know how
things were going, if there was anything he should know,
prepare for, in order to protect his family.

Sharon said he would've done anything to protect us.

Then the government created Brightside. They started rounding up Thought Thieves. Soon we'd all be on the

mountain or dead. Sharon and a few others arranged for friends to turn them in. To infiltrate. Only a few were selected, the ones with the strongest ability, able to quiet their thoughts, block everyone out, so their secret would be safe. The selected offered themselves up, settled in, got chummy with the Boots as hundreds of people from all over the country arrived by helicopter. These secret agents never let on, never aroused any suspicion, just quietly put themselves into positions of power.

I'd moved out years before and Mom hardly came home, so Dad volunteered to help the cause. They turned him down though, because when they tested him, he couldn't keep it in, the secrets. He would have broken, slipped up, and all this would be for nothing.

Months went by and Dad kept trying to join the fight. There was talk that Brightside wasn't sustainable. Too expensive. Soon they'd have to start cutting rations, supplies. Eventually there'd be only one alternative: execution. Quietly, of course. America would never hear a word, although they probably wouldn't care if they did.

That's when Dad decided to offer me up. Since I didn't know anything, I wouldn't be a liability.

My entire head felt like it was about to implode. I couldn't feel my hands or legs. Just this throbbing in my brain. Why would he...

Michelle, Sharon thought.

And slowly, it all fit together, just like Grandpa's shotgun.

A week before I got to Brightside, Michelle said Dad had come over looking for me. She said he seemed panicked, asked for a drink. She said he sat there for an hour waiting for me, but I was working late, trying to boost my bonus. She turned on the TV, a newscast about Brightside. Michelle said she was just trying to make conversation, talked a bit about how dangerous these people were. Dad said he agreed, but kept asking these strange questions. She thought he was just afraid like the rest of the country. But here in Sharon's office, I knew Dad had been testing her.

Michelle would've turned me in without hesitation, even called up her brothers to take care of me first.

Michelle's mind made up Dad's.

I couldn't breathe. Everything closing in, the walls. Sharon's stupid waterfall was all I could hear, sounded like someone was pissing in my ears.

I went for her desk, ready to tell Sharon to inject me, to make everything calm, like Rachel was in The Cabin.

"Joe, you need to calm down."

My words to Rachel coming out of Sharon's mouth.

I'm sorry, she thought.

I saw my father's face, that big, dumb grin. I yelled at her and pressed my thumbs into my closed eyes, shoving them back into my skull.

The door flung open. Demarius ran in, tackled me into the chair. Pinned my arms. I kept fighting. Demarius pulled tighter.

Enough! Sharon thought.

I told you he was going to crack.

Sharon bent down, touched my face like I was a child. *No, he's not. Isn't that right, Joe?*

I thought about Mom, rubbing butter on my face.

"Joe, what's it going to be?" Sharon asked.

"Let's just send this motherfucker to The Cabin."

"Quiet." Sharon forced my eyes to hers.

What's your decision?

My father's voice flowing through my brain. *Whatever you need.*

I found myself ten minutes later in the lobby. I don't even remember taking the elevator. People were gathered outside the double-doors. There were whispers about a death. I entered the fray wondering if they were talking about me.

Robert was four feet in front of me, his big black microphone held to his throat, the wire traveling down to the brown box at his waist. He said, "Hey. Joe. You. Know. What's. Going. On." The lack of inflection made it so you couldn't figure if Robert was asking or telling.

"No idea."

"Wayne. King. Escaped."

The reason for the accelerated news, why Sharon and Demarius said we had to do this tomorrow night, the end of Day 100. Their plan, my gun.

"I'm. Going. To. Catch. Him," Robert said. "Want. To. Join. My. Team?"

Robert kept talking, but I couldn't hear with the helicopter directly overhead. The woods were only a few blocks away. Part of me wanted to say fuck it. Take off out the cave. Sharon, Demarius, and Dad could eat a big bag of shit.

I hadn't meant to think it so close to Robert, but his eyes widened, knew what was rattling around my head.

I started walking. The helicopter kept circling, scouring the town for Wayne. I kept thinking about taking off now, but knew I wouldn't make it fifty feet before they caught me. I also couldn't leave Rachel behind. Not like this.

She deserved better. All she did was believe in me. Love me. Wanted to take care of me. And I repaid her by ripping out her broken heart.

I turned left, The Cabin up on the hill, its windows open, all warm and inviting.

Come on in, have a seat. Let your problems disintegrate.

Rachel's building was up ahead. Sharon said to let her be, said I needed to get some rest. Sharon loved to talk. Just like Dad. The two of them plotting and scheming to stick me up on this goddamn mountain.

I knocked on Rachel's door, kept knocking until her neighbor, Frances, came out and told me to shut the hell up or she'd call the Boots. Frances looked like a man with her chiseled jaw and thick, bushy eyebrows. I almost told her to go ahead, they'd never show. But I just walked out and headed for the diner, then Oscar's, then the park. I asked if anyone had seen her. No one had, except Nathan, the guy who proudly came to Brightside a virgin. Then he met Krystal.

"She wasn't looking so hot," he said about Rachel. "That was a couple hours ago, though."

I thanked him and continued my search. I needed to find Rachel, apologize, beg her to take me back. We could escape tonight, leave Sharon, everyone in this fucking town.

I kept moving, never stopping long enough to think about anything but Rachel. She was going to be pissed, but I'd tell her all the things she needed to hear. I'd mean it, too. At least for the moment. That'd be enough.

Sharon had given me a special cell phone, one that couldn't be traced. She told me to only use it if there was an emergency. I wanted to call Rachel, but she didn't have a phone. No one did but me.

I wandered through the Square, even went back to Rachel's place, but she still wasn't there. I started thinking maybe she'd found some guy and they were busy getting sweaty paying me back.

I didn't even notice the storm rushing in, but soon the sleet felt like needles. Thunder boomed.

It was midnight and I could barely stand. Freezing, wet, and weak, I headed back to my place. The hallway light fixture was filled with so many bugs I could hardly see, but my nose was working fine. There was a new smell. A little ripe, like sweat and something else. It grew stronger as I got to my door.

That smell.

The door did its usual creak, just a lot louder. The kitchen was dark, blinds keeping out most of the moonlight. I emptied my pockets onto the table, then locked the door.

A sliver of light lit the first bit of hallway that led to the bedroom where the blinds were always closed.

Everything looked normal, as normal as it can in the dark. It sounded like it should, too. Quiet. Everything was fine.

Except for the smell.

And that sliver. The tiny slice of light that made it hard to move.

Someone was here. My first thought, Wayne, but the door had been locked.

I went for the light switch, but it just flicked up and down.

I said Rachel's name but it came out soft and pathetic. I said it again, louder this time. Rachel was the only one with a key.

No one answered. Just more nothing. Then the tiniest plop.

It took forever to move away from the door and get into the hallway. I stopped after two steps because the smell was all wrong.

The next step was the hardest. The next one after that even harder, the wall still blocking most of the bedroom.

The wall ended with my next step. My hand fumbled around for the switch. This one worked, threw light all over the room. I wish it hadn't. Oh God, I wish it hadn't.

A body on the bed. But lying the wrong way, legs hanging off the window side. The plaid skirt bunched up around her underwear. Rachel's favorite Love-A-Lot Care Bear ones she liked to dance around in. Her matching t-shirt that used to be white, the bear and its big heart drowning in blood.

The outfit told me it was Rachel. Rachel without a face.

The top of her head was gone, her hair clumped beneath the ragged, hollowed out bowl, a stream sliding down the comforter, onto the carpet.

I asked the stupidest question. "What the hell did you do?" I asked it again and again but the answer was right there.

I turned. The whole room was red, it started to spin. Slow then fast. I held onto the wall and it helped a little, but it was wet with something I wiped off without looking.

"Goddamn it, Rachel! What the hell did you do?"

Rachel didn't respond, didn't have a mouth.

But on the floor I received my answer.

The shotgun beneath her dangling feet, the stock lying in the puddle of piss.

The lightest rain fell from the ceiling. It drip, drip, dripped onto the bed, her body, what was left of her head. I wondered if the roof was leaking.

But it wasn't rain. Up on the ceiling, Rachel left me a gift. She'd painted me the perfect Pollock.

I fell onto her body, my face smashed against that bloody Care Bear. Thunder boomed outside the window. I wondered if that's what covered the blast. If someone had heard it, they'd be here.

The bracelet her daddy bought her was half submerged in a puddle by the pillow, the diamonds splattered crimson. They matched her ring, the only thing better than her diploma because the school couldn't take it away.

Rachel didn't have a pulse. I was stupid to check. Her wrist still warm, still soft. Her hand so small, not squeezing back to say everything would be okay, that we could still leave together, sprawl out on that beach.

Something creaked in the hallway outside. Bootsteps.

I pressed my cheek into the bedspread as if I was actually hiding. Like a child who doesn't understand the physics of hide-and-seek.

More bootsteps. Muffled voices.

Rachel's hand went back into the puddle. I pulled the rest of her closer. Saw her jaw. The lower half on Love-A-Lot's smiling face. The top half shards on the ceiling.

I waited for the knock, waited to see their expressions when they saw me cradling Rachel without a face.

The light switch. I needed to turn it off, make them think I was sleeping, but I couldn't move. Every neuron dead, just like Rachel.

The chair had a chunk of hair draped across the armrest.

The Boots getting closer.

I closed my eyes, squeezed Rachel's chest, squeezing so hard I thought I might sink into her ribs, disappear forever.

Why did I ever come here? The Cabin was so close. All I had to do was walk in, and the nurses would take care of the rest. I'd never know about Rachel. Never...

Suddenly, the Boots were running, but not towards me. Each step softer, further down the hall until there was nothing.

It was hard to stand without one hand on the wall. I looked around, needing a way to explain this in case they came back. There was nothing on the nightstand, the TV, the bathroom counter. No paper, something that said no one was to blame.

But Rachel would never leave a note. That's what she'd told me one night at Oscar's. She said people only wrote them to make other people feel better, which was bullshit. If she ever did it, she wanted everyone to know it was their fucking fault.

Why did they ever let you out of The Cabin, Rachel?

Sharon had to know she was unstable, that this was a possibility. She didn't make the call on Rachel's release, but she gave her recommendation. Was this part of the plan? What the hell did Rachel have to do with our escape?

I fell back against the wall, slid down until my ass was on the floor. Something was digging into my leg. The cell phone. I pulled it out, started to dial Sharon, but stopped. What if this was all a setup? She could just be waiting for me to call, so she could send Palmer and the rest of the fucking Boots.

But why tell me about the plan then? Why tell me about my father if it was just to set me up for Rachel's death? She could've sent me to The Cabin. I even offered.

My father, the man who turned me in, was the only person I could trust. Laughter sprayed from my lips. I looked over at Rachel's body, the blood and chunks of brain and just lost it, doubling over, cracking up because there was nothing left. I didn't need The Cabin. I was already fucking gone.

But it finally lost its amusement. The awfulness settling back in. I started dialing.

"Hello?" Mom said.

I couldn't speak, so tired, shattered.

"Joey? Is that you?"

I took a deep breath, wiped back my hair wet with blood. "Hi, Mom!"

"Joey, what's going on?"

My whole body shook. "I fucked up."

"Joey, come on, you're scaring me."

"Yeah, I'm scaring me too."

"Tell me what's going on. Are you okay?"

"No, I'm not." I sucked air through clenched teeth.

Mom sat there, breathing, waiting. We both did until she finally asked what I'd done.

"Oh...I don't have enough minutes for that. Can I just talk to Dad? Please. I really just need for him to get on the fucking phone."

"I'm going to call the doctor, okay. Is that what I should—"

"NO, MOM," I said, my voice not my own. Wild and crazed like a man covered in his girlfriend's blood. I took a deep breath. "I just need you to get Dad. Can you just move and fucking grant me this one simple—"

She sounded scared out of her mind when she said, "He's not here."

Big inhale through the nose. "Okay...when do you expect him? Soon?"

"He went..."

"Where? He went where?"

In the smallest voice, she said, "Fishing."

I felt like the top of my head was going to eject like some fighter jet, like Rachel's.

"He went...fishing?"

"Joey, he needed a break. Since you – since he...did this, it's been eating him alive. He's not well. It's killing him."

My father's not well. I'm sitting on the floor covered in Rachel's flesh, and my father needs a vacation.

"Joey, whatever you've done, can you make it okay?"

"No, Mom." I laughed. "No, I don't think I can."

"Joey! Listen to me. Are you listening to me?" That voice from my childhood, the one that said if I didn't shut my mouth she was going to smack me.

* * *

I was five years old, sitting in the back of the Buick, my face burned and peeling. We were parked out in front of the school, all the kids filing in, but I wouldn't budge.

"I don't wanna. I feel sick. My stomach."

"You're fine," she said. "You just don't want to go with your face all messed up."

But that was only part of it. I couldn't go back to all the voices, the thoughts, everything so loud I'd piss my pants. I didn't say any of that to Mom, she wouldn't have understood or she'd think I was even crazier than she already did. That's why I just sat and scratched at my cheeks.

She snapped, "What did I say about that?"

I shoved both mittens back in my jacket. "I forgot."

"Do you want to look retarded? You think they aren't going to make fun of the kid tearing off his face?"

The slushy gray playground was right outside my window. All the kids were out there, but I wasn't moving. I blew on my window, fogged it up with a white cloud, slunk down so low I couldn't see out. I knew what was waiting, all the laughter, the vicious taunts. I'd start crying and they'd call me a little baby and that would be even worse.

Mom was back to smiling at herself in the rearview, her eyes not quite making it. She was back to sounding nice, too. "Come on, Joey. You know the drill."

The drill was Mom pulled over, I got out. There was no holding hands, walking together to the gate. No kiss goodbye. But the drill was different this morning. I wasn't moving.

Mom got something from her purse, brushed red on her cheeks until they matched her hair. "You need to get going. Go learn your ABC's. We're not doing this anymore."

My safe spot was warm. It wasn't totally safe, but far enough away so Mom would have to climb over the seat to swat. She wouldn't do that in front of the school. Not for a few more years.

"That's enough," she said. Mom flicked her eyes, played with the lashes, never once looking my way. "I'm wasting time. And gas."

I tried not to sound like a baby when I said, "I hate school. I don't want to go."

Mom turned the mirror, gave her you-little-shit five-second stare. "You think I want to drive you here? You think I want to dress you in the morning or make your Lucky Charms?"

I knew a lot about Mom, way more than I wanted. I thought I knew her buttons, how far I could press them. That's why I said, "Don't then."

Mom spun around, gripped the back of her seat. "Goddamn it, young man. If you make me get out of this car..."

I said, "They're mean to me."

Mom moved quicker than I'd ever seen, getting out and slamming her door, jerking on mine to see it was locked. She stood there in her purple leotard, banged the window with her fist. "Open this right now."

Mom was about to break through the glass. I slid across the seat, pulled the knob up, went right back to my spot.

Mom opened the door, lowered her voice so other parents couldn't hear. "It's freezing. Get out now."

I looked away from Mom's chest, put my boots on the seat. "I'm not going."

Mom started talking way too sweet, like her god-damn perfume, didn't care how much they both bothered me. "Sometimes there are things you don't want to do, but you gotta do them anyway."

Tameka's dad walked by which explained Mom being nice.

Mom turned toward him and waved.

When Tameka's dad was far enough away, Mom snatched my ankle like it was some kind of snake, squeezed my boot like she was trying to choke it.

"You're hurting me," I said.

Mom kept her grip and yanked me across the seat. "Stop being such a sissy. Is that what you want all the other kids to think?"

I stomped my foot as hard as I could, splashed yucky gray snow all over Mom's leg.

Mom took a deep breath and blew it out, put those eyes on me. Made me stare back.

"What do you want, Joey?" She stood there, hands on her hips, nipples pushing out that purple silk for everyone to see. "You want me to lie to you?"

What I wanted didn't matter because Mom was holding up her don't-you-dare finger.

"I'll lie to you, if that's what you want," she said. "Say you look fine. That no one's going to make fun of you. That the world is the most wonderful place."

Her one-woman pep rally wasn't making me feel any better, but that didn't slow her down. "You looking like this is nothing," Mom said. "You're gonna get teased. You're gonna get picked on. You're gonna get beat up."

I tried to say enough, I was ready for school, but Mom kept talking.

"You're gonna fall in love. You're gonna have your heart broken. Your dreams are gonna be squashed. That's life," Mom said. "That's the truth. So it's your choice, Joey. You want the truth or not?"

If I knew what was coming maybe I could prepare for it. I said, "The truth."

Mom bent over at the waist and put her face close. Gave guys driving by something nice to stare at.

Her eyes weren't trying any more. The fight was over. But Mom still smiled when she took hold of my jaw and turned my face side to side. She ran her ice-cold fingers over my cheeks, brushed flakes of me into the slush. "When life sucks and gives you things you don't want, you've got to keep your chin up," Mom said. She kissed the top of my head. "And keep it up no matter what, you hear? Because people are depending on you."

* * *

That's what Mom was saying on the phone, me on the floor, Rachel's faceless head on the pillow.

"You can never quit," she said. "Never."

CHAPTER FOURTEEN

It's lunchtime and Sara still hasn't come back. I'm at my desk with the door closed, lights off, acting like nobody's home.

I'm on no sleep and little food. I know I can't keep this up, but how can I eat? Not when all I can think of is Rachel and what's left of her, the saddest secret I've ever held.

Cleaning up Rachel's body was my form of grief. I was crying, holding her in my arms, remembering the good times. I kept stroking her neck, because her cheek was gone, just cradled her in my arms, rocking back and forth, apologizing for all the things I'd done, for the things I wouldn't say. I told her she was beautiful, especially her nose, the one she hated, the one somewhere in pieces behind the nightstand. For some reason, I sang Dad's stupid song about fish heads. I told Rachel, Dad would have liked her, even though he probably wouldn't have. It was okay to fib. The part of her that knew if I was lying was splattered all over the ceiling, the wall, the bed. It was the part she just wanted gone.

I wondered what was going through her head when her thumb pushed down on the trigger. Besides the buckshot. I hoped it wasn't about me, prayed she didn't go out on such a sour note. I wanted to believe she was picturing that tropical beach, just her and the surf. No one around for miles. Not a single soul with all their fucked up, twisted thoughts. Just her, the sand, a giant piña colada.

I kept rocking, picturing her turning the shotgun around, getting her fingers curled under the handle between her knees. Her thumb fits perfect.

The barrel's so long, the hole so big and black and forever. To get this right she's leaning forward, bending her head, mouth open.

The metal's cold but clean. The barrel digs into the roof of her mouth, the front sight splitting her lower lip.

It doesn't matter. Nothing matters any more. It never did.

Her eyes water when she pushes the shotgun higher, tearing into the flesh so she knows exactly where it is, making sure the angle's just right. That's all she wants...something to be right. For once. *Please.*

All she needs is ten pounds of pressure. Ten pounds and all of her pain will be gone. No more thoughts ever again.

She's got the meaty part of her thumb on the trigger. She's closing her eyes.

Ten pounds isn't much. Just a quick shove. A quick shove and everything stops. No more Brightside.

A bead of sweat's running down her nose, the one that's now in pieces. Her mouth's filled with saliva. It's dribbling out the corners, down her chin, just like when I tried to make her drink in The Cabin. She needs to hurry. Almost there.

She's thinking goodbye, no one around to hear. She's thinking sorry for all the men who put her through hell. She's picturing me, her father, the lacrosse team. She's putting more pressure on the trigger.

It's now or never...

The loudest bang, but she only hears one-tenth. All her problems blasting out of her head. Then silence. Peace.

Holding Rachel got me thinking about Steven. A few days after he passed, his parents had a funeral. There was some old Chinese lady playing a harp, the women wearing veils, the men holding them tightly, rubbing their arms for comfort. Steven's mom even rented a swan to waddle around and stretch its neck as they lowered Steven's little casket into the ground.

I'd begged Dad not to make me go, but he said every man needs to face death, it's coming whether we like it or not. Steven's mom threw herself on the casket. Steven's dad pried her off. I'd never heard such screams. The swan apparently hadn't either and started attacking Steven's aunt. Dad told me to help, and the thing bit my hand and took off for the pond.

Still, Steven got a proper burial. Something I couldn't give Rachel. If I had called anyone, they'd find the shotgun and they'd drug and interrogate me until I cracked. Dad would finally get his wish to be in Brightside, but no one else would ever leave. They'd find the cave, seal it off, and we'd all be stuck. Things would change. They'd bring more Boots, more cameras, making sure none of us tried anything like this again.

I stared into Love-A-Lot's eyes. "I'm sorry, I'm so sorry. But people are depending on me, and I've already let too many people down."

I lifted what was left of Rachel into my arms and carried her to the closet. Then, with my parent's voices telling me time was running out, I started cleaning, put on some yellow rubber gloves. I started with the big chunks, tossing them into a black trash bag, each piece plopping onto the one before. I ran out of paper towels, had to use the extra set of sheets. I kept pouring bleach, scrubbing the floors, never really getting all the blood and bits, just sort of swirling it around and around.

I took two showers, dug my nails into the soap, scrapping out the little flecks of Rachel. I scrubbed so hard at my skin I thought I'd reach bone. Then I air-dried because I'd used both bath towels on the floor. I brushed my teeth and combed my hair like it was any other morning here in Brightside. Everything's fine. Just going to work.

I swept the last puddles towards the kitchen, made sure there was nothing left that could leak into the hall. I stood in front of the open closet, told Rachel I was sorry, that this would all be over soon. Someone would take her to the cemetery, bury her like she deserved. Then I closed the door.

The sun was beginning to rise, soft reds and yellows sifting up from the darkness. Day 100 had officially been going for hours, but it wasn't until the sun took its place above the horizon, that this really began.

* * *

Sara finally comes back into the office right after lunch. She looks like she's just witnessed an execution. For a second, I wonder if I'm thinking about Rachel, but I'm not. I'm just staring at Sara, wondering what the hell happened. She picks up the rose off her desk, the one meant for Rachel, the one from Alex.

"I'm going to be going away for a while." Her voice so soft and confused it's as if she's still refusing to believe it. "The Council decided I need some time in The Cabin."

"For what? You haven't done anything."

"The roof is off-limits and I broke the rule." She turns to me, already in my head. She smiles. "Don't worry, you're fine. Sharon informed them it was part of your treatment. You've been cleared of all infractions."

"Sara, you don't have to go. I can talk—"

She shakes her head like she's trying to fling out every single thought of mine, every moment we shared. "Don't!"

"Sara..."

"No, Joe, you've done enough already. And it's my fault. My fault for thinking..."

Sara, you don't understand. Everyone's leaving. Tonight. This place won't be safe. It's your last shot.

No, Joe. It's yours. I'm not coming.

Sara wipes the mascara running down her cheek. "Now, I have a few hours to spend with Danny so I'm going to go." She gets to the door, opens it, but stops. She's thinking of asking me to stay, to put an end to this before I get myself killed. Then she wonders if things wouldn't be better that way. She clicks her teeth, upset at herself, at me. She leaves, never once looking back.

* * *

I find Sharon in her office. She's with this frail Spanish man, one of the new Brightsiders.

I shout at her, "What the hell did you do?"

"Hello, Joe, as you can see I'm with a patient."

The little Spanish man stares at me with his sad eyes, but mine are locked on Sharon's. "You can't do this," I tell her. "You can't send Sara—"

"Let's lower our voices." *Unless you want to go with your girlfriend? That can be arranged, you know?*

I realize the Spanish man speaks no English. He says, "Debo ir?"

"No," Sharon says. "Joe's leaving."

"No, no estoy," I tell her. Then I turn to the man and say, "Salir!"

The man picks up his hat from his lap and scurries out of the room.

Sharon forces a smile and closes the door. "Glad to see those tapes are paying off."

"You can't lock her away in—"

Quiet! You want us all to end up in there? Now, just let—

Why did you do this?

Because she was never going to come.

You don't know that.

Actually, I do. And she knows too much. It'll get her hurt. She'll be safe there.

Safe?

Yes.

And Danny?

He'll be joining her shortly.

Sharon and her perfect plan. I realize I have no idea who this woman is. First she's spewing New Age bullshit. Now's she's the leader of a revolution.

No one's ever what they seem on the surface.

"You need to go back to work," Sharon says. "Finish the day."

I picture my office, Sara's desk, the one that used to be Rachel's.

Rachel...crumpled in my closet like some disfigured sex doll.

Sharon's eyes widen, horrified. She has no idea. It wasn't part of her plan. Sharon's not perfect after all. She just made herself believe she could handle things. Just like I made myself believe I could pull this off.

Joe...

But I want nothing to do with Sharon's thoughts. I walk out, head back to my office.

People pass by my door, which is thankfully closed. I hear Carlos so I click out of solitaire. I can't tell how many people are with him, but I guess three or four. The high heels either Frances or Gloria. That laugh, all Alex. Poor Alex, thinking his rose is going to win Rachel's heart. I consider telling him he can have it. It's just sitting in my closet, inside Rachel's chest.

Carlos and the others start laughing, wanting every-one to hear how happy they are. I open my sales spreadsheet and customer list so it looks like I'm working. I don't even know why I'm still pretending, but I'm on automatic. Shock does that to me. It's keeping me from losing it. I start rearranging pictures of condos into regions. The two-bedroom with the kitchenette is South America. The pent-

house with the hammocks on the balcony go in the Austral-
ia/New Zealand pile. Everything in its little place. Everything separated like Brightsiders from normals; Sharon's
secret club and those better off in The Cabin. People like
Sara and Danny.

Alex speaks way too loud, same as always. "What do
you say, Carlos? Oscar's for dinner?"

Carlos is right outside my door. "I don't want to
make plans yet," he said. "I have a feeling about today."

I sit up and wonder if Carlos is one of Sharon's elite,
the chosen few who get to leave. I asked Sharon why not
everyone. She said there were too many liabilities, too many
who'd already become institutionalized. Part of that was her
fault. Her Zen bullshit actually convinced some of these
pathetic souls Brightside was for the best, that they'd never
want to leave if they just opened themselves up to the
possibilities, the wonder of this mountain town. Sadly, that's
exactly what is going to happen to these poor fucks. They'll
never leave, not after today.

Carlos knocks, I put the phone to my ear. He pops his
head in, sees me nodding.

"...Yes, right on the beach, where you can rent jet
skis," I say to my imaginary client.

Carlos whispers, "How's it going?"

I give him the thumbs up.

Carlos winks, closes the door. His shirts are always
vertical stripes. Today's is red, makes him look like a candy
cane.

I have to piss, but they're all still standing there, asking what everyone's plans are for the weekend. I want to go
out and say a few of us will be dead at the bottom of the

mountain. Might even get a few bullet holes if we're up for it. The rest can forget about sleeping in. They'll be in The Cabin soon enough.

My bladder's throbbing, but I wait until the laughter's gone. I take a peek, see a clear shot to the hallway bathroom, start humming to block everything out. My pace makes me more conspicuous than if I set myself on fire, but I make it to the urinal in the back corner, away from Lenny popping a zit in the mirror. I aim at the drain, counting off random numbers so I can't think about anything else. Lenny leaves. I stuff myself back in my pants, walk over to the sinks, and do my best not to look at the mirror. Men don't cry in bathrooms, at least when there's a chance another dude might come in.

I wash my hands and notice a small dribble of blood where my thumbnail disappears into the skin. I scrub and scrub and scrub, seeing Rachel's faceless body, my hands swirling around the contents of her head on the floor. When I take my thumb out from under the water, I realize it's my blood, not Rachel's, because the blood dribbles out again.

I'm drying my hands when Wendell, top salesman for the past three months, hurries in, all four hundred pounds of him between me and the wall, saying excuse me as he sticks his hands under the faucet, his massive paws splashing water all over the counter.

There are three paper towels left. I wait for Wendell to finish and hand them to him, so he can finally take a piss. Wendell won't touch his dick unless he washes his hands. I have no idea why, just his thing.

Wendell's spraying the blue cake, thinking about the weekend, possibly barbequing a nice burger in the Brightside park.

There's no way Wendell's a part of Sharon's plan. I suddenly feel sorry for him, that big dumb bear. Stuck here with all the rest of the ones Sharon decided are too risky.

Wendell still hates me for what happened at the bar when I let out all my thoughts about everyone, all my judgments. I give him a smile to apologize, to say goodbye.

He looks at me like I'm hitting on him and quickly exits, not even thinking he should wash after handling himself.

The emergency exit is down the hall on the other side of the bathrooms. I consider heading for it, taking it to the roof so I can perform Paul's plunge, but with the helicopter still hovering, I won't even make it to the ledge.

This is the helicopter Sharon says I have to take care of, as if I have any chance. Most likely, I'll end up in smaller pieces than Rachel. That's probably what Sharon wants. After barging into her office, I'm proving to be the biggest risk of all. It's probably just another part of Sharon's clusterfuck of a plan, to use me as a scapegoat. Everything's accelerated because of Wayne. Since he broke out, the Boots have been patrolling, searching for anything amiss, for his crazy ass.

Sheriff Melvin has disabled a lot of the cameras, according to Sharon. It's why they haven't found Wayne. It's buying us time, just like all the bleach in my room. But the Boots will eventually fix the cameras so we have to be ready. A big spotlight will be put on every nook and cranny. The whole town won't be able to sneeze without someone watching. They'll see us gathering, find the mineshaft. Our one dumb shot at escape will be gone, and anyone in Sharon's special club will be locked away, some in The Cabin, the others down with the orange jumpsuits.

Sharon and I will end up together, most likely underground. The rest of my days with that fucking lunatic, who truly believes she's a revolutionary. I can't deny she's been impressive. For almost two years she's integrated, assimilated, wedged her skinny butt into everything Brightside. I can't imagine trying to pretend for that long. I couldn't even keep Sara from Rachel, couldn't tell Rachel I loved her. I'm the fucking coward Dad always warned me about.

"The crazy leads the men to battle, but the coward gets them killed."

I'm not going to make it if I keep thinking like this. I have to stay positive, get through the day. That's what Dad also said. "Worry about tomorrow, tomorrow. And if it doesn't come, then your worries are over."

I can't do anything but worry. It doesn't help being trapped in my office, hearing my coworkers out there bitch about the coffee, the cold weather, the lack of selection in the vending machine. They have no idea what's happening around them, but it's probably for the best. It's the little things that keep us from putting a shotgun in our mouths and blowing out our wonderfully gifted brains.

That's what I'm thinking as the clock refuses to budge. Rachel ran out of distractions, the inconsequential crap that keeps us from seeing how awful our lives really are. She knew I didn't love her, that no one ever would, not like she needed. So she took control, found the only foolproof way out of Brightside.

I keep picturing the night I visited Rachel in The Cabin, her sitting there so quiet and peaceful, each moment a gentle breeze. Not like now, the wind gone, everything still, Rachel shoved in next to Dad's broken fishing pole.

Broken Rachel, broken gifts. I just can't stop breaking things. It's what I do.

Yes, Rachel was broken when I met her. Then The Cabin broke her more. But I had to go and finish the job.

Next, it'll be Sara. Then Danny. Stupid, happy Danny, the only person who's truly able to find good in anything. But The Cabin will end that. They'll inject him, make him swallow the meds, and they'll kill the only spirit in Brightside worth saving. The idea of them destroying that gets me to my feet. I still have an hour left of work. Carlos might call the Boots, but fuck it. Let them sound the alarm. This is the only chance I've got to make things right.

* * *

The wind cuts across my face and makes my eyes water, so it looks like I'm crying as I walk through the Square. I have my headphones on and the people I pass think I'm on one of my strange walks, only now I'm apparently working out to music that makes me weep. I don't care. I just need to get to Danny, need to tell him to talk some sense into his sister. He's the only one who can get through to her. I'm sure he's scared right now as Sara tells him she's going to The Cabin. She's probably telling him to be strong, that it's the only way they can get through this.

Lodge Two is just up ahead. I start to slow my pace. There's a car parked out front, and an ambulance. I'm too late. I start running. I can imagine Danny fighting off the Boots trying to protect his sister. I see the gun pressed to the side of his head, him screaming for Sara as they drag her from the room. I see the Boots crushing his ribs, kicking in his belly.

But as I rush in, there's only one person in the hall-way. Blue jeans and black windbreaker, cell phone to his ear. He's pacing outside of a room near the stairs, the opposite end of Danny and Sara's room.

I usually stay away from the Boots, but this guy's young and doesn't look that dangerous with his aw-shucks face. Plus, morbid curiosity is all I seem to be seeking these days.

I pass the elevator when he turns my way. He holds the phone to his chest and points over my shoulder. "You need to turn around."

I've never seen him before, but it's obvious he's weirded out. Whatever is in the room isn't good. I walk closer.

The guy tries to use his big boy voice. "Did you not hear me? I said turn around."

I stop four feet from him, close enough to know he isn't counting numbers or singing songs. He can't get the image of the rope out of his head, the rope on the other side of the door. I nod past him. "Whose room is that?"

"None of your damn business." He's not good at this and thinks of Robert.

I reach for the door and he jumps back like I'm at-tacking. His right hand slips inside his jacket. "Stay back."

This poor kid's shaking, has no idea what he's doing. He's scared, and it's going to get me shot. Light reflects off his wedding band a few inches below the gun's barrel. "D-d-don't take another step."

My voice gets real calm, like I'm trying to put him to sleep. "I know him," I say. "You don't need to point that at me."

He starts counting to himself, just like they trained him, to keep us out of the loop. He realizes he looks like an idiot aiming at a shithead like me and his fear gets washed out by embarrassment. "Calm down, sir," he says, even though I'm the calmest I've been in months.

"There's a situation here," he says, "and you don't need to see this."

I should've kept my goddamn mouth shut, but still said, "I just saw Robert this morning." There's no reason for me to be here at all. I came here for Danny, not Robert.

The guy sees my nerves showing and tells me to wait. He says he'll be right back, slips into Robert's room. I think about running, but if I do, I might as well just run straight to The Cabin. I need to just stick, see whatever is behind that door, start crying, act like I'm getting sick, then leave.

The guy didn't close the door behind him. I see a shadow swaying across the wall.

I hear a voice. "Who saw him?" It's Palmer, the asshole who put the gun to my head, the fucker who wants to finish the job. I'm already turning, realize I've made a huge mistake, when Palmer's dirty fingers grab the door, his face, those mirrored sunglasses pointed straight at me. "What's this all about?"

I have no choice but to turn around. Palmer sees me and that creepy smile spreads across his acne-scarred cheeks.

"Can I help you?" he says.

"No. I just..." *The truth. Just stick to the truth.* "I saw Robert yesterday."

"I thought you said this morning?"

"I did, but I meant yesterday."

Palmer lowers his sunglasses, studies me. I've made such a swamp of shit and I keep diving deeper and deeper.

"Look," I say, "Robert was talking about Wayne King. He said he was going to find him. He..."

The door opened a little more and the smell of actual shit hit me.

"Yeah, pretty nasty stuff."

Palmer opened the door all the way. He wanted me to see. Wanted to look me in the eyes when I did.

The newbie stood a few feet from the window, the wooden chair lying across the kitchen floor, the giant square of plastic right in the center. The puddle of piss and shit on top of it. He was thinking Palmer was the coldest dude he'd ever worked with, worse than his uncle that used to show him snuff films.

I don't know why, but I'm walking in the room. Robert must have learned from Belinda, who fell from the fan when it couldn't hold her weight. He cut away a section of sheetrock in the ceiling. One end of the rope is wrapped around a two-by-four, the other around his black turtleneck, covering that hole in his throat. He's swinging with his back to me. Palmer looks at me and pokes Robert in the ribs with his small baton, sends Robert swinging a few inches.

Kind of low, Palmer says, "So when did you see him last?"

"Yesterday. He was looking for Wayne."

Robert's black microphone is dangling off the kitchen counter, no final words from Robert.

"What do you know about Wayne King?" Palmer asks.

I quietly remembered the first time I saw Wayne. It was after Krystal had kicked me out and I was thinking about Mom.

Palmer's smile somehow gets creepier. There's no way a Boot could be one of us, but I wasn't taking any chances. In case he was listening, I keep thinking about Wayne, about my mom, about Krystal. As disgusting as it is, it wasn't going to get me in trouble.

Robert spins. His face is bigger than I remember, his skin all puffed out, tinged the lightest blue. Just like his eyes, wide open, squiggly red lines surrounding them. But it's his tongue that paralyzes me. It's so big, pushed out all the way, the tip halfway down his chin.

Palmer's walkie-talkie goes off, but he keeps staring at me, waiting for me to slip.

"Palmer, where the hell are you?" a voice says. It sounds like Sheriff Melvin, but I can't be sure.

Palmer's jaw clenches, that muscle just below the ear flexing like a little tumor. Finally, he answers. "Investigating the Madison case." He wants me to know I'm not going anywhere. "I got Joe Nolan here."

Melvin tells him they think they've got a location on Wayne King, that he needs to get his ass over to the Square.

Palmer's still staring at me and I'm just humming, trying to plug the leaking boat I call a brain. I'm trying not to think about Melvin, Sharon, her fortunate few.

I close my eyes, breathe in the shit and piss puddle under Robert's swinging feet.

The newbie runs over to Palmer and accidentally bumps Robert, sending him swinging again, spinning him like a giant marionette. This time another drop of piss lands on the floor, right next to my foot.

The newbie just wants to get out of there. He says I obviously didn't do this, that they need to get to the Square.

Palmer extends his baton with a snap of his wrist. "You got five seconds to tell me what happened here," he says to me.

I can't look at Palmer anymore. I stare at Robert spinning. And I don't know how in the hell I didn't notice it before, the front of Robert's briefs poking out, his little boner all that's left to say hello.

"You really don't know?" I ask, suddenly kind of cocky.

Palmer tilts his head, knows I'm hiding something, but Melvin is telling him to hurry. Palmer pokes me with the baton. "I'll be seeing you real soon. Count on it."

I keep humming, staring at Robert's face, all big and blue.

CHAPTER FIFTEEN

In twenty-eight years, I've seen death. Lily and Sunny, the countless fish that died in the hands of my father. And all the loved ones that people carry around in their heads. Their parents, war buddies, their best friend from college.

But I'd never seen human death in person. I'd never been face-to-face with a human corpse. Steven, my first real friend, was dying, not dead, and when he passed, I only saw the casket, his school picture. Not like the past twenty-four hours. Robert and Rachel. Two people who made the mistake of coming into my life.

Without question. Rachel was my fault, and even though I don't have any hard proof, I'm sure Robert's death is also on me. Robert heard my thoughts of escape, knew about my plans. I didn't know him very well, but I can't believe he took his own life, even by accident. One final jerk-off before his hunt for Wayne King. Wayne must have set up his death, made it look like some perverted attempt to get off that simply went awry.

Robert's black microphone keeps flashing in my mind as I walk out of the room. It looked like it'd been thrown, ripped out of Robert's hand, the red burn line on his lifeless palm. Robert probably tried to call out for help when the man he was hunting simply showed up at his door.

I have no idea why, but it's the only reason I can find.

I'm heading to Danny's room. My footsteps slow and staggered. His door is cracked open, and I fear Wayne has gotten to him as well.

Danny's door is third on the right. I force it open, waiting to see Danny hanging there like Robert. I call out Danny's name, but it's so quiet, I know he couldn't hear me, even if he's alive.

I step inside, eyes straight ahead, every inch of the far wall covered with my drawings.

The kitchen is the same, the fridge displaying my first drawings. Billy Bass, mouth open, sits on the counter next to an angel food cake. My favorite. A sign below it, Danny's scribble, CHEER UP JOE inside a happy face. The cake looks like it's been here for a while so I know it has nothing to do with Rachel or Robert or any of the other fucked up shit I've just been through.

I walk to the counter, tears falling down my face, onto the drawing of the small boy escaping through the wall. Danny added two large arrows on the picture, names next to each one. Danny is the little boy, Joe for the hand pulling him through.

But I've failed. Danny and Sara are already gone.

I'm suddenly on the floor, looking at everything, at nothing. I'm too late. They've taken them, and there's nothing I can do. Even if I somehow break into The Cabin, I'm only locking myself in. They'll never let me leave with

Sara and Danny. We'll all be in there when Sharon's exodus goes down.

My watch says I have less than an hour. That's when the sun's going to set and Sharon's club will be filing down the mineshaft on their way to freedom. At least that's the plan. I'm supposed to take care of the helicopter. If I don't, no one will make it out alive.

But fuck them. I'm not moving. My only two reasons are locked away, and if Danny and Sara can't escape, then no one should, especially Sharon, the woman Dad trusted enough to turn me in.

* * *

It was before I met Michelle, a year before Brightside. I'd just broken up with Chloe, this waitress I'd been dating for about six months. Chloe never liked me, thought I was annoying, and knowing this, I just became more annoying to piss her off. I thought it was funny. She'd get so red and flustered, and would tug at her hair until it tore free from her scalp. I listened to her thoughts, figured out exactly what bothered her the most. Then I'd perform each one to watch her squirm. I drummed my fork on the dinner plate, just like her brother used to do. I'd scratch my scalp like her stepfather did every morning at breakfast.

I was bored, destructive, pissed off at the world. I was so tired of hearing everyone's thoughts, knowing I'd never find love, because I'd always get the truth. That's why I set fires, wanted to watch these assholes burn. People like Chloe, who never deserved it. Finally, she had enough and moved out. She never told me, but I knew all about the abortion. It wasn't a tough decision. She knew I'd make a terrible father, wanted nothing to do with me ever again.

That's what sent me into the darkness, the bleakest state I found until Brightside.

Chloe had been gone for a week, and Dad showed up because I hadn't been answering his calls. He found me in the living room just sitting in my underwear. Unshaven, filthy. Plates of dried food everywhere. Lily licking at the scraps.

"Jesus Christ, Joe," Dad said.

I must have left the door unlocked because he was just standing there.

"What the hell happened here?"

I went back to watching Lily lick the dried rice and beans. Dad picked up the plate, told Lily to stop. He stacked a few dishes, put them out of her reach.

Dad said my name, but I couldn't look at him, knew if I did, I'd start crying.

With Dad I didn't need to speak. He knew everything, about Chloe, about the abortion. He cleared off some space on the couch and sat, neither of us saying a word.

"You know," Dad said, "your mother and I considered..."

"I know," I said. I'd heard Mom thinking it more than once, how she should have just ended the pregnancy.

"Your mom couldn't do it."

I finally turned. I'd always assumed it was Dad who'd talked her out of it.

"We were at the doctor's, already in the examination room, and she just couldn't do it. We both knew you might turn out like me, but she didn't care." Dad pictured the first time he held me in his arms. "And then you showed up, and I knew you were meant to be here. That you'd do great things one day."

The wreckage of my life suddenly came into focus. The dirty clothes, the sacks of fast food wrappers, the half-empty bottle of whiskey.

"Guess you were wrong," I said.

"No," Dad said, "I wasn't. You just need to pull yourself together, stop feeling sorry for yourself."

"Yeah, that's all I need to do." I laughed.

Dad grabbed my face and squeezed my chin, forced my eyes to his. "You want to destroy yourself, go ahead. But there are people out there who could use your help. You can still do great things, Joe."

I don't remember exactly what was said after that. I know I didn't want to hear his pep talk, knew I just wanted him gone. He finally left and I sat back down on the couch. Lily crawled over and plopped down on my feet. She needed to be walked, and while nothing inside me wanted to see the outside world, I took her around the block. Dad's words started to sink in. My dog needed me.

The next day I went into BMW and convinced Saul to hire me. A few weeks later I met Michelle. The money poured in, and even though I knew my father was wrong, that I'd never do anything great, I thought I was at least doing some good. I was going to buy a house with a big yard for Lily. I told myself Michelle would accept the truth, that things would work out.

Then Dad paid Michelle that visit, learned she'd never accept who I was. He must have known I'd crumble, just like I had with Chloe.

That's the only reason I could come up with. That Dad sent me here before it was too late.

He must have believed this was the only way for me to reach my potential.

If only he could see me now, sitting on Danny's floor, pathetically weeping over Rachel and Robert, the guy I barely knew. Weeping for Danny and Sara, the only people here worth saving. Everyone dead or locked away because of me.

Grandpa's shotgun flashes in my head. The gift my father sent in pieces, a puzzle like my Rubik's Cube. I had to go and solve it so Rachel could blow off her face.

"Joe," a voice says.

It sounds like Sara, and I figure I must already be in The Cabin. They must have found the body in my closet. But I don't remember them taking me.

Sara's face is right in front of me.

The slap stings too much for the medication I must be on. It sends little crackles up and down my head.

"Where's Danny?" she says.

I'm not in The Cabin, still in the room with all my sketches. Danny's room. Sara's room.

"Was he here?" she asks.

"What?"

She just about screams, "Was Danny here?"

"No. The door. It was open."

She paces back and forth, says, "Shit."

I get to my feet and ask what's going on, why she's not in The Cabin. Sara says she went looking for Danny, but he wasn't at work. He didn't even show up today.

"They've already got him," I say.

"Who?"

But she already knows. "Why? They said they were only taking me! Danny didn't do anything."

"It's Sharon. She wanted him out of the way."

Sara's head shakes back and forth, like she's trying to get rid of every horrible thought. She has Sharon's throat in her hands, crunching her windpipe.

I think of Robert, the rope digging deeper, his face turning purple, his tongue dangling down like he was trying to get a crumb off his chin.

Sara turns to me disgusted. She hadn't needed all of that.

I try to apologize, but she wants to know what the hell is going on. I tell her I don't know. I touch her arm, expecting her to push me away, but she just collapses, huge sobs filling the air. Her mind only on Danny, the brother she swore she'd protect.

Finally, the shove comes. Then her tiny fists ball up and beat at my chest. "YOU DID THIS TO HIM! YOU!"

I take each blow, wishing she were stronger, wishing her fists were holding knives.

"He can't..." Sara's picturing a catatonic Danny, the joy completely drained from his eyes. "I have to go," she says.

My hand is around her wrist. She's pulling away, but I grip harder, yank her back. "You go there, and you won't be able to do anything. They'll do the same to you."

"I don't care. I'll be with him."

"Sara, no. They'll never let you leave. You know too much."

I hear Sara thinking before she even says it. "Then I'll tell them everything. I'll tell them and they'll have to let us go. They'll know Danny and I..."

Part of me wants her to do exactly that, to put a stop to Sharon's plans, to end all this before we all end up comatose or dead. But I remember what Sharon said, that Brightside couldn't last forever. It's not sustainable, and sooner or later, the funds would run out and they'll have no choice but to eradicate us. They'll say it's what's best for the country, the normals will never know the truth.

I know Sara thinks a little time is better than none, but there is another way. We can break Danny out and make the escape on our own.

I tell Sara to wait by the pond, that I'll handle everything. Sara refuses, says she's coming with me. I tell her fine, but we have to stop by my place first. We're going to need Dad's gift.

CHAPTER SIXTEEN

Sara makes me promise I'll turn myself in if Danny has already been drugged. She says we'll never get him out of there. Medicated, he'll be too heavy. I tell her I will, but I'm still thinking of other options, thinking about the ambulance, how we could steal it, load him up, drive right out. But the Brightside entrance is locked by a steel gate that not even Sheriff Melvin has access to.

We exit Lodge Two and I see the helicopter hovering over the Square. I'm praying they don't find Wayne, not until we can free Danny. Every Boot is preoccupied, but the moment they have Wayne in cuffs, their attention will shift back to us. Danny and Sara are supposed to be taken in the next thirty minutes.

The sun is falling and it's blinding on the way to my place. I can barely see the sidewalk. I almost trip off the curb. Sara grabs my arm, yanks me back.

I tell her thanks, but she still hates me and my insane plan. She doesn't see how we'll ever pull it off.

Still, Sara wants it to work. She wants Danny to be free, to have a life, to be normal, even if it's only a little.

There aren't any Boots outside my building. The place is quiet, almost too quiet. Everyone is at work, all that remains are the smells, especially the bleach growing stronger as we near my door. The bleach covering Rachel.

Faceless Rachel, still in my closet.

I tell Sara to wait here, even though she's seen everything in my head, me cleaning, sweeping the broken bits of gifts, broken bits of Rachel. Sara's eyes get real big, she's looking at my door that's open just a crack.

The Boots must be in there. I start to tell Sara to run, but she's stepping towards the open door. There's something on the floor, just inside my apartment. It's Danny's hat.

Sara shouts for Danny and throws open the door.

The pitch black room could hold anything. I try to pull her back, but she's already in. I have no choice but to follow.

Sara keeps calling for Danny. I'm flicking the light switch, but it's still broken. Someone's feet crunch over the tiny pieces of plastic and metal. I can't tell if it's Sara or someone else.

"Danny, it's me," Sara says.

The bleach is making my eyes water, but I can still smell Rachel. My hand feels for the closet. It's closed.

"Shut the door," a voice says.

Sara asks who's there, but I know that gravelly voice coming from my couch. It's the sound of insanity, of someone who has seen far more death than me.

The next sound is just as familiar. I've heard it since I was a kid. The shotgun being racked.

"I'm not going to tell you again."

I reach out for Sara, but she's moved. I can't see anything, know the only way to find her is to either rip open the drapes or close the door.

Let in the light or adjust to the darkness.

The drapes are too far and I hear Sara's panicked breaths. I close the door. Slowly, my eyes gain focus. Shapes, faces, the apartment spread out before us.

Wayne sits there on the couch, shotgun resting on his lap. He looks at Sara and says, "You must be Loverboy's new gal."

"Where's my brother? Is he here? If you've hurt him..."

"He's safe," Wayne says, "for now."

"Tell me where he is."

Wayne smiles, looks to me. "Bossy like your mom, huh? You do have your type, don't you, Loverboy?"

"Tell me or I'll scream," Sara says.

Wayne laughs, the sort of cackle I imagine his victims heard before he drove in the knife. But Sara isn't backing down so Wayne lets us hear his thoughts, how he found Danny in their room, how he didn't have to touch a single hair on that boy's head, simply told Danny if he wanted to see his sister again he needed to follow. Danny obeyed, followed Wayne right out the door. Wayne ends it there, not letting us know where he took Danny.

Like we'd come over to his house to play cards, Wayne says, "Why don't you both have a seat."

Sara says she's fine, but I take her arm, guide her to a chair. Pissing Wayne off isn't going to get Danny back.

I actually start wishing Danny was in The Cabin. It's better than this. At least we'd know he was still alive.

Wayne removes one of his hands off the shotgun, scratches at his beard. "You really should take better care of your place, Joe. You're kind of a slob. I mean, just cramming everything into the closet like that. It's lazy."

Rachel...

"But I suppose Mommy used to clean up after you. I never had that luxury."

I ask Wayne what he wants and immediately regret it when he starts smacking his lips. I tell him, "We just want Danny back. That's all."

"And you'll get him. Unharmed. Mostly." Wayne waits for Sara to speak her violent mind, but I touch her arm. Wayne is loving this too much. Silence is our only option.

Finally, Wayne gets bored, lifts the shotgun, aims it at me then Sara, then back at me. I close my eyes, suddenly more fed up than Sara.

"Just do it," I say.

Sara shouts my name. *What the hell you doing?*

"No, if he wants to pull the trigger, fine. But he'll never make it out of here alive. He knows that. Don't you, Wayne?"

I let this hang in the air until it lands. I hear Wayne shifting in his seat, suddenly paying attention to every word out of my mouth. "It's why he staged Robert's death the way he did. He's trying to draw attention, keep everyone busy. He's trying to get out of here, just like us. And if he fires the gun, that deafening blast, it's all over and he knows it."

"Rachel did it," Wayne says, "and no one came running. Not a single soul."

I figure the storm covered the noise, but his grin says there's more to it than that. "And that's why you killed Sheila," I say, not really knowing, but trying to put this together. "You killed her to distract everyone."

"Why would I do that?"

"You knew what Rachel was going to do. You must have heard her thoughts when she left the office. You must have—"

"Well, Loverboy, then why didn't I stop her?"

"Because you're a sick bastard. Two deaths were better than one."

I have no idea why my mouth won't close. I'm not a detective. I don't even know if any of it's true, but my heart's racing like I'm jacked on caffeine.

Wayne's teeth click. "Loverboy's using his big brain."

The satisfaction of being right is erased when Sara thinks what an asshole I am. What is this accomplishing?

I ask Wayne what he wants. "You obviously came here for a reason, and it's not just the shotgun."

Wayne's smiling again, pushing out his lower lip like a little kid. "I wanna be in your club, Joe."

Sharon's chosen ones. The lucky group I've somehow joined. Seems Wayne has been eavesdropping, listening to more people than me. Who knows where he's been lurking?

"It is a small town," Wayne says.

I realize Wayne could've escaped the moment he broke out, but he knows he can't last, not with the helicopter, not with every Boot on his trail. He learned Sheriff Melvin had disabled most of the cameras or put them on a loop of old footage. But it won't last. He knows the only way off this mountain is with my help, because Sharon isn't going to let him join in. Her club obviously has a better way down the two hundred foot drop than my stupid rope. They probably have a getaway car. Sharon didn't tell me, but I figured the same. Still, Wayne's here because I'm the only one who can get him in with Sharon.

"Do you feel special, Momma's Boy?" Wayne asks.

He's trying to intimidate me, but he's already shown his cards.

"Why would I help you?" I say.

"To save that Bob Dole retard, of course."

I can hear Sara's teeth digging into her tongue, that squishy sound of saliva the slow trickle of blood.

I ask, "How do I know you won't just—"

"Kill him?" Wayne cocks his head. "You don't know. Hell, I could kill all three of you."

I start humming to drown out the bad thoughts, the ones of Sara and Danny, both faceless, both piled on top of Rachel like some expired orgy.

Wayne stands, his nose blowing puffs like a weary Grizzly. He knows we're wasting time, that if we can't come to an agreement, we're all fucked. So he tosses me the gun. I can barely see in the dark, but somehow catch it. My first thought is to aim, pull the trigger, end this piece of shit's life.

Wayne says, "Remember, it'll be loud, Loverboy."

Still, my finger finds the trigger, my left hand under the pump, the grooves, everything Dad taught me. Never be afraid to fire the shot.

I'm stepping closer, the hollow end only a foot from Wayne's chest, but Wayne doesn't flinch, his nose breaths still coming at the same steady rate. The gun's getting slick.

My hand's sweating. I start to feel my finger slide off the trigger. I'm worried if I adjust, I'll crack off the shot.

Sara's hand gently touches the barrel, forces me to lower the gun. *We'll never find Danny if Wayne's dead. He could be locked away somewhere suffocating. We need him just as he needs us. At least for now.*

"Listen to your girlfriend, Joe," Wayne says. "She's smart."

Firing would sound the alarm, send the Boots storming, but I can't let Wayne just walk away without a nick. My trigger finger slides off and back towards the butt, my hand gripping the wood, which I crack into Wayne's chin. He stumbles back, bends over, almost drops to a knee, but stays on his feet. He laughs, spits blood all over the floor. He slurps up the rest and that laugh of his comes back, but only for a second. It's followed by this icy stare, the "I'm going to fucking love watching your girlfriend squeal under my knife" kind of look.

I tell Wayne I'm not doing shit until we know Danny is alive. Wayne says they'll be at the mineshaft at sundown, says if I don't like it I need to end this right now. I don't even realize he's just prying my mind until it's too late. I'm already picturing the path to the cave. My hand grips the butt of the shotgun, but Wayne's not going to let me hit him again. He gave me one and that's all I'm going to get. He says if I don't fulfill my part of the plan, it'll be the last sunset Danny ever sees.

Everything's too goddamn tense. I force a smile. "Guess I'll tell Sharon we need room for one more," I say.

"That's the boy Momma raised."

Wayne pushes me out of the way, peeks his wild eyes out the door. The coast is clear so Wayne slips out and disappears back into Brightside.

I stand there shaking, my hands going numb on the Mossberg 12-gauge.

Sara takes the gun, tells me I need to calm down. I have no idea why she's being so rational, but I figure it's all for Danny. Some people can lower their pulse to save the ones they love. My heart feels like it's going to rip at the seams.

So what do we do next? Sara thinks.

"Nothing really," I say, "I just have to take out that helicopter."

"Oh," she says, "that all?"

* * *

When I was thirteen, Dad told me there was no honor in killing anything over a hundred yards away. If you can't see a man's features, then he's not a man at all, just a target, which lessens the consequences of taking a life. Consequences are necessary. Without them, this fucked up existence has no value at all. That's why he never showed me how to use a rifle or anything else long range. The Mossberg 12-guage could shatter your skull across a football field, he said, but move twenty rows into the stands, and you'll just end up with a bruise or blind if you're not smart enough to blink.

Dad's lecture worked in theory, but it didn't do much to inspire confidence in my part of the plan, the part where I have to take down a fully armed chopper hovering in the sky.

When I was nine, I used to point my finger as a gun and take out the airplanes flying over Columbus. I didn't realize I was playing terrorist, never imagined one day that's what I'd be called. Thought Thieves were deemed the most dangerous people on the planet by the President, the government, every school board across the country. All because we knew everyone was lying.

The politicians weren't a surprise, but the pastors and priests; the little league coaches and lunch ladies threw everyone for a loop. It was just easier to get rid of us, ship us here to this mountain, than to face the truth that our society was based on the ability to lie. Parents tell their kids they're special, that they love them. Teachers tell students they can achieve anything. Bosses want their employees to know they're valued, that they aren't just a warm body underpaid and abused. It's how everything keeps moving. Without the lie, people have to fix shit, face conflict, come to terms. Lying is the buffer that keeps us all from ending up like Rachel.

Thought Thieves aren't any better. We told ourselves Brightside could be worse, we bought into the bullshit, even though we'd been ripped from our homes, stripped of our jobs and families. We were banished to this prison in the clouds, but we told ourselves we'd just relocated. We had jobs, went on dates, fucked coworkers and the last person left at the bar. Lies have kept this town intact. They give us a reason to shower, brush our teeth, make our beds.

But none of it was real. It was no different than when I was back in the outside world. The other salesmen at BMW were just like us. We worried about paperwork, what we were going to have for dinner. We wondered if we should move the couch to the other side of the room. Little tasks and stupid nonsense kept our minds busy, but also kept us from realizing all of it was shit. Our lives, jobs, the people we called friends.

I've been hearing other people's thoughts for as long as I could remember, but no matter how many times I heard their lies, their excuses, their justifications for doing horrible stuff, I never realized that I was no better. Until Day 100. That's when I saw who I really was, a coward, a fraud, a waste of potential.

I could have been anything, could have used my gift to get elected to office or the head of a company. I could have rubbed elbows with the rich and powerful and had my own island. But I pissed it all away, told myself I was better than those cheats, even though I did nothing but swindle. I stole girls' hearts, told them what they needed to hear to get them in bed. I sold luxury cars to unsuspecting souls. I convinced people I was sensitive, caring, when I was simply regurgitating all the things seeping out of their heads.

It was easy to keep secret because no one was like me. Not like Brightside, where secrets are more precious than life. I still can't believe I've lasted a hundred days. I guess I'm lucky Wayne escaped and Sharon accelerated the plan. Another week and I'd be locked away in The Cabin or in a cage with the orange jumpsuits. I've been cracking, letting too many people in. Now Danny's with Wayne and Sara's involved. Then there's Rachel, poor faceless Rachel, shoved in my closet, her version of a suicide note still stained on the ceiling, the floors.

Sara's in the bathroom, so I decide to take the opportunity to say goodbye. I open the closet and crouch down next to Rachel. I tell her I'm sorry again, imagine she forgives me. I tell her there's a good chance when this is over I'll be joining her. I wonder if they'll put us side by side in the cemetery.

If the rumors are true, we might all end up there soon. Wendell and Carlos; Krystal and Phuc. Every Brightsider buried to keep the world safe. I honestly don't know how they ever thought this could last. Selling timeshares and other crap over the phone was never going to keep this place going. Just another lie we told ourselves to keep one foot moving in front of the other.

I just keep thinking about Wendell and all the people we're going to abandon, the ones too risky for Sharon's club. If I succeed and take out the helicopter, there's going to be panic and chaos, bullets ripping through bodies. The Boots won't know who's with Sharon and who just happened to be taking a walk. It's all a part of Sharon's plan. The distraction, the confusion, the melee that follows. It's going to buy us time, keep the Boots one step behind.

Collateral damage is just another detail in this fucked up scheme.

Sara comes out of the bathroom and says she wants to know how I'm going to pull this off. There's no point in lying. I haven't a fucking clue. Sharon had suggestions, like climbing a tree or throwing rocks to get the pilot's attention. Our brilliant leader is an idiot.

Sara asks how close I have to be. I tell her under fifty yards, but probably under twenty to be safe. It's been over ten years since I've fired this shotgun, and I know I'm going to be shaking and scared out of my mind. I've only hit a few birds, but that was because of the buckshot spray. It only took one tiny pellet to take out a quail. The helicopter's going to take a hell of a lot more.

Sara says she wants to come with me, but she's only being polite. She also needs to stay hidden. The Boots are busy looking for Wayne, but if they find her they won't hesitate to take her in. I tell her she needs to stay here until it's time to make a run for the cave. Sara refuses, says there's no way she's going to just sit here while I'm out there risking my life. Plus, she wants to find Danny. She says she saw a flicker in Wayne's thoughts. It was just a blip, but she saw Danny near a tree. I tell her Wayne isn't dumb enough to slip up like that. In all likelihood he's trying to get her caught, giving the plan another distraction to keep the Boots off our ass. Still, she's definitely not staying here, she says, so we make a compromise. I tell her she needs to make sure no one sees me go to the office. She can help me get in so I can get to the roof.

CHAPTER SEVENTEEN

I promised Wayne I'd talk to Sharon, but there's no point telling her shit. If I do and she agrees, there isn't a damn difference, but if she freaks, like I know she will, then I'm only putting Danny in more danger. Wayne's going to be there whether I talk to Sharon or not, and his big ass isn't going to climb down a rope by himself. And he's going to want in on the getaway vehicle, whatever that might be. I'm such an idiot for not asking Sharon for more details. I was too caught up in arguing about Sara and Danny being sent to The Cabin and my father turning me in.

Still, I have to call her. Sara and Danny have to be included in the getaway. I take out the cell phone, the one Sharon said couldn't be traced.

"There a problem?" Those are the first words out of Sharon's mouth and I almost tell her there are more problems than she can handle.

"Just one," I say. "Sara and Danny are both coming."

"Absolutely not."

"Then I'm not firing a fucking shot and that helicopter will be sitting right outside the mineshaft. You can kiss your little plan goodbye."

Sharon's breathing, and while I can't hear her thoughts, I know that damn mantra is on full blast in her head.

"It's your call," I say. "But I'm not doing shit until I know they're in."

Sharon's teeth click a few times. She says, "Fine."

"Yeah? I have your word?" As if her word means anything.

"Yes, but if they get caught on the way to the cave or if they're one second late, we're not waiting."

"Okay."

"And Joe?"

"What?"

"If you fail, the deal's off."

"Yeah..." I start to ask how we're getting off this mountain if we actually pull this off, but Sharon's already hung up.

I know Sharon has something waiting for us when we get out, a bus or car or even a plane. She told me there were others in the real world, ones yet to be discovered, willing to help us. Unlike Danny, Sara, and me, there were a lot of Thought Thieves rolling in cash. They broke into banks already knowing the security codes. They bought stocks on silent information. They took down casinos one table at a time, knowing exactly what the dealer or other players were holding. Unless they were stupid or too goddamn greedy, there are probably hundreds, even thousands, still on the outside.

It makes me wonder how many Thought Thieves are still sitting in power. The President himself only signed the law after the panic had gotten out of control. I like the idea of the Commander in Chief being one of us. It would explain his second term, how frequently he fires top officials. I imagine the White House is filled with people looking to take him down, but he'd know every move before they could make a grab at his job.

Even Carl Pepper, the man who supposedly saved the President's life, never seemed to be fully responsible for stopping the assassination. When they played the scene on the news, the President definitely ducked before Carl clobbered the gunman.

Carl was one of the first sent to Brightside, but no one has seen or heard from him since. He's either dead or locked up so tight he's wishing he were. I can't imagine what Carl must be going through. He was a hero for a week, then a villain for life. I'm sure there's not a second of the day he doesn't wish he would've let the gunman fire the shot. The President he saved banished him for being a traitor and I can't fathom how that must feel. Even though my own father turned me in, at least he tried to offer me a way out. Carl is just fucked, same as all the other Brightsiders we'll leave behind.

I need to stop thinking about pointless crap. Who cares what Carl is thinking or if the President is a Thought Thief? Neither is going to help me one bit. I have a job to do, and I need to shut off my head. I know I'm doing it to distract myself, to keep from thinking about the chopper's gun spinning and firing fifty rounds into my chest before I even take aim, but if I can't control my thoughts, I'll for sure end up dead.

Sara's wearing a stocking cap, parka, and these huge sunglasses Rachel left at my place on Day 39. I'm wearing my puffy jacket wishing I had a trench coat. The shotgun is practically sticking out the bottom of my pants, and it's making me walk like someone who's trying to hide a gun. There's an elastic drawstring at the bottom of the jacket, and I pull it tight to keep the Mossberg in place. But I just keep picturing it sliding down and blowing off my leg. Sara asks if I have a duffle bag or something, says this just looks stupid. I run to the closet and have to pull Rachel forward to slide out the bag. It's covered in blood, which is only going to draw more attention.

I rummage through the closet, through all of Dad's boxes, when I find a backpack. It's too small to hide the Mossberg, but it's better than keeping it in my pants, so I fieldstrip the gun. Not all of it, just break it down so it'll fit. Assembling it is going to take more time, time I don't know if I'll have, but it's the best option I've got.

* * *

The walk to the office is freezing because the sun is about to set. I'm wearing headphones, but my iPod is turned off. I'm just silently talking to Sara as we move down the street. Most people are at work or locked away in their apartments. Wayne has set everyone on edge.

The building where I work has a small crowd out front, but I don't see any Boots. Neither Sara nor I know how many people heard she's being sent to The Cabin, but we can't take any chances. I have to go in alone. We keep our distance and switch up the plan. It's better this way, because Sara needs to draw the helicopter to me.

She slips off through the Square. I watch her and have the fear this might be the last time I ever see her. I want to chase her down, tell her how sorry I am she got pulled into this, but again, it's not going to help me do what I have to do. I flick on my iPod, crank it as loud as it can go before entering the building. There are a few people getting into the elevator so I take the east stairs. The shotgun pieces clang around in my backpack as I climb. Luckily, no one is in the stairwell, though, I sort of wish there were. I want someone to catch me, to make me go back to my apartment. The Cabin doesn't seem like such an awful outcome right now.

My hand goes to the door handle, but I can't open it. It's not locked, I'm just freaking out. I keep thinking about how I almost plummeted off the side. Sara had to pull me up to save my life.

I'm leaning against the wall and I can feel the sweat soaking through my clothes, which doesn't feel all that bad because it's so fucking hot here in the stairwell. I decide to put the shotgun together. If the helicopter flies over while I'm assembling it, they'll kill me.

Sara also needs time to get to the Boots. She's supposed to say Wayne is in this building. I told her to keep her distance to let others spread the word, but I know she's not going to risk Danny to save herself. I just hope they don't recognize her before they head this way.

The barrel clicks, and I pull out the shells. Slide two in. I have another dozen in the backpack, but I'll never get the chance to reload. It's one shot.

The Mossberg is in my hands, and I keep thinking about Rachel. If someone were to see me, I don't know what I'd do. I guess I'd have to shoot, but that's only going to alert the Boots, the helicopter, and the gunner.

I suddenly realize this plan's already fucked. Sara's going to tell them Wayne's here, meaning they'll already be looking to kill him, meaning as soon as they see I'm armed, I'm dead.

I'm starting to think this really is all a setup. Melvin could get a hell of a lot closer to the helicopter than me. But Sharon said I was the only one for the job.

They're probably already at the cave escaping, while I'm up here like an idiot holding a shotgun that will draw all the attention.

I'm hating my father right now for trusting that lying bitch, for giving me a shotgun instead of a rifle, which I could fire from cover, instead of standing right out in the open, making it so easy to take me out.

Plus, I don't even have an escape plan. The helicopter will definitely beat the Boots here, but it won't be long before they secure the building.

At least Sara's not with me. Danny either. They might still have a chance. This is what I'm telling myself as I hear the distant *thwump* of the chopper getting louder and louder. I don't even have to put my ear to the door to know it's almost here.

Sara's supposed to meet me at the pond. I know she won't wait forever. I told her she can't be late to the cave. It's Danny who's important. I just hope she doesn't hold out too long. Sharon won't hesitate to leave her and Danny behind.

I wonder what's going to happen with Wayne. When Sharon sees him, she's going to shit herself. I wish I could be there to see her face. I just hope Wayne doesn't get Danny killed.

My hand is on the door handle and my heart feels like it's the size of my head. The Mossberg's at my side, my finger just above the trigger.

Everything's tunneling. I can't breathe.

It sounds like the helicopter is circling. I need to time this right, wait until it's on the other side of the building before coming out.

Voices fill the stairwell, but they're not coming up. Everyone's fleeing, meaning the Boots are probably already here. They'll sweep every floor. I've run out of time.

The chopper is as loud as ever. I wait for a couple of seconds until it's a little quieter, hoping I can make it to the wall next to the air conditioners before the gunner sees me.

My hand presses down. The click of the door. At least this will be quick.

I throw open the door and I'm practically blind from the sun. I stayed too long in the stairwell and my eyes can't adjust. The chopper's coming around and my finger goes to the trigger. It's so loud and bright. I press my back against the wall, hold the shotgun to my chest. I'm closing my eyes picturing Lily and Rachel and my parents. Dad's telling me I can't be afraid to pull the trigger.

But I suddenly realize that fear might be the only way out of this. The chopper is less than two seconds from seeing me with this shotgun. There's no way I can pull this off, not like this.

So I drop the gun, kick it so it's under the metal folding chair. The one I used to salute the flag and sing like a goddamn lunatic.

That's exactly what I have to look like. A man who has lost his mind.

I take off running, waving my arms, screaming at the top of my lungs. "HE'S IN THE STAIRWELL! WAYNE KING IS COMING DOWN!" The gunner's hands are wrapped around steel, ready to open fire, and I have no idea if he can understand a word I'm saying. But I just keep screaming that Wayne's heading down the stairs and start pointing over the edge. I'm right up against it, looking over, seeing the ground, but somehow with all the adrenaline, I'm not afraid. I'm just screaming, "DOWN! DOWN!"

The gunner must understand enough, because he's saying something to the pilot, who starts to circle around to the front of the building. He's descending, the rotor now even with the ledge. They're looking in the windows, looking for Wayne.

I turn back to the wall, where the shotgun is and take off running. I try to pick it up, but my hand smacks against the folding chair. The chopper sounds like it's starting to pull away to get a better view. I flip over the chair, grab the gun, and run back to the ledge. The crowd down below is staring up at the chopper. I see them through the spinning blades, moving so fast it's just this translucent swirl.

I tell them to fucking move even though they can't hear me. I raise the barrel and aim it right at the center of the blades. One shot. That's all I get.

I hold my breath, just like Dad taught me. One eye closed. Shoulder's relaxed. Arm steady.

Someone down below sees what I'm about to do and screams something. The crowd looks up and I'm waving my hand to tell them to get the fuck away from there.

The pilot must see them, because the chopper begins to rise. I don't have a choice. The gunner is going to have me in his sights any second.

My finger curls around the trigger, just like Rachel's and Grandpa's before everything went dark.

The blast is louder than the rotor and the kickback practically separates my shoulder, searing pain shooting down my arm. But I don't move. Just watch the buckshot spark off the blades, which slow down to the point I can see all four. Then the chopper begins to tilt. The pilot's trying to pull up or set it down. I can't tell. I just see the crowd running and the blades grinding and carving into the street. Sparks and metal spray into the air and sidewalk. The fire isn't instantaneous, but it doesn't take long before the entire helicopter explodes.

Two women are thrown back. A guy is holding his face, obviously burned and ripped up by the shards of metal.

The gun is still in my hands as I back up, nearly trip. I stare into the sun as the crackling sounds mingle with screams.

What the hell have I done?

The door closes behind me as I enter the stairwell. I'm against the wall and shaking. The backpack is on the floor and I just stare at it, knowing I need to break down the shotgun, but I hear voices coming up from the first floor.

The Boots are here, and I have nowhere to run. They're going to open fire. My fingers fumble for the shells, but I can't keep a grip. It's like they're covered in oil. I look over the side. Someone is definitely coming. A seven-floor climb and it's all over.

I see the next level down, the door that leads to my office. I grab the pack and race down the stairs. The voices are getting closer. I stay against the wall. My foot misses a step and I nearly fall, my ass almost hitting the stairs, but I keep moving, flinging myself towards the door. My hand finds the handle and I quickly slip in, expecting to see Carlos and Alex and all my coworkers ready to tackle me, but the floor's empty, everyone evacuated.

My office is right there and I think about hiding, crawling under my desk, curling into a ball, curling so tight that I wake up and find myself back on the couch with Michelle and Lily. The TV still on *Letterman* and my ears fine. No flashbang. No gunshots into Lily's ribs. All of it just a terrible dream.

But hiding in my office isn't going to keep me alive. I need to get to the cave, find Danny and Sara. If Wayne's holding Danny and Sharon refuses to let them join her, Sharon won't hesitate. She'll tell Melvin to take them both out. I'm sure by now they have guns. I have to keep moving.

When I get to the elevators I see the red numbers rising. If the doors open, I might get off a shot, but it stops one floor down.

My lungs start working again. I lean against the wall, trying to figure out how the hell I'm going to get out of here. I can see Carlos's office, think about just climbing out the window. It's one less floor than Paul fell. Maybe I'd just break an ankle.

Then I hear the stairwell door open. Whispers. They're checking offices. Looking for Wayne, for me.

My finger goes to the trigger, but I remember I didn't load it. I'm digging around in the backpack. An office door opens. A voice says, "Clear."

I'm picturing the floor plan. There are only three offices between the stairwell and the elevators.

A different voice, another, "Clear."

I finally get a shell in my hand. I'm sliding it in. Trying to click the barrel closed as quietly as possible.

Then a voice whispers, "Joe."

I turn, ready to fire, when I see Wendell peering out from the bathroom. He's waving me in with that big, meaty paw. He seems friendly, more friendly than whoever is searching our offices, so I step towards him. I'm ten feet from the bathroom. I hear bootsteps. I turn around and back in to the bathroom so I can still take a shot if they come around the corner.

Wendell shuts the door without making a sound, holding the handle so there isn't a click. Then his fat finger presses to his lips as if I need to be reminded to stay quiet.

The whispers are at the elevator. I can hear them through the door. I push Wendell back and put my ear against the wood and listen. They must be giving hand signals. It's quiet, but I know they're coming.

I look around the bathroom. The stalls aren't going to keep me hidden for more than a few seconds. They'll just kick in the door.

A walkie-talkie goes off. A voice tells them someone is on the roof.

Bootsteps running, fading until I hear the faint sound of the stairwell door slamming shut.

Wendell exhales, thinks we're safe, but I know we're not. I only heard one set of boots running. There were definitely two whispers. I silently tell Wendell to get back against the wall. I press myself against the sink, the small puddle of water on the counter seeps into my pants. The gun's aimed at the door. I see the handle slowly turn. Sweat drips into my eyes, but I'm trying not to blink. The door begins to open. I see the barrel of the revolver, the eyes of the newbie, the Boot that was guarding Robert's door so no one would see him swinging from the ceiling, his dick still hard.

The newbie enters. He's shaking, staring down the Mossberg. He's telling me to drop it, but I'm not moving. Wendell's against the wall. The newbie doesn't see him. He just keeps telling me to put it down. His voice trembles. His finger tight against the trigger.

I know he's going to fire, whether he wants to or not. I stay real still, knowing even a twitch will get him to take the shot.

"Okay," I tell him. "I'm putting down the gun."

"Yeah, yeah, that's good."

I bend forward, gently placing the shotgun on the wet floor. He tells me to kick it towards him. I do it.

"I just want to get out of here," I say.

He looks confused, as if I'm telling him I'm from another planet. He stretches out his leg and puts his foot on the Mossberg, slides it back. The revolver still aimed at my chest. He takes one hand off the gun and goes for the walkie-talkie, his eyes never leaving mine. He fumbles the walkie, nearly drops it.

Wendell's inching forward, and I can hear his fucking breath from here. The newbie starts to turn, but Wendell drives his shoulder into his stomach and plows him into the paper towel dispenser. I grab the newbie's arm, pry the revolver from his hand. Wendell's got him against the sink now, and the newbie's flailing, his hand finding Wendell's face, trying to force the big fellow off.

Wendell lifts and the newbie is off the ground for a second before Wendell slams him down. The newbie's head cracks against the sink. His body slumps to the wet floor. I can't tell if he's dead or just knocked out. Wendell's breathing in clumps, like he's about to have a heart attack. He drags his sleeve across his lips, just stares at the newbie.

I want to tell him thanks, but the whole thing is just too crazy. I keep my eyes on Wendell until he finally turns. He's more shocked than me.

"You okay?" I ask.

Wendell nods.

"Okay, okay," I repeat, trying to think. The newbie's body is still splayed on the floor and there's no way we'll be able to explain it to the Boots.

"You, uh..." Wendell takes a second to catch his breath. "You have to get my sister."

"What?"

"You have to help her escape. She's working in the deli."

I didn't even know Wendell had family here. For a second, I think Wendell might be a part of Sharon's club, but he tells me he just learned about it, overheard someone's thoughts. He says Sharon would never let him in. He says, "I'm too fat."

A voice comes through newbie's walkie-talkie. The voice says there's no one on the roof, says he's coming down.

"Her name's Becky," Wendell says. "She's at the deli. You have to get her. You have to." Wendell's eyes are as wide and pleading as I've ever seen.

"Okay," I tell him. "We'll go get her."

"No," he says, "just you."

The ding of the elevator.

One set of boots.

I grab the shotgun. Wendell picks up the revolver.

You know how to use that?

Wendell shakes his head no.

Just squeeze and don't close your eyes.

Wendell nods, but he's so out of breath he can't hold the gun still. If someone walks in, I'm going to get shot from both directions.

The stairwell door opens and shuts.

The bootsteps are moving, but not towards us. There's a muffled conversation.

I decide to peek out, figuring they're going to come here eventually. The elevator doors are still open.

Follow me.

No.

Goddamnit, just do it.

I'm staying, Wendell thinks. *Just go.*

There's no time to argue. I take off, angle my body to slip in just before the doors close. My fingers mash the button. I hear the Boots, the bathroom door click shut.

"He's in there!" one of them says.

Their yelling is muffled. I can't tell if one of the voices is Wendell. The lower the elevator goes, the harder it is to hear. But the next six quick sounds are unmistakable.

The elevator slows, it's about to hit the first floor. I shove the shotgun up under my jacket, angle it so it's not poking me in the chin. Then the doors start to open and I immediately regret it. I should've kept it out. Who knows what's waiting? Luckily, there are people everywhere, everyone jostling towards the front doors. I keep my head down and sink into the crowd.

Two of the Boots are on walkie-talkies. I stay hidden behind a few Brightsiders. We're almost out the door when the voice over the walkie-talkie says they got the guy.

Wendell's dead.

CHAPTER EIGHTEEN

The smell of burning metal, leather, and flesh. Everyone is circled around the wreckage so I can't see the pilot or the gunner, just the one single blade rising towards the purpling sky. The sun is starting to creep under the horizon. I move through the crowd. Some people weep; others just stare in shock. Harry, my hermit neighbor with his little toupee, is barking out instructions in his thick Boston accent, telling Brightsiders to take off their coats and carry them across the street. They lay them flat on the ground and start scooping handfuls of snow, piling it right on the coats. Two people, one on each end, lift each coat like a hammock and shuffle back, flinging the mounds of snow onto the flames.

I don't know what I expected, but definitely not this. They're trying to put out the fire because of the pilot, who's still moving. His charred, blistered hand reaching out through the broken glass and twisted metal.

The prisoners desperately trying to save their captor.

Stockholm Syndrome is the first thought in my head. But these people genuinely want to help. They're praying they'll get him out before it's too late. They're good and decent. They don't want the man to die. They just see a crisis and want to do what's right. The government calls them Thought Thieves, but these people are definitely not terrorists.

Unlike me.

My stomach's climbing up my throat and I try to escape the smoke, but can't. The wind swirls it, covering me no matter which way I move. I bump into a woman and feel the shotgun almost slip out of my jacket. I tell her I'm sorry and keep my hand on the butt of the gun.

More Boots are arriving, but no one notices me. The pilot is all that matters, the pilot I shot down.

Everything is telling me to run, but I keep it slow and steady. I can't draw attention, that I know. I'm not even watching where I'm going. I'm just moving down the street and I can't stop picturing the pilot's hand, the desperate, pathetic reach, each black finger pleading for help.

I've never actively taken a life. Rachel died because of what I couldn't say. Lily, because I stayed in one place too long, let the Boots close in. I stopped being Steven's friend, but I didn't give him cancer. And Robert just heard my thoughts, but Wayne was the man who strung him up.

The gunner, the pilot...this is completely on me. I aimed the gun. I pulled the trigger.

Sharon's voice is echoing my father's. *You're going to do great things, Joe.*

So fucking great. I actually thought I was doing the right thing. The Boots were evil; they needed to be put down.

But if that's the case, then why do I feel like shit?

I don't even realize I'm near the pond, but Sara's calling my name. She comes running out from behind some trees.

"Oh, thank God. I didn't think you were going to show. I didn't know if something..."

"Sorry."

"Are you alright?"

"Yeah..."

"Holy shit, I can't believe you did it." Sara keeps looking past me, staring at something in the distance.

I can't look back.

Sara smiles. "Well, we both made it."

"How'd you get away from the Boots?"

"They were searching a building near the Square. Questioning people, seeing if anyone knew anything. I just ran up and told them someone spotted Wayne in the office. There were only a few of them and they took off running, called it in, I guess. I just walked away." Sara laughs, still freaked out.

"So you saw it? The helicopter?"

She nods. "You sure you're okay?"

I picture the crash, the explosion. "I only had one shot and... They're still trying to get him out from...he's trapped..."

I see the pilot's hand reaching.

"Joe, you didn't have a choice."

I finally look back and see the huge cloud of black smoke. It's still rising. I hear the sirens. The ambulance must have arrived. They're going to have to cut through the metal.

"Joe, come on, we have to hurry."

But I'm moving back towards the wreckage. Sara yanks my arm. "What are you doing?" She spins me a little. "Joe? Hey, listen to me." She grabs my face. "We have to get to Danny."

Even with her holding my face, I can't stop looking at the black smoke rising up from the carnage, the flesh.

"Joe! Come on!" She's pulling me, but I'm fighting it. She says, "Danny needs us. He needs you, Joe. He's your friend, remember?"

It's like I've just been slapped awake. "Right. Yeah... Sorry."

I start for the woods, holding tight to the image of Danny, of Wayne. I tell myself not to look back, just get to the cave.

The sun's halfway under the horizon. Streaks of red splash across the sky and dissolve into the darkness of night.

I can hardly see and am unsure which way to go.

"Joe, what are you doing? Why are you stopping?"

"I can't remember." I look left and it seems kind of familiar, but so does the right. But it's all just trees and snow and I have no fucking clue.

"Joe!" Sara shakes me. "Relax, okay?"

I'm trying, but she's still shaking me. Finally she stops.

"Just clear your head and think. Which way is the mine?"

I close my eyes, try to remember the first time I found it, the huge tree crashing down and uncovering the entrance. I picture the rusted metal tracks.

"Hey, come on, focus. Where were you before the mine?" Sara asks. She's pissed and needs me to get this.

I remember I just got off the phone with Mom. She'd said my father had turned me in and I just started running, lost one of my shoes in the snow.

"What else?"

It takes me a second then suddenly it's clear. "I went to the tree!" The one where I'd carved Michelle and Rachel's names, which later I scratched out because I can't stop hurting every woman I meet.

Sara doesn't have time for my bullshit, but it reminds me it's not too far from their names.

I take off running, and the shotgun starts to slide out of my jacket. I pull it out, carry it in one hand. The snow is halfway up our shins, but we keep plodding. Even when Sara gets stuck, I grab her hand and pull. Twenty more yards, the carving just visible. We just need to angle right, then head up the hill. The fallen tree is at the bottom, wedged against a few towering pines.

"It's up here," I say and help Sara keep her balance up the rocky, snow-covered slope.

The cave is still covered by rocks. Completely untouched. But there's no one here. Sharon and the others should be waiting, that was the plan. I walk around the cave, looking into the woods. The gunmetal is freezing on my bare hand, so I set it against the rocks and keep looking around. Sharon and the others must have seen the helicopter crash, or at least heard it. I start to wonder if they've already escaped, but they couldn't have put back the rocks. They're covered with too much snow.

I tell Sara it doesn't make any sense.

Sara's not paying attention. She's looking at the trees, turning around in circles, anxious and panicked. I know she's not talking about Sharon when she asks, "Where are they?"

I tell her to be quiet. There's something coming from far away. It sounds like gunshots, but it's too faint to be sure.

A voice rings out. "Sara."

"Danny?" Sara turns around and calls his name again, but there's no answer. Seconds tick by and I start thinking I'm going insane.

Then Wayne, with a knife to Danny's throat, comes walking out of the trees. Wayne's eyes dart around the forest. He sees we're alone.

Danny's pencil is gone, fist empty, his thumb rubbing up and down on his knuckle. His eyes are filled with tears ready to burst and stream.

"Let him go!" Sara says.

Wayne just brings the knife closer to Danny's neck. They're in the shadows so it's too dark to see, but Danny's gasp says the blade's piercing skin.

"Stop it! You're hurting him!"

Wayne's jaw clenches under that nasty beard, his eyes gleaming at me. "Shut her fucking mouth or I take the retard's head."

Sara starts for Wayne, but I pull her back, tell her to stay calm.

"Wayne," I say, "now, we had a deal."

"Oh, I'm aware."

"And I did my part so let Danny go."

Wayne sticks out his neck, swivels it left then right. "I don't see the rest of the party?"

"I don't know where they're at."

"Then you broke the deal."

"You said I had to take out the helicopter."

"No, that Zen cunt told you to do that. I said you had to convince her to let me tag along."

"I don't know where she is!"

"Then you didn't live up to your part of the bargain." Wayne takes a fistful of Danny's hair and snaps back his head, the knife pressing hard against Danny's throat.

"Please," Sara says. "Please don't."

"Wayne, you don't need to do this." I'm trying to keep my voice steady. "We don't even need Sharon. We can go on our own."

Wayne clicks his tongue. "Yeah, I don't like that idea. Unless you got a car waiting?"

There's no point in lying, not with Wayne, so I tell him I don't. But I remind him we're out of options. The helicopter's down, but another one could be here any minute. So unless he wants to head back and turn himself in, we need to go now.

Wayne mulls it over. I know he's going to slit Danny's throat no matter what, so I keep my eyes locked on his. I don't even blink.

"You kill him," I say, "and I'm not lifting a fucking stone. And there's no way you'll get down by yourself."

Wayne laughs. "Momma's Boy wants to be a man." Wayne turns towards Sara, the tip of his tongue sliding over his lips. "Maybe I'll just stick here, enjoy your lady."

I blow out Wayne's sick fantasy. "We're running out of time. We can do this quicker with Danny."

Wayne seems disappointed. He lets Danny go with a shove. Danny runs into Sara's arms. She squeezes him with everything she's got, pats his hair, asks if he's alright. Danny gulps and nods. She checks his neck. It's bleeding, but not bad.

"Well, let's get to work," Wayne says.

I look to Sara and tell her to go on, let her know this is our only play. Danny moves to the cave and starts pulling away rocks. Sara and I help while Wayne wipes the bloody knife on his shirt. I drop a rock and look at Wayne, ask him if he's going to just stand there.

Wayne slides the knife in his belt and lifts a huge stone. I can tell it's hurting his back, but he turns and chucks it to the ground.

Sara tries to lift a big one, too, but can't. She starts to move to a smaller rock, but I tell Danny to help his sister. He's got a small stick in his fist but works around it, grabs one end of the rock and they pry it out, both of them stepping sideways a few feet.

Wayne's staring at me. I just lift another huge rock, focus my thoughts on the weight. I drop it as Sara and Danny drop theirs. Then I see my opportunity. Sara and Danny are out of the way. I run and grab the shotgun, but before I can even take aim, Wayne says, "Now, Joe, why do you have to complicate things."

Still, I point the hollow end right at his face and wedge myself in between Wayne and Danny.

Wayne's cocking his head, sizing me up. He says, "Momma didn't raise a killer."

"Fuck you, Wayne. I already broke my cherry." I'm trying to sound tough, but Wayne's inside my head.

He rubs his beard. "But you didn't like the taste, did you?" Wayne narrows his eyes. He's burrowing around inside me. "How'd you do it, Joe? How'd you take down that chopper?"

I'm trying to hum, to block it all out.

"You look those men in the eye, like your daddy told you? Huh?" A grin spreads over Wayne's face. "Or did you wait until they were down below and shoot them in the back?"

I can't get the pilot out of my head fast enough. I'm humming as loud as I can, and Wayne's still grinning. I tell him to back up, but he just keeps coming, not even moving his hands, just presses his chest against the barrel.

Wayne's breath pours over my face and I jab him with the gun to push him back, but Wayne leans in so I'm practically holding him up, the hollow end digging into his ribs.

"I'm right here, Joe. What's it going to be? You a coward or man?"

I hear my father's voice telling me to stop being such a goddamn baby, and Wayne's laughing. My finger's on the trigger. I can feel it fine against my skin. But Wayne keeps leaning, his eyes wide and psychotic. I just can't squeeze.

Wayne grabs the barrel, swipes it away from his chest. I'm holding onto the butt of the gun, both of us yanking, pulling, grunting. Then Wayne gets his other hand on the gun and slams me into the rocks, knocking everything out of me. He's using both hands, one on each end of the shotgun, forcing it against my throat. I push back on the barrel, and Wayne pulls me away from the rocks then crushes me back against them, my head smacking, nearly splitting. My legs give out, but he's holding me up with the Mossberg on my neck, cutting off air. I close my eyes and try to kick, but Wayne throws out his knee and blocks it.

"Look at me, Joe. This is how you do it. You look them right in the eye—"

Danny's roar only lasts a second, but it's enough to get Wayne to turn, just in time to see Danny's hands coming at him. The stick punches through Wayne's cheek, Danny's fingers digging into Wayne's eyes. They spin.

The Mossberg flies out of Wayne's grasp and cracks against a rock. I'm on all fours sucking air. Wayne and Danny are pulling and pushing and punching, a snarling violence that collapses to the ground, probably close enough to touch, but I can't lift my head to know for sure.

Wayne's laugh almost covers the sliding of metal on leather. Sara screams. I look up and see Wayne holding the knife high above his head, ready to drive it through Danny's chest. I look for the gun, but can't find it. It's somewhere buried in the snow. So I dive into Wayne. We start tumbling, rolling down the hill. This sharp pain carves into my side, but I can't tell if it's the knife or just a rock. Finally, we stop rolling and Wayne crawls on top of me, a ragged hole in his cheek. Spit falls from his lips and onto mine. He wipes the snow from his hair and sniffs, sucking up blood and snot. He flips the knife around in his hand so he can get a better grip.

"Please," I hear my voice squeak.

Wayne's thinking how good it's going to feel to slice through me. The cartilage and fibers shredding and spraying blood like warm rain.

Then comes the *crack!* And I see the hole in Wayne's head, all dark and hollow. It's about the size of a dime.

Wayne's eyes are focused on something behind me until there's no focus at all. He falls to his side, his face half-swallowed by the snow, which dissolves and turns crimson.

I force off his legs and expect to see Danny or Sara with the shotgun. Instead, I see Sheriff Melvin, Sharon and about forty other people.

Melvin is holding a revolver. His uniform is covered in blood. Same goes for a half dozen of the Brightsiders. They look like they've just been through a war, bruised and broken, their bodies still carrying fragments of lead.

Melvin stands over me and asks, "Can you get up?"

"Yeah."

"Good, 'cause I ain't carrying your ass."

I get to my knees and feel the pain shooting down my side. My jacket is torn and I unzip it, peer in and see the blood. My fingers feel the wound and it's not very deep. The jacket took most of the damage.

Danny and Sara run over and help me to my feet. Sara asks if I'm okay and I tell her I'm fine. Danny keeps apologizing for not stopping Wayne.

"It's okay, Danny," I say. "You saved my life."

That simple joy returns to Danny's eyes. "I did good?"

"Yeah, real good."

We walk back to the cave where the Brightsiders are ripping down the rest of the rocks.

Sharon gets in my face. "Who knows about this place?"

"No one, just Sara and Danny."

Sharon looks at Wayne's lifeless body.

I say, "And him, too."

Sharon doesn't find it funny. Apparently, her little club has a leak. The Boots found out about the escape. There was gunfire in the Square. A few people died.

"Joe, I need you to think about this real hard," Sharon says. "Is there anyone else that's not here who knows about the cave?"

Rachel knew, but she's dead. Same went for Robert.

I didn't tell another soul.

"Did anyone see you on the roof?"

"A couple of people, but no one could've known about this place. They were down on the sidewalk. They only saw me fire the shot."

"What about afterwards?"

I picture the stairs, the office, the elevator. That big paw waving me into the bathroom.

Sharon's face squinches up. "Wendell?"

"Yeah, but I didn't tell him anything. He already knew. He heard it from someone. But he didn't tell anyone, at least not after he saw me."

"And how do you know that?"

"Because he's dead."

"Still, he heard it from someone? Who?"

"I don't know, Sharon. Could be anyone. I mean, this operation isn't exactly a well-oiled machine."

Sharon glares at me then walks over to the cave. "Alright everyone, listen up! We've got ten minutes to get off this mountain or else our ride is gone. So let's move!"

Sharon's chosen ones keep hurling rocks. A few have torches, which they douse with gasoline. Carlos and some guy who works at the deli carry this giant spooled up ladder.

Danny says, "I wanna help."

Sara tells him okay and Danny heads over to the cave and starts chucking rocks. Sara looks at my torn jacket, but doesn't ask about the cut. She's listening to my thoughts about Wendell, another unlucky soul who made the mistake of running into me. He didn't need to die. He was just trying to help me, even after all the awful shit he heard me think about him.

"It's going to be okay. It will," Sara says. "We're getting out of here."

"Yeah, lucky us."

All Wendell wanted was for me to help his sister, Becky. He gave up his life because I promised him I would.

"Joe, you need to let it go. We only have ten minutes to get out of here. The girl will be fine."

"No..." Once we're gone, the people left behind will never be safe. They'll lock it down and turn it into a zoo.

Carlos and the guy from the deli set down the spooled up ladder. I walk over.

Carlos looks up and says, "Joe!"

I don't have time for him. I say to the other guy, "Do you know Becky? Wendell's sister? She works with you, I think."

He says he does, feels like shit about it. The girl's only sixteen. She has no one left.

"Do you know where she is? Where I can find her?"

"She was at the deli earlier, but there's a curfew now. Might be at home. Lodge Two, I think. Yeah. Second floor."

I nod and turn back. Sara's right there.

"Joe, come on, let's just go help Danny, okay?" Sara takes my arm. But I'm not going with her. I'm looking for the shotgun.

"Are you crazy? If you go back there with a gun, they'll kill you."

Sara's right, I have to go unarmed. One shotgun isn't going to stop every Boot. It's only going to draw them in.

"Joe, please don't do this."

I look at the cave. They're only halfway done with the rocks. I'm already backing down the hill. Sara begs me to stay.

I tell her, "I'll be back in time. I promise."

"Yeah? And if you're not?"

"Then leave and don't look back."

Sara is still yelling as I take off into the woods. I'm running down the hill. Trees fly by and I jump over a log, dodge holes, angle left at my carvings. I pump my arms as fast as they go. The pond is less than twenty yards away. My left foot slides out beneath me and gets caught on something in the snow, my ankle cracking. It's not broken, but it's definitely sprained. I don't have long before it swells. I put most of the pressure on my right leg, but keep moving. My left foot barely touches the ground as I head towards the Square.

CHAPTER NINETEEN

Most of the lamp posts in the park are lit, but a couple have been shot out, glass scattered beneath them. I make it to the Square. The streets are so quiet and empty it's creepy. It must be because of the curfew, which makes me realize trying the deli is pointless. No one is going to be there so I head for Lodge Two. I have to cross the street, but otherwise I try to stay up against the buildings.

There's a Boot up ahead. He's scraping something off his sole. Gum or something.

I crouch as low as I can without putting my ass on the ground. It puts pressure on my ankle, but I can't be seen. The Boot is hopping on one leg, losing his balance. I slip around the corner, cross in between two buildings. I start to take a left when I hear this faint buzzing sound.

There's a security camera somewhere. They must have realized most of them had been disabled. I wonder how many are back on.

There's a fence to the left. It's about five feet high. I check both ways then take off and run, but my ankle gives out. My hand goes to the pavement. I'm completely exposed so I spring up and hobble onto the grass. I climb the fence, flinging my body over the top and land on my side to protect my ankle.

Lodge Two is just over a small hill. I creep towards it, see two Boots out front. They're armed and trying to look real serious, even though no one is around. I figure there must be a camera on the front door. They're being watched, which means I need to find another way in. I swoop around towards the side and look up at the second floor. There's no way I could climb up, even with two good ankles. But the first floor offers opportunity. There's a window and it's slightly open, which is odd in this cold.

I move closer and hear voices inside the apartment.

A woman says, "I told you I was sick."

A man says, "Oh, believe me I know, and it's disgusting."

I duck walk the rest of the way, praying there isn't a camera. I get to the ledge and slowly lift my head up over the sill. The living room is empty, just the same shitty furniture as every apartment in Brightside. The bedroom door is closed and so is the bathroom. They both have lights on, which spills out under the doors.

My breath is streaming fog and I can barely feel my fingers. I look at my watch. I only have five minutes to make it back. I'm already behind schedule and I haven't even made it to the second floor. Instinct tells me to turn back. I can still make it if I hurry, but Wendell keeps popping into my head. His big giant body splayed on the wet bathroom floor. The holes in his chest, his face.

The window gives the slightest creak as I lift it a few inches. Luckily, the couple is still arguing from different rooms. I don't think they can even hear each other because they're saying the same thing.

I press up on my right foot and hoist myself through. My stupid coat is getting stuck so I have to wiggle a bit. I nearly propel my face to the floor, but my hands spring out and soften the blow. I'm heading for the front door when I hear a flush.

The knob begins to turn and I nearly trip over the coffee table, my hand frantically reaching out for the door. The bathroom light flicks off and I turn the knob, slip out just in time.

The hallway's empty. The stairs are at the other end. I hobble and hurry and use the handrail to keep weight off my left foot. There are at least eight doors on the second floor, and I have no idea which one is Becky's. I don't have time to try them all, so I just knock on the first one. A middle-aged woman, with dry, frizzy hair, answers. I think I've seen her washing dishes at the diner.

"I'm looking for Becky," I say.

"No Becky lives here."

"Okay, but she's on this floor. Do you know which one is hers?"

The woman scratches her scalp and something comes off in her nail. She pinches it and studies it.

"Please. Her name's Becky. Wendell's sister?"

"Oh," she says, drawing out the word like it has fifteen letters. "Yeah, weird girl. She's over there." The woman points to the last door on the right. There's still a piece of scab under her nail. I tell her thanks and start hobbling.

This floor seems so familiar, but I can't remember ever being here.

I knock on the last door.

A girl says, "I'm in bed." She sounds frightened, like she's been caught doing something bad.

"Becky, I'm a friend of your brother's. Please, just come to the door." I hear her moving around. I also see the middle-aged woman peering out her door. But as long as she's peering, she's not calling the Boots.

Finally, the door opens and I see Becky, a frail, freckle-faced girl with big brown eyes that look like she's been crying.

"You don't know me," I say, "but your brother sent me."

"My brother's dead."

"Yeah, I know, and I'm sorry, but he asked me to make sure... Can I come in?"

It's like she knows she's being watched. She says, "No. I can't have visitors."

I'm not trying to get you in trouble, but your brother asked me to come get you.

Why?

So you can leave Brightside for good.

"I...don't know what you're talking about."

I know she's lying, but she's also scared.

She starts to close the door, but I block with my left foot, pain ripping through my ankle.

I grit my teeth. *He risked his life for me, Becky. He did it so I could escape and so you could, too. Your brother wanted you to get out. He made me promise I'd come get you. Now, I can't force you to do anything, but I gave Wendell my word. I owe him. That's why I'm here. But you*

have to make up your own mind and it has to be right now.
We don't have any more time.

Becky stares at nothing, trying to process what I'm telling her, but she's also thinking about Wendell. She knows her brother would've done anything to help her escape.

The door behind me opens and I hear this awful voice I know too well.

"What the fuck are you doing here?"

Krystal.

And it all comes back. Lodge Two, second floor.

I stay focused. *So what's it going to be, Becky?*

"Oh shit." Krystal laughs. "You're a fucking pervert. She's sixteen!"

Becky, you have to decide right now. Yes or no?

Becky keeps staring at the floor. She's unable or unwilling to comprehend what I'm saying. I start to think this is a mistake. Here I am trying to convince a girl I've never met to run off with me into the woods. And Sharon's ride is probably already here, about to leave, and I'm going to miss it.

But then Becky looks up with those big brown eyes and nods.

I silently tell her to get her coat, that we're already late. She asks if she can pack a bag and I tell her there's no time. Sharon's club is leaving as we speak.

I shouldn't have thought it, regretted it the moment it flew out of my head.

"You're the ones causing this shit?" Krystal's voice fills the entire lodge. "That's why we have a curfew? So you idiots can try to escape?"

Krystal is shoving me, prodding her fingers into the back of my head. Other doors start opening, people popping out to see what's going on. I try not to look at them, but I catch a young man's eyes. He wants to know if it's true. If there really is a way off this mountain.

I don't mean to picture the pond, the carvings in the tree, the hill, and the cave, or maybe I do. I have no clue what I'm doing anymore.

Then another familiar sound, far worse than Krystal.

The faint sound of bootsteps.

And they're getting louder and louder.

I jump into Becky's room, slam the door, lock it. Krystal's banging and screaming and telling everyone the traitor is right here.

Becky puts on her coat, her boots. I hobble to the window and open it. There are some bushes and it looks like a snow bank has blown up against the building.

Krystal's outside the door telling the Boots to hurry up.

I take Becky's hand, tell her it's going to be okay. She ducks her head under the window and slips out first, her fingers gripping the sill. She's terrified.

"It's okay. Just jump."

Words I never thought would ever leave my mouth.

But Becky lets go and falls, and I stick my head out to see her lying on her back. I can't tell if she's breathing, but then she smiles.

The key slips into the lock. The bolt turns. I stick my leg through the window, duck under and look back to see the doorknob turn. I let go. Just falling in the dark. The snow breaks my fall, but not really. I'm heavier than Becky and she already smashed a lot of the powder. I can barely breathe, but I pull myself up, keep most of my weight on my right foot as we run for the park.

I'm running, hobbling down the path, shouting for Becky to keep up. I hear voices in the distance. Someone says we're heading for the trees.

I take Becky's hand so we don't get separated. She's so light she's not sinking in the snow like I am when we step off the path and into the woods.

I practically drag her between two enormous pines, the needles scratching our faces and clothes.

Someone yells, "Stop right there!"

But I don't look back, just keep moving as fast as my ankle will let me.

"Are they going to shoot us?" Becky asks.

"No," I tell her. "They have to warn us first."

A cloud slides over the moon and I can hardly see all the rocks and dead logs. I nearly trip. So does Becky. I say, "Keep going, that's all we have to do."

I think I see the tree with my carvings, but I can't be sure.

Gunfire erupts behind us, bullets blowing through branches on both sides.

So much for a warning.

Another bullet whizzes by. It's so close my entire body is covered with goose bumps.

Carvings or not, I yank us right. My ankle's practically numb from the snow and we sprint through a bunch of trees and start moving up the hill. Becky's frail, but she's a fighter, keeps churning, running, even when it sounds like she's about to have an asthma attack.

Other than her labored breaths, I don't hear anything. No more shots. I wonder if we somehow lost them. It's
only thirty yards to the cave. I squeeze Becky's hand and
keep pulling her up the hill until we hit the rubble.

I look back expecting to see a dozen Boots storming
like it's the beaches of Normandy, but no one seems to be
coming.

I realize Wayne's body is missing, too. I know he
didn't just stand up and walk away though. I saw the bullet
enter his psychotic brain. There's a three-foot wide path that
leads to the trees. The Brightsiders must have dragged him
away to keep the Boots off our trail.

I lift Becky over the few remaining rocks blocking the
cave, set her down in the darkness.

"What is this?" Becky asks.

I silently tell her to be quiet.

I'm not holding her hand, but I know she's trembling. I reach into my pocket for my keys, but my fingers are
so frozen I can't keep a grip. They clang on the ground. I
kneel, put my hands on the cold dirt and sweep around and
around until I hear a jingle. I pick up the keys and hold them
in front of my face, but I can't see anything but black.

I wanna go home, Becky says.

Hold on…

Danny's little flashlight clicks and shines across the
ground. I see the rusty steel tracks. *We just have to follow
these. Come on.*

Becky wraps her hands around my arm and we start
moving. The wooden beams creak as we descend down the
belly of the mountain. The tunnel splits after a few hundred
yards. I take us right. I silently tell Becky what part of the

mountain we're walking under, even though I'm not entirely sure. I just know she loosens her grip a little. She asks if this could collapse.

Out loud, she asks, "How would anyone find us if it does—"

I cover her mouth. There's someone coming. They're a ways behind us, but not that far.

I silently tell Becky we have to run. I'm pretty sure she's nodding even though I can't see her face. I quicken our pace, remind her to tread lightly, to keep quiet, even though I can't. The numbness in my ankle has worn off, and the pain is searing. I keep dragging my left foot no matter how much I try not to. It's scrapping across the rocks and dirt and echoing so loud.

Becky takes the flashlight, which lets me balance better. I put one hand on her shoulder.

How much farther? she asks.

I honestly don't remember. It's been two weeks since I've stepped foot in the mineshaft, but I don't think we have far to go.

But the Boots are getting closer. I can't tell how many of them there are, but it really doesn't matter since I don't have the shotgun.

Suddenly, more voices. Familiar ones. But not from behind. They're just up ahead. I see the end of the rope ladder anchored into steel plates under the tracks. Each rung gets a bit brighter. The exit to the mine is ten yards away.

And we have company.

Danny and Sara are standing at the edge, a hundred stars twinkling behind them. It's the most beautiful sight I've ever seen, but I'm still mad. *What are you doing here?* I ask.

"Joe!"

I slam my hand over Danny's mouth and turn back to the darkness. I can't tell if the Boots are moving quicker or not.

I turn to Sara. *I told you to go.*

Danny refused.

Yeah, I refused.

I step up to the edge and look down two hundred feet. The last of Sharon's club is loading into the back of a huge moving truck. Sharon walks up to the driver. I can't see his face, but he's clearly pissing her off. Her arms swing wildly as she screams. But the guy's not budging, and Sharon looks up at us. I can barely hear her saying, "Fucking move!"

Come on, we have to go, Danny. Can you do this?

Danny nods and gets down on his knees. He grips the rungs. Little by little he crawls backwards, down over the edge.

Sara is telling him to be careful. He's almost vertical when he just stops. Sara's eyes pop.

What's wrong? she asks.

Danny must think since he's outside now, hanging off the edge, that he can talk as loud as he wants. "I found your gun, Joe!"

Danny, be quiet.

Danny's face turns red. I silently ask him where it is and Danny's head jerks towards my left. I fear he's going to fling himself right off the ladder.

But there it is, up against the rock wall of the tunnel.

American metal. Dad's gift.

I walk over and pick it up.

The Boots are getting closer. We all hear it.

Danny, you have to hurry, Sara thinks. *But be careful!*

Danny keeps climbing down and I tell Becky to go next. I don't know why I think she's going to have a problem with this after she jumped out her window, but it's a short fear. She drops to her knees and descends like she's been living in a circus. She even has to slow down to keep from stepping on Danny's head.

Sara and I lean over and watch them like two proud, nervous parents. But reality comes screeching back when I see the flashlights.

Sara, you need to go. Now!

Sara struggles more than Danny or Becky, but soon she's over the edge. I've got the shotgun aimed down the tunnel. I give a quick look back over my shoulder and see Sara staring up.

Joe, come on!

I'll catch up. Don't worry. Keep going.

My finger's tight against the trigger, and it feels good. It's not just a gun anymore. It's our savior and protector, and it's going to make sure Sara, Danny, and Becky make it to the truck.

I hardly know Becky, but I'm glad she made it. I only wish I could've brought more. It feels wrong to leave so many behind, but there's nothing I can do.

I slide over to the rock wall and lean against it, try to stay out of the moonlight. I don't want the Boots to see me and duck back, turning this into some prolonged gunfight. I'm too tired and sore, and I don't have enough ammo.

Two hundred feet down, that's all that stands between me and home, wherever that might be.

The Boots are arguing with each other. They're telling one to shut up. They must see the ladder, because they've stopped moving. The flashlight clicks off. I was hoping they'd keep it on to let me know where to shoot, but it probably would've blinded me.

One eye closed. Shoulders relaxed. Barrel up.

The Boots are trying to tread lightly, just like I told Becky, but those hard heels can't be silenced.

I clear out my thoughts, focus on the sounds. There's at least three, maybe four. I assumed there'd be a lot more, but I bet half of them took the other path when the tunnel split. I just wish I could tell if they are walking single file or side by side.

My hand slips into my pocket. I've got four more shells. The only problem is there isn't any cover, so the first round can't miss.

Inhale slowly. Exhale slowly. Inhale and...hold.

The first Boot comes out. He's not even looking at me, just marveling at the stars. I wait an extra second to see if another one is going to follow. Sure enough, one Boot does. They're standing so close I'll hit them both even if I only aim at one.

I crack off the shot and the kickback slams me into the wall. It fucking kills. I should've given myself space, but at least both Boots are on the ground. One's dead, and the other's well on his way. I click open the barrel and load two more shells when a bullet rips into the rock by my head. Little jagged shards cut into my neck. My eyes are closed when I start to take aim at the third Boot, but they're wide open by the time I get the gun parallel to the ground. The next shot tears right through his neck. It looks like his whole head might come clean off, but it stays intact as he falls onto his dead partners.

I load another round and try to be as quiet as possible. I don't hear any more bootsteps. I don't hear breathing or even someone cocking the hammer. It's just silent.

I take a quick look back over the edge, see everyone waiting inside the truck. I know they aren't going to wait much longer so I get down on my knees and crawl towards the ladder. I keep the shotgun aimed for another twenty seconds or so, just in case the last Boot has more patience than the others.

But there's not a sound. I need to go.

I slide the shotgun down my back, inside my coat, and I use one hand to shove it in the back of my pants and into the crack of my ass. The rungs are cold on my fingers. I start to back up. The rungs are getting slippery, but I know it's just my sweat. My heart is thumping in my chest. I realize that in the last hour I've stood on a high rooftop and jumped out a window, but there's just something about facing the fall backwards that throws my guts up towards my throat. I keep telling myself just don't look down.

My ankle throbs, but I keep moving. I'm almost halfway down when the rock next to my face explodes, spraying bits into my eyes and mouth.

Another bullet. But not from above. It came from somewhere off to the left in the distance. My cheeks and eyelids feel like I just dove into a pool of needles. I grip the rung with my right hand, while my left wipes away the little shards in the corner of my eye.

I hear Sara and Danny screaming from below, but I still can't look down. I turn left and see this twenty-something Ranger posted up on the hill, the muzzle of his rifle aimed right at me. Palmer, the dickhead Boot, gets out of his car, stands beside him, hands behind his back like he's watching a tennis match.

Melvin fires his revolver, which has no chance of doing anything except add to the noise, because he's too far away.

Danny screams for me to hurry and I'm trying, but my ankle keeps giving out and I can only come down with my right foot. I'm halfway down. A hundred feet from the ground.

The next crack of the rifle is almost as loud as the crunching sound the bullet makes as it blasts through my clavicle. My left hand just flies off the rung so now I'm holding on with only my right. I finally look down.

Fuck me...

I force myself to look up, which isn't any better. The Ranger takes aim, the barrel of that rifle pointed right at my skull. If I don't move, I won't even hear the crack. My brains and blood will just rain down on Sharon's chosen few.

I try to swing my left arm up to a rung to give me some stability, but all I feel is red-hot pain searing through my shoulder. I can't even squeeze a fist.

Palmer smiles and cocks his finger at me. The Ranger fires off a shot and I curl my body back under the ladder. The bullet zips by my neck as I slam into the rock. The ladder is all twisted now and I try to flip it back before the Ranger reloads, but my right hand slips. I don't know how many rungs I try to grab on the way down before I finally get one, my legs wrapping around the ladder. Everything's tangled and the shotgun falls and cracks against the rocks below. I force myself to look. Need to know exactly how far I have to fall. It's at least another fifty feet. I have to drop if he fires again, even if I shatter my legs.

I look out and see the Ranger and Palmer enjoying themselves. But I'm enjoying something, too. Melvin has moved into position.

They don't see him. The Ranger reloads. Palmer gives him the signal. I see my left leg is over the rung, meaning even if I let go, I'm just going to flip upside down. I try to pull out my leg, but it's impossible with only one hand. My left is just hanging at my side.

Another shot fired. Then another.

I squeeze my eyes, wait for death, but it never comes. I finally peek and see Palmer and his Ranger both slumped over, both dead.

Sheriff Melvin is making his way back towards the truck.

My right hand is starting to lose its grip, but my left leg is still over the rung. I pull up with everything I've got and jerk my leg up and free myself. I take a second to catch my breath. It's just fifty feet. I can do this. It's slow and painful, but I'm coming down rung by rung. Only twenty feet to go.

I take a small break, look out at Danny and Sara, expecting to see smiles or them running towards me, but everyone is just staring up. It's not good.

Six Boots all poised at the edge of the mineshaft. Each one armed and pointing at a different target. Sheriff Melvin is running, but he's still too far away.

I just start to laugh. Why I thought the worst was over, I haven't a clue.

"Fucking do it!" I yell. "Just fucking shoot me!"

Then comes a low rumble. A stampede of a hundred feet mixed with wild howls. It just keeps getting louder and louder until the entire night is filled with this primal roar.

The Boots come flying off the ledge. Arms and legs flail against the laws of nature. They pass me one by one, each smacking like slabs of meat on the rocks below.

I look out at Danny and Sara. I've never seen them so happy. Then the ladder starts to shake and I look up, see a pair of feet coming down. I lean out and see more feet following.

Brightsiders climbing down from hell above.

I have no choice but to get moving. I drop two rungs at a time, knowing if I don't I'm going to get kicked off because they're all coming. I drop the last few feet and rip more tendons in my ankle, but Danny and Sara are there to help me to the truck. Sharon's yelling at the driver to go, but he gets out and runs over to us.

I finally see his face, and I can't decide whether to hug him or punch him. He smiles and thinks, *We'll have time for both, Joe.*

Dad tells Danny to grab my legs. "Come on, we have to get him in." They fling me into the back of the truck, crammed in with the others.

Brightsiders run for the truck, but the roll-up door clangs down. They bang on the back and beg to be let in, but their cries fade as we pull away. Their chances aren't good on foot, but they have ten hours of darkness. If they split up and hide, some should slip away.

Sara eases me into her arms, careful of my shoulder. She kisses my head and tells me not to close my eyes, that I have to stay awake.

I think about the ones we left behind, lost and wandering this desert valley. Most are probably cursing us, but as I look around, I know we couldn't have fit more than one or two. The others would have flipped the truck, torn us to shreds.

I pray they see the sunrise, that they live long enough to tell the tale to their grandkids. I pray the Brightsiders that stayed behind aren't punished for our sins. I hear my prayers echoing in the minds of everyone around me. We're the lucky ones. Sharon's special club.

But I realize it's my club too as Becky slides her foot against mine and Sara pulls me into her arms.

Sara whispers, "You did good."

I nod and try to tell myself she's right, but I can't stop thinking about Rachel and Wendell and Krystal and...

"Shh," Sara says. She's pointing at Danny, sitting by the door, eyes closed, humming along to the sound of the tires. He's not thinking about anything, just humming. His mind as tranquil as the farthest reaches of space.

I don't even realize I'm laughing, but I can't stop. My head flops back and Sara has to move out of the way.

The others stare at me like I've lost my mind. Maybe I have, I don't know, but I'm not alone.

Sara's chest is shaking into my back. She's trying to control it, but I hear her giggle. It spreads around the truck.

Becky starts to ask what's so funny, but it takes her too. She covers her face and throws her head into Danny's arm. He snorts and what started as a little stream is now a raging river. All of us doubled-over, wiping our tears. Cackling like maniacs. And no one has any idea why. All we know is that right now there's not one single thought in this truck.

For once, we're actually free.

25 Perfect Days

A collection of short stories in which massive overpopulation, food shortages, contaminated water, and an ultra-radical religion lead to the passing of the Reduction Act. The twenty-five interlinked stories, each written from a different character's point of view, focus on the love, strength and self-sacrifice displayed when facing the Act's extreme measures. Scheduled for release in early 2013.

Ain't No Messiah

"Most my life, I've been saying I ain't no Messiah. All my life, Father's been swearing to God that I am. And now I'm here on this couch, not knowing what to think, figuring it probably don't matter either way." Look for it in 2013, the first in a five novel series.

Unlocking the Cage

Mark's first nonfiction project scheduled for release in 2014. As a former fighter, Mark could never answer why he stepped in the cage. Through an extensive survey and interviews of hundreds of MMA fighters from across North America, Mark hopes to answer who fighters are and what they have in common.

www.marktullius.com

MARK TULLIUS

I'm a father and a husband, a brother and a son. I'm an Ivy League grad who worked in a warehouse, an MMA fighter with too many defeats. I'm the bouncer and body-guard, the drunk guy in the fight. The jailer and the jailed, the guilty and innocent.

I'm a writer shaped by influences, too many to count. I grew up on King and Koontz while force-fed the Bible. I narrate Dr. Seuss and Disney nearly every night. Like you, I've seen things I wished I hadn't, heard some truths I won't forget.

Writing is my heavy bag, the sparring partner that doesn't punch back. It's where I shed my armor and cast off the blindfold, take a look at myself and the world around me. The writing takes me wherever it wants. Dark alley or dinner table, classroom or morgue. I go along for the ride and try to capture the moment, show life like it is.

ACKNOWLEDGMENTS

I owe special thanks to the following people:

Tom Spanbauer and Michael Sage Ricci, who taught me to believe in my writing and embrace my true voice. I will forever be grateful.

Anthony Szpak, the genius editor I plan on working with for as long as he'll have me. Every time someone tells me they can't put down *Brightside,* I feel the need to credit Anthony. He's great at understanding what I'm attempting to do then working his magic until that's what I'm doing.

My classmates at UCLA Extension Writers' program and the dedicated readers who suffered through early versions of *Brightside*. Your input has been invaluable and I hope the wait has been worth it.

My wonderful wife, Jen, for her constant support and unwavering love.

Sincere thanks to all of the people who showed support early on and let me know what Brightside meant to them.

"Wow!!!! I was gripping the couch as I read the last chapter...I felt like I couldn't read fast enough. Brightside is absolutely amazing!!!!" Olivia Hillcoat

"My faith has been restored, great story tellers are still alive! Brightside grabbed me from the first page and kept me to the end." Laura L.C. Williams

"It was an amazing exhilarating book that I was not able to put down. Filled with twists and turns and horrible sadistic things..." Gerardo Aguirre "Jerry"

"I'd recommend this book to anyone! Amazing thriller that will keep you engaged to the very end!" Shari Lindsay

"The tension builds with every risky encounter with another thought thief until you're frantically churning through pages to reach the ending - which comes not with a whimper but a wailing scream." Stephanie Heath Price

"An excellent book on all levels. It tapped into many feelings and emotions... so many real truths pertaining to real life." Marie Hensche

"Truly couldn't put it down and didn't want it to end. Page after page of suspense." Suzette Morris

"I really enjoyed not only the story but the idea of thought readers and how that would change communication and life." Rolando Delgado III

"I couldn't put it down, I always had to read it no matter what." Zachary King

"All I can say is INCREDIBLE!!! The style and flare make the material impossible to put down." Liz Ann Levesque

"Darker than Dean Koontz." Nancy White

"Most exciting, thrilling conclusion of any book I've ever read. I found myself racing to the finish." Michael Tullius – (My dad. The coolest review I'll ever get.)

The entire Tullius clan.	Lorraine Gonzalez
Jason Stanley	Evan Scott
Eugene Inozemcev	Richard King
Ian Vollmer	Cheyann Reagan
Andy Birskeugh	Houston Stout
John Holland	Monique Johnson
Glenn Cantillo	Brandie Light
Krisserin Canary	Sabrina Lee
Karl Dominey	Chris Zanderholm
Anthony Caso	Joe Worden
Brian Esquivel	Darryl MarcAurele
Dan Wills	Carrie Cressy
Mattie Leto	Lisa Lindsay Tooley
Paul White	Florante Ortaliza
Mat Santos	Daniel Teach
Diane Farmer Watzek	Nena LB
Dana Schneider	Rob Cipriano
Ryan Couture	Andy Law
Michael Polvere	Velma St. Pierre
Motu Ili	Andy Hillcoat
Bruce Boyington	Joe Chavez
Dave Curtis	Vic Torres
Terri Riker	Ru-Yi Yalich
Jason Gallagher	Ademo Freeman

Special thanks to the following bands whose music helped inspire *Brightside*.

Machine Head	http://machinehead1.com/
Fear Factory	http://fearfactory.com/
Puscifer	https://store.puscifer.com/

CHAPTER NINE

Demarius had a big mouth. Day 66, he heard me thinking about Belinda, the woman who lived in my apartment before me. Everyone said Belinda seemed nice. Kept to herself. I never met her, but every time I saw my tub, all I wanted to know was what she was thinking.

That tub was the reason for my two-minute showers, why I did most of my washing at the sink. I'm not superstitious or any of that, but I didn't like going in there. I had too good of an imagination.

Was the water real warm, your body relaxed? Had you always known it was the right thing to do? Did you question it when you held that razorblade? When you realized all you needed was sixty cents of steel? Not even that because all you really needed was that tiny little tip. Just dig it in and drag it back. And let it go. Let yourself flow away because you finally did it. You did what you should have done such a long time ago.

Demarius told Sharon everything. He had to. It was the rule. The Council said everyone had to report thoughts of suicide. It wasn't to be taken lightly. Too many people had died. Some ended up in wheelchairs, like Paul.

Paul said he was up on the roof because he used to be a gymnast. He liked the freedom. The total control. He said he slipped, caught his toe on the ledge. He said someone'd have to be crazy to do what he did, risk ending up like him, confined to a wheelchair.

But everyone knew better. Paul couldn't control his thoughts, the truth rolling around in that damaged brain. His wheelchair was electric. He controlled it with his mouth. He worked in the same building as me. The Council created a special job to keep him busy. No one knew what he actually did. Everyday he'd just roll around in his fancy chair. He had a live-in caretaker, who'd dress him in a black sweat suit and matching baseball cap to cover the part of his skull permanently sunk in. I didn't know Paul before the fall. Didn't know if his eyes were always bugged out like that or if that was just the way anyone's would be after freefalling eighty feet.

* * *

Sharon told me to take a seat, then said, "I know it's difficult."

"I'm not suicidal."

Joe...

I got loud when I said, "I'm not. Yes, I thought about Belinda. But she killed herself in my bathroom. It was just a thought."

"Calm down."

"I'm not going to kill myself."